P9-CAD-244

Trudy Krisher

Delacorte Press

Published by
Delacorte Press
Bantam Doubleday Dell Publishing Group, Inc.
1540 Broadway
New York, New York 10036

Library of Congress Cataloging in Publication Data

Krisher, Trudy.
    Spite fences / Trudy Krisher.
        p.   cm.
    Summary: As she struggles with her troubled relationship with her mother during the summer of 1960, a young girl is also drawn into the violence, hatred, and racial tension in her small Georgia town.
    ISBN 0-385-32088-4
    [1. Race relations—Fiction.   2. Mothers and daughters—Fiction.   3. Georgia—Fiction.]   I. Title.
PZ7.K8967Sp   1994
[Fic]—dc20   94-8665   CIP   AC

Manufactured in the United States of America

November 1994

10 9 8 7 6 5 4 3 2 1

BVG

For my father,
   who has taught me about the ties of history;
For my mother,
   who has taught me about the ties of family;
For my children,
   that they may discover the ways in which they are
   bound to both.

Chapter 1

Mama had the spoon in her fist. She was waving it in Daddy's face. They had started fighting again. First thing in the morning.

"A salesman's supposed to *sell* things, Henry Pugh," Mama said. "Not give 'em away *free.*" Daddy had lost his job as a salesman with Johnson & Johnson this summer. Mama blamed it on his sample policy.

I escaped to my room and picked up the camera. I held it to my chest, peering into the viewfinder. It was a used camera but a good one, given to me by Zeke. He had dug the camera out of his trading sack, passed it to me, and insisted that I take it with a nod of his head. "I won't take nothin' for it," he'd said. It was one of many times I'd been grateful to Zeke.

The camera had two lenses, one for the viewfinder, one for the film. One was on top of the other, like a figure eight. I peered down into the viewfinder, the voices in the other room making pictures in my mind.

1

I heard Mama yelling again. "First it's a sample of baby powder, Henry," she said. I imagined her shaking a can of baby powder under each armpit. *Aim. Click.*

"Then it's a bottle of baby oil." I could see her on the film, running drops of oil down each forearm, rubbing them in. *Advance the film. Trip the shutter.*

I could see her pinning Daddy to the wall, shaking the spoon in his face. "And finally," she shrieked, "you're lettin' 'em take that nice pink baby soap in the silver foil, which they're probably savin' for the wife for Christmas."

I heard my daddy too. "Stop bein' such a hard one for happiness, Izzy," he said. I peered into the lens, imagining him there, mopping his forehead with his red bandana. "The Lord loveth a cheerful giver." *Focus. Click.*

I needed to escape. Not just today. Almost every day since last summer. I didn't want to think about Mama and Daddy, but most of all I didn't want to think about what happened to Zeke. What happened last summer wasn't something I could talk about or even look at yet. The memory of it was like a picture you took when the people wouldn't hold still. I tried to keep that picture from coming into my mind.

My room was one way of escaping. The pecan tree in the corner of our yard was another. But my favorite way of escaping was going on a sneak with Pert Wilson. Nothing could get my mind off things like a sneak with Pert. On one sneak we had biked all the way to Troy for the double feature at the drive-in. Neither one of us had a red cent, so we stood outside the back fence, watching the picture even if we couldn't hear it, making up dialogue as we went along. Pert made the big strong cowboys in the John Wayne movie talk in high squeaky voices, and I made barking dog sounds for the people in *Old Yeller*.

Once we snuck over to Clifton Hill, where the rich folks live, to see Phillip Jubal Adkins's great-grand-daddy's leg. P. J. Adkins's great-granddaddy had his leg blown off at Chickamauga in 1863. He carried it back to Kinship in his saddlebag and had it stuffed by the local taxidermist. It was mounted with the boot still on because P.J.'s great-granddaddy had stole the boots off a dead Yankee and wanted to prove it. Pert and I snuck into Adkins's house and saw it, sure enough. It was inside a glass case with a brass lock, and the spurs on the boot looked like the cockleburs that clung to my jeans when I ran through Lem Patterson's cow pasture. I knew for sure it was an Adkins leg; Adkinses had fat knees even back then.

On another sneak we took Daddy's old can of red paint, putting our red handprints up all over Kinship. On the trash can near the base of the Civil War statue of John B. Gordon. On the trunks of the trees at Pearl Lake. When Mama found out, her own handprint rose up red on my own bottom.

But I could see that I wasn't going to be able to escape on a sneak with Pert Wilson today. Mama had plans. She had started up right after breakfast.

"Get on in here, Maggie Pugh," Mama called to me from the front room. "I'll bet you're in there a-fiddlin' with that ol' camera again. You'd best be puttin' it away now, girl. We got dustin' out here. And dishes."

I put down the camera and picked up the dustrag, heading into the living room. As I worked, I watched Mama out of the corner of my eye. I saw her pacing, rubbing her hands, and tying her scarf up tight around her bobby pins. They were familiar gestures to me. They meant she was set on work.

Gardenia had been concentrating on the strings of a cat's cradle when Mama hoisted her up, plunking her down on the kitchen stool. "Hey, Mama," Gardenia wailed, "you're knottin' my cradle strings."

"Now sit still and stop your squirmin', angel," Mama said. She was looking Gardenia over the way she looked over meat in Shriner's meat case. The announcer on the radio, got on a trade with Zeke, was saying how the coloreds in Alabama could use the city parks same as white now and how a private school was opening up in Atlanta for kids whose parents were members of the Ku Klux Klan. After that he announced the price of bush beans and the number of board feet of sawlogs this year.

Then Mama snapped her fingers and pointed to me. "Get the comb and brush from the bathroom cabinet, Maggie."

First she brushed all over the top of Gardenia's yellow head. Next she brushed the left side, and then she brushed the right, mumbling to herself. "That fool daddy of yours might have lost his job and that fool sister of yours ain't got no future better'n housework, but Izabelle Pugh's still got her baby Gardenia, and the

Hayes County Little Miss Pageant's next week. An angel as pretty as this one's as good as money in the bank."

Gardenia's blue eyes got round as globes. I stopped my mopping and looked into them.

Then Mama took the comb, parting Gardenia's hair in three sections. "Don't you think french braids would look nice, Maggie?"

She didn't wait for my answer. She was plaiting Gardenia's whole head lickety split, the comb clamped tight in her teeth like a pirate's knife. "Yes, sirree, Bob," she said. "The winner gets fifty dollars, an all-day shopping spree, and a chance to compete in the state pageant in Savannah."

The top of Gardenia's head looked like a braided basket. Mama pulled a daisy from the vase by the sink, sticking it behind Gardenia's ear. "Ohhhh-eee!" Mama said. "Ain't you somethin' else, baby!"

Then, just as quickly, she was ripping the whole thing out.

"Maybe we should try pigtails. I do declare pigtails with two big white ribbons might just do the trick," Mama was frowning. She was never satisfied.

"But I *hates* pigtails, Mama," screeched Gardenia. "Pigtails is for pigs."

First Mama had ripped out the braids. Now she scowled at the pigtails. This time she had decided on curls. "Curls," Mama declared, pulling out the big white ribbons, "is a sign of favor from the Lord. Curls is evidence that God put some extra time and attention into a person." I held my tongue, thinking of yet another way that Mama's God had ignored the Pughs. We had straight hair, every one.

Mama had rooted through the tithing box, pressing the change in my hand. "Now you run on up to Byer's Drugs, Maggie, and get me one of them Tonettes. I'm fixing to give your baby sister here a permanent wave. Take the extra, Maggie, and get you some film. We're gonna need pictures to show them judges at the beauty contest."

I was happy at the thought of the film, happier still at the thought of escaping Mama.

To get uptown from my house you had to go over ten blocks and down three, and you saw the way Kinship was laid out like a baseball diamond. Dividing it in two were the railroad tracks, running west to east through third base and first. Years ago Reginald Fenwick had tried to get the railroad to run through Kinship. Almost did too. They'd laid the tracks and built the depot before the railroad bosses changed their minds, routing it through Macon instead. Because they went right through the middle of Fenwick Street, the tracks were a daily reminder of what it was to live in Kinship: things you hoped for always threatening to run out.

Mayor Cherry still pushed hope. He liked to mention how a branch of the Troy School of Stenography had been started up in an old brick warehouse and how the Trailways made regular stops in town now. But Mayor Cherry was running for reelection this fall, and most folks knew that what there was of promise in Kinship now was mostly on account of Fenwick Acres.

Fenwick Acres was on the east edge of town in the direction of Troy, the county seat. Like first base Fenwick Acres was the place you were always trying to get to. Fenwick Acres was patio tables with umbrellas in the middle that looked like whales spouting water. Fenwick Acres was houses that were paid for with benefits that came from VA loans and GI bills. Most of all Fenwick Acres was people who had steady paychecks for TVs and washing machines. For that reason it was Mama's idea of heaven.

The houses in Fenwick Acres were followed by the shopping center with the new Piggly Wiggly, the drive-in up by Troy, and the shop that sold nothing but TVs and hi-fis. Not everybody liked Fenwick Acres. Especially Uncle Taps, Daddy's brother. He laughed and called it "Fertile Acres" since all the young couples who lived there had three or four babies. Mama sniffed whenever he told that joke.

Uncle Taps was my favorite relation. He got his name when he was in the Army. He was always going AWOL, so they made him play taps every morning. He was handy like Daddy. He worked jobs when, Mama said, he wasn't passed out in the hammock dead drunk. Uncle Taps had taken work over at Fenwick Acres and claimed the houses were made bad. Said he'd never trust a contractor from a big city like Charlotte who could throw up a whole house in two weeks. It didn't much matter what Uncle Taps or Mama or anybody else of our kind thought about it. Pughs would never get a pitch that could land us in Fenwick Acres. Even if we did, we'd swing and miss.

At the north end of town on higher ground was the rich part of Kinship. This was where Fenwicks and Adkinses and Matlacks lived. They had sloping lawns and maids and wills done up by fancy lawyers. The women had fair skin that burned in the sun when they went boating at the country club in Troy; the men wore their suit coats buttoned whatever the temperature and checked with their banker every day. Their money was passed down the family like their houses, and they made it in turpentine and pecan groves and pine boards and textiles from the sweat of people like Pughs. I secretly suspected that they got to second base the way most players did: by stealing it.

Our end of Kinship was on the west side of town. Like my own family our relations struggled to stay north of the railroad tracks. Uncle Taps lived near us, of course, and his wife, Aunt Ella, who cooked all day long. Mama's sister, Aunt Lolly, and her husband, Uncle Bunny, lived just a block from us. They were caretakers for Memory Lane Cemetery, the white cemetery. The colored cemetery was just a stone's throw away and didn't have full-time caretakers even though they had the most famous dead person in Kinship there. He was Dixon Mason, a male witch who once visited Queen Victoria and put her in a trance. Aunt Lolly and Uncle Bunny also ran a small business selling plastic flowers and memorial markers outside the gates of Memory Lane. They were rich as kings at Easter and poor the rest of the year.

Uncle Bunny always talked about the people who were buried in the cemetery like they were still alive.

His favorites were Mary Anthony, who was hired to teach the actors in *Gone With the Wind* to talk like us, and Bud Parker, a safecracker who ran with the Dalton gang. Uncle Bunny and Aunt Lolly were proud of their job because they said they got to keep watch on every member of the family. Baby Edgar Pugh, who died when he was an infant, and Cousin Milton, a Merritt on Mama's side who had smoked cigars and kept a mynah bird that whistled "Dixie."

All four of my grandparents were buried in Memory Lane, and I was always glad that Aunt Lolly and Uncle Bunny could look out for everyone, especially Grandma Pugh, my daddy's mama. Grandma Pugh loved to crochet. She crocheted afghans for everyone in the family. She'd come to your house and sit a spell and ask you what colors you liked and then she'd go off and make one for you. Just before she died, she was working on Gardenia's afghan. Since Gardenia was the youngest in the family, Gardenia's afghan had been the last one for Grandma Pugh to make. Daddy kept it in a special place at the foot of Gardenia's bed. He left the crochet hook exactly in the place where Grandma stopped.

Aunt Lolly was always fussing over Gardenia and me, spitting into her hanky and wiping the dirt from our cheeks or inspecting our necks to see if we had washed. Uncle Bunny could wiggle his ears and do magic tricks. You never could tell that he worked in a cemetery all day long. Their kids, our cousins Willie, Sally, and Lester, were a lot like Gardenia and me. Not counting Willie, who had three front teeth, there wasn't anything much to notice about them, so nobody ever did.

The people at our end of Kinship lived in small frame houses huddled near the turpentine plant and the textile factory that made raincoats for Sears and Roebuck. We filled up the trailer park and the local schools. We looked over the used-car section of Matlack's Ford dealership and bought the do-it-yourself kits from Bucky Gleason's hardware store. Except for Newell Puckett, who had a window air conditioner, there's not much to say about our end of Kinship. It was out in left field. Even so, the west part of Kinship was a darn sight better than south. South was on the other side of the tracks. South was colored.

I knew near about everybody in Kinship and passed half of them on the way to town. Olive Shriner worked out on her porch, beating rugs hung over the railing. She gave me a wave with her carpet beater. Martha Leonard was running her broom across her front porch. Martha lived on Madison Street with Charlie, her retarded boy. Every morning she swept not just the sidewalk but the curb. When Jim Bob Boggs held up the First National Bank of Kinship, they parked the getaway car in front of Martha's house. When she knocked on the windshield and asked the driver to move so she could sweep the curb, he did.

Boyce Johnson was painting his house. He painted one side of his house every summer. You could write the calendar from it. If he was painting north or south, it was an odd-numbered year. If he painted east or west, it was even. I used to think it was a clever way to mark the calendar, but after what he did to Zeke, I decided it was a dumb way to mark time. Boyce gave a frown in my direction; it was his way of saying hello. I wouldn't even look at him. I wasn't going to give a fellow like Boyce Johnson the time of day.

I missed seeing Zeke. There were still plenty of coloreds uptown. Missy Moses still sold sweet summer fruits from her apron in front of Shriner's Grocery. Rocker still passed out religious pamphlets in front of the bank. Reverend Potter still wore a straw hat when he walked the streets, and he still conducted prayer sessions for the lonesome people at the Trailways station who were just passing through. But I missed Zeke.

Ever since I was small, Zeke had been uptown, his trading cart stuffed with old sheets, aluminum foil, church keys, and broom handles. After last summer he kept to his side of town more and more, and I saw his creaking wheeled cart less and less. The thought of it wrenched my heart.

Zeke and I went way back. At first it was the cart that led me to Zeke. The drawers and compartments Zeke had made himself bulged with pomade and iron skillets and rhinestone dog collars. There was a statuette of a Chinese lady, her head tilted slightly, her hands folded quietly in front of her red kimono. There was a plastic flyswatter in the shape of a green frog. There was a pink bed jacket that matched a pair of pink mules. In my mind Zeke's cart was the closest thing Kinship had to the circus.

After that it was more than the cart; it was the things Zeke did for me. The summer before I started school,

Cousin Lonnie Burris, who was visiting from Milledge-ville for a few days, dropped the collection plate in church. It made a sound like heavy chains laid down link after link. On the scramble back into the plate a few dimes found their way down my socks. After all, it was Daddy's birthday the next Saturday, and I didn't have two nickels to rub together.

On Monday morning I headed straight to Zeke's cart. I had my heart set on the shaving mug on the corner of the second shelf. I held up two dimes.

Zeke looked over at me and squinted. "Where you be gettin' that money, Maggie Pugh?" he said.

"Found it, Zeke," I lied.

Zeke had been folding a white chenille bedspread. His big hands were making short work of it when he let a corner slip and bent to me. He smiled, his white teeth gleaming. He looked like he was fixing to laugh.

"Found them dimes just laying around on the street, Maggie?"

I nodded.

Zeke's mouth broke into a full grin and his big shoulders shook. "Is that money laying around on the street any relation to the money that's 'sposed to be growin' on trees, Maggie?"

I hung my head. It was filled with Baptist sin. That I stole was bad enough. But then I had to go and lie about it.

Zeke put his face right next to mine. "Never be afraid of the truth," Zeke said, his eyes locking mine. Then he wrapped my fingers around the handle of the shaving mug, pressing it into my hand. "It's yours, Maggie. No charge."

I wasn't sure that I'd ever be able to speak the truth without fear, but I was sure that I was grateful, and it was the first of many times that I'd be grateful to Zeke. Pughs never got anything free.

After that it was the things Zeke told me that bound me to him. "Lordy, Maggie Pugh," he'd say, dusting a cracked china cup and saucer, "the things folks think. Don't give a lick that Lem Patterson got drunk on corn likker and beat LouAnn. All's they can talk about is the way he left his cows in the field, mooing to be milked." Once I saw Zeke trading Reverend Potter a bookmark for a pair of nail clippers. Afterward he said, "Reverend Potter's a real fine gent'man. Don't put on no fancy airs. Shaves with the same soap he takes a bath with."

I loved the stories Zeke told me of how things arrived at his cart. My daddy's new shaving mug, for instance. Zeke said it was sold at the estate sale after Lawrence Fenwick died and bought by the Alhambras, who started a taxi service, which Mama thought made them uppity coloreds. The Alhambras gave the mug to the Tabernacle Baptist Church white elephant sale, where it was bought by Joey Stoddard, whose daddy ran the white barber shop and surely didn't need another shaving mug. It was given to Zeke along with razor straps, old cloths, cracked combs, and half-used ends of soap when Douglas Stoddard did his spring cleaning. And then it ended up with me. "Things in Kinship get swapped around like rumors," Zeke said. "Truth don't go out much."

In the end it wasn't the cart or what he did or what he said that tied me to Zeke. It was finally just Zeke himself. Thinking about him reminded me of what Mama said about the difference between milk glass and cut crystal. Said you could always tell when crystal was real. Crystal rang with a sound that was pure and high. Mama knew because she had run her fingers around the rim of Tillie Fenwick's water goblets at the UDC get-acquainted tea while Tillie was filling her silver platter with squares of raspberry crumb cake. When Mama heard the proper ring, she declared those glasses were real. It was the same with Zeke. Everything Zeke said rang true to me. I swear to goodness that I missed him.

Although the first thing I looked for in the center of town was always Zeke, the first thing most folks noticed was the bank building. It sat in the center of Fenwick Street and faced north. Like the pitcher's mound it was smack dab in the middle of things. Every day the fortunes of Kinship passed in and out of its heavy brass doors. From the same solid oak desk were written the foreclosure notices when the Shriners' cotton fields were ruined by boll weevils and the improvement loans when the Matlacks expanded the car dealership. The daily deposits from Russell Simmons's pecan factory and Clarence Adkins's sawmill and the daily withdrawals that went into Raymond Niedermayer's gambling and Ira Gaines's pretty women were made from the same bank window. Into the big black safe of the First National Bank was deposited the money for Pearl Jackson's Christmas fund, the start-up costs for

Frank Alhambra's taxi company, and the Sunday collection from every church in town. First National was about the only place in Kinship that didn't care about your color.

From the steps of the bank you could see the statue of General John B. Gordon to the east at one end of Fenwick Street and the top of the cross of Thaddeus Adkins's cemetery plot to the west at the other. Straight across from the bank was Byer's Drugs, which faced south. It sat between Gleason's Hardware, where Bucky Gleason tied crepe-paper streamers to his electric fans to beef up sales, and Millie's Curly Q Salon that smelled of nail-polish remover and permanent-wave solution. Down a block was Shriner's Grocery, the Bijou Theater, and the Texaco station. Over one was the feed store and the Trailways depot.

Elmer Byer had hung a set of jingle bells from his front door ever since I could remember, so the door to Byer's Drugs gave a little jingle every time you went through it. When the bells jangled behind you, they made you feel like buying stuff. Today I really could.

I liked nearly everything about Byer's Drugs. The beauty aids section. The pharmacy. The comic-book rack. The fact that my friend Pert Wilson worked the lunch counter. The only thing I didn't much like was Hazel Boggs. Like most of her family she was mean and lazy. When she worked the register, she made you wait while she finished filing her nails or looking through the pictures left off for developing that were none of her business. I gave Hazel the money for the

Tonette and the film, and she gave me a dirty look with my change. Then I headed on home.

When I returned from Byer's, Mama whisked an old white dishcloth under Gardenia's chin, fastening it at her neck with a clothespin. Mama bent over Gardenia's head all afternoon while I dusted and mopped.

"This stuff's icky, Mama," Gardenia said, holding her nose as Mama splashed her crown with waving lotion, the sharp smell of ammonia piercing the air. The radio announcer was singing the praises of Vidalia onions in between bits of news.

"Shut that dern radio off, Maggie," Mama said. "I can't stand all that news about the coloreds. All that stuff about using the public parks when their own is twice as good as what white folks got. And the Kennedys. John Kennedy this, and John Kennedy that. If the American people's stupid enough to elect a Catholic, we'll be takin' orders not from the President of the United States, but from the pope of Rome."

I flipped the dial, watching Mama out of the corner of my eye, thinking how she never took orders from anyone. She examined the thin squares of white endpaper, holding them reverently to the light. Next Mama rolled each strand of hair onto rollers that wiggled and squirmed in her hands like pink worms, fastening each to Gardenia's scalp with a pinch, a sigh, and an "Owwww, Mama! That hurts!"

When she had finished, Mama brushed out the curls, training them into separate ringlets around her bony fingers. Then she stood back, admiring her work. "Go get your camera now, Maggie," she said.

I struggled to open the camera, grateful for the film. I'd checked out a photography book from the Kinship Public Library to study how to take good pictures and to see how you loaded the film in case I ever got any. I'd been practicing with the camera, snapping pretend pictures, ever since Zeke had given it to me. I'd head out by the depot, composing the lines of railroad track through the viewfinder, noticing the way they disappeared at the horizon line. I'd head up to the feed mill, composing the piles of feed sacks through the lens, snapping imaginary pictures again and again.

I finished loading the film and closed the camera. I peered down into the viewfinder, focusing on Gardenia. Through the glass I saw that everything about Gardenia was small and delicate. Her clear white skin, filmy as the gauze from Daddy's sample case, stretched across the high bones of her cheeks. The blue lines of veins along her neck looked like underground streams, giving her a cool, fresh look. A bridge of light-brown freckles ran across the top of her cheeks, forcing your eye to travel back and forth between the two blue pools of her eyes. Her nose tilted up at the end, fragile as glass.

I felt my blood rush the way it did whenever I looked through a lens. "Hold still, Gardenia," I said. "Say, 'Cheese.' "

She moved at the last moment, the instant I tripped the shutter. She had scratched her nose, wrinkling it as she scratched.

I knew the image would be blurred.

My hand shook as I remembered the blurry images in my own mind and tried again.

"Hold still, angel," Mama said. Mama fluffed Gardenia's curls while I refocused. "Watch the birdie!"

The images came rushing back, black and white all mixed together like a double exposure. The patterns of light and dark swam up from last summer, and I concentrated on the images in the viewfinder, willing away the images in my own head.

As I tripped the shutter, I wondered why.

Chapter 2

I asked, "Why?" all summer long. Why was I standing before this pile of dishes? Why was I in this stranger's house? Why did I have to live in a hateful place like Kinship, Georgia?

The dishes were the easiest to explain. I had always been good at cleaning. Mama said so herself, and Mama was always right.

What Mama had really said was "You ain't much to look at, Maggie. It's a good thing you can work." Mama gave a compliment the way she gave spankings. With the back of her hand.

The stranger was something different. Lord knows I needed the work. Mama stuck a card up at the Piggly Wiggly. *Big Strong Girl Likes to Clean, Etc. EXMOOR 6281,* it read. Mama even took some extra cards to her once-a-month canasta club. I hated the thought of being passed around like cookies.

But in the end it was Zeke who got me the job. I

told Mama that her ad had worked, that a new couple over in Fenwick Acres needed someone to clean. She never knew Zeke was the one to get me the job.

Things had changed in Kinship this whole year, and it seemed most of the changes had something to do with Zeke. The change you noticed most, of course, was the way Zeke was hardly ever uptown. He'd been in the center of things there for as long as I could remember. He knew the number of drunks on Saturday night and the amount of the collection plate on Sunday morning. He knew the state of Martha Leonard's rheumatism and Waldo Rumple's gout. He knew which relations had come to town and which ones had got mad and left. He knew that if Alf Linderman had just made a move in the continuing checker game in front of the feed store by the time you left for the bank, then Ray Snowden would still be thinking over his next move by the time you got back. But even though Zeke knew everybody's business, he never let on about it unless you asked and he decided to tell. Zeke was different from Lucy Tibbs, Kinship's switchboard operator. She knew everybody's business and blabbed.

So naturally Zeke knew my daddy had lost his job and naturally I was pleased as punch at the chance to make some money, but, Lord, the job itself didn't sound so all-fired natural.

He spied me at Edmonia Jennings's tomato stand. Edmonia Jennings grew tomatoes every summer at the patch at the side of her house. She had dozens of bushes, and the red tomatoes and green vines all mixed up together put me in mind of Christmas. Once her tomatoes got ripe, Edmonia moved back and forth between the side yard and the front porch all summer long, growing and picking and selling her tomatoes in what struck me as a handy way to run a business. Mama sent me to buy some of Edmonia's tomatoes because they were always the best early tomatoes in Kinship. That plus Mama wouldn't be caught dead trading in person on the south side of town.

I was digging down into one of Edmonia's tomato baskets when I heard Zeke's voice. I'd know that voice in the dark. It was deep and trembly like a slide trombone. "Heard about your mama's ad, Maggie," he said. "Still need work?"

I stopped my digging and smiled up at Zeke, hoping my smile said it was sure fine to see him. "Sure do, Zeke," I said. "Work and money are the same things to Pughs, and I don't have either one."

I started rooting in the tomato basket again. Some of the tomatoes were still attached to fuzzy lengths of vine that felt like caterpillars when they brushed my fingers. I picked up a big firm tomato, pushing on it to feel how ripe it was.

"I think I can get you somethin', Maggie," Zeke said.

I stopped pushing on the tomato and looked at him. "Sure 'nough, Zeke?"

"But it's real special, Maggie. It's a job for a real special person."

"What do you mean by that, Zeke?"

"Well," Zeke said, looking around, waiting to finish until Edmonia had gone back into the house and the screen door made a little slap behind her. He began talking again when he saw that only Lewis Jennings, Edmonia's son, was left on the porch. Lewis was climbing on and off the front porch railing; after he tired of climbing, he began jumping off the porch onto the grass below. "It requires someone who can clean real good," Zeke said.

"That's me, for sure, Zeke," I said. "But being able to clean's not anything *special.*"

"It's special to your employer, Maggie. But there's something more to this job than just cleanin'."

"How you mean, Zeke?"

"Well, you might have to deliver stuff."

"What kind of stuff?"

"Oh, letters to the post office. Packages to me. Maybe a few things to Reverend Potter."

"Zeke," I said, "what's so special about that?" I had decided that the big tomato in my hand wasn't ripe enough. I bent back to the baskets. The tomatoes still gave off the sharp green smell of their vines.

"It's special to your employer, Maggie," he said again. "It's special to me."

"Well, Zeke," I said, "I can't see what's so special about cleaning up somebody's mess and taking a few things to the post office."

Zeke's big hand pulled a tomato from the basket next to mine. His entire palm closed around it. "I want you to listen to me, now, Maggie," he said, tilting his head in my direction. "The job requires cleanin' and deliverin' a few things. But that's not really what makes it special."

22

"What does, Zeke? What does make it special, then?" I wasn't understanding him.

"What makes it special, Maggie," he said, looking around again before he went on—Lewis had run next door and was throwing sticks at the neighbor's dog— "what makes it special," he said, "is that the job requires you to keep secrets."

"Secrets?" I asked. On the ground lay split tomatoes seeping juice.

Zeke grinned. "These secrets is so secret, I can't even tell you, Maggie. Best I can tell you is that for every question that might come to your mind, the right answer is 'Don't ask.' "

"Well, now, how to goodness can anybody in Kinship expect to keep anything a secret? You know that this is the nosiest place in the world."

"Sure is," Zeke said. "That's why I want you for the job."

"Me?"

Zeke nodded. "One thing I know, Maggie, is that Maggie Pugh knows when to talk and when to keep quiet. Been knowin' that for a long time now."

Inside I felt myself swelling up just a tiny bit. I knew Zeke was right. If there was anyone in Kinship who could keep a secret, it was me. After all, I'd been living with Mama for almost fourteen years.

I'd work two days a week, Zeke said. I'd get five dollars each time.

"What's the name of my employer?" I asked.

"Don't ask," Zeke said.

"What will the messages be about?" I asked.

"Don't ask," Zeke said.

"Why is this job so all-fired secret?" I asked. This time I gave a little stamp with my foot. "Zeke," I said, "something's fishy. Seems to me you're asking me to keep a secret when I don't even know what the secret is. So what is it I got to keep secret about, Zeke?"

"Don't ask," he said. Zeke looked at me and smiled. I smiled back, and then we both busted out laughing.

Before he left, Zeke pressed the key in my hand and gave me directions. He warned me to enter by the side door so I couldn't be seen. He told me I could start on Monday. Then we shook hands to seal the contract. I wondered if I had done anything wrong. White folks said you weren't supposed to shake hands with coloreds.

When I got home with over a dozen ripe tomatoes and change to boot, Mama never even thanked me, but inside I quietly gave thanks to Zeke, wondering about my employer all day Saturday and Sunday while I swept the porch, cleaned the tiles in the bathroom, and washed the downstairs windows for Mama.

When I headed for work on Monday, I almost missed my employer's house. Zeke was right. You could miss it if you weren't looking. It was south of town, but it was way west, almost all the way to Fenwick Swamp. I could get to it on my bicycle most of the way, but when the paved road turned to gravel and then to dirt, I had to walk. I had thought the only thing out there was swamp grass and mosquitoes, but the place looked like something someone had once used for a summer cabin, a place where they could try to rest up from all the trouble that was Kinship.

My employer's house was up on stilts and set back from the road. All but the front porch was cloaked in woods. Spanish moss hung from the trees, draping the unpainted slats of the house. The house crouched under the branches the way I felt all summer long. Hiding. Keeping secrets. I couldn't see the fuss about coming in the side. You'd miss the house if you didn't know it was there.

I stood at the threshold of the side door, looking around. There was a tiny mudroom before you got to the main part of the house. Muddy footprints were caked all over the floor. Didn't my stranger know about wiping his feet?

One rain boot drooped by the door, its partner nowhere in sight. Hadn't my stranger heard that pairs were meant to be kept together?

Scattered piles of *The Atlanta Constitution* were thrown all over the mudroom. Didn't my stranger know about folding things neatly? Lord knows what Mama'd have to say about that. Her eyes spit nails after Daddy folded a road map.

I peeked around the door to the main part of the house, sniffing the odor of cough syrup. I remembered Gardenia with the croup last winter, barking like a seal, milking Mama's sympathy for all she was worth. I wondered about my stranger. He was messy, Lord knows. Was he sick too?

The kitchen was off to the right. There were dishes everywhere. In the sink. Beside the drainboard. Piled on the tops of kitchen chairs. A line of ants marched around empty Coke bottles that looked like miniature glass bowling pins.

What are you going to do now, Maggie Pugh? How are you going to manage this?

Mama would have glared at this mess and blamed the closest person.

Daddy would have cast his eye to heaven, searching for a line of Scripture.

Gardenia would have turned on her patent leather heels and scurried back into her bedroom to play with her dolls.

And me?

I did what I knew.

And what I knew was work. Scrubbing a sink with Bon Ami. Wringing a mop like a chicken neck. Dusting knickknacks with diapers that had hugged my own bottom.

The detergent foamed under the rushing tap, and I put on the gloves lying on the counter. The rubber gave a little snap as I pulled it over my fingers.

Mama had an order to everything. Even dishes. You did glasses first. Then plates and cups. Next silverware. You saved pots and pans for last. Setting things straight was Mama's passion. "A straight house, a straight life," Mama said.

I stared at the scraps floating in the sink: dried egg yolks, bacon ends, coffee grounds. They made me think of this summer in Kinship: Daddy out of work, Mama taking in rich ladies' laundry, me washing dishes for a sloppy stranger, Zeke handed shame like it was supper.

I washed pile after pile of dishes, following Mama's orders. I heard the glasses squeak under my fingers, watched the dinner plates gleam in the light. I scrubbed carefully between the tines of the forks the way Daddy scrubbed between my toes when I was small. I dunked the Coke bottles under the suds, hoping to outsmart the ants.

I set the last pot on the drainboard and snapped off my gloves, hunting for a towel to start the wiping. A single soppy towel sagged by the sink. I searched for a dry one in drawers, on shelves, in cupboards. My stranger was hopeless. I'd even have to remember to bring my own towels next time. But I perked up, remembering Mama's rules. "Dishes got to be air dried, Maggie. Towels carry germs."

I moved to the trash can, overflowing like Zeke's cart. Tiny flakes of cereal crunched under my feet like snow. An empty tin of cherry pipe tobacco stuck out of the trash, explaining the sickroom smell. Empty soup cans littered the counters. Every single one was chicken-with-rice. Mama disapproved of people who ate from cans. They were temporary people, people who didn't take life serious. Hoboes. Gypsies. I tossed the cans into the trash.

As I stomped the trash down with my foot, a leaf of S & H stamps stuck to my heel. So my employer was rich, rich enough to throw out trading stamps. I thought about wiping off the stamps, taking them home to Mama. She needed an electric skillet, and it was ten and a half books. But Pughs didn't steal, even though they were poor enough to need to. I laid the stamps neatly on top of the stove.

After I had bundled up the trash and swept the kitchen floor, I moved to the living room. It was like one of those white elephant sales Mama dragged us to. Piles of books climbed to the ceiling. Ashtrays were heaped with flakes of tobacco. But the desk beat everything hands down. Why were there so many stacks of papers, so many pencils, so many bottles of ink?

I wiped my sweaty forehead on my sleeve, taking a closer look. There were dozens of letters, some hand-written, some typed. They were ragged at the ends where my stranger had opened the envelopes. There was a bill from Hayes County Electric & Light, a bill from Southern Bell. They were both unopened. Didn't my stranger know that when a bill landed in your mailbox, you opened it straightaway and then squinted over it to make sure it was right?

There were reams of paper all over the desk. Some of them were filled with complicated mathematical symbols. The only one I recognized was "pi." It looked like the mark Mrs. Parello put on my compositions when I needed to start a new paragraph. Some of the papers were torn from legal pads, words scribbled all up and down the yellow pages. A law book, thick as a Bible, lay open on the chair at the desk. There were bottles of fountain-pen ink in every color. Blue, black, blue-black, red, green.

My eye buzzed like a fly over the contents of the desk, landing on a note at the right-hand corner. It was written on official-looking paper. At the top of the paper was a seal from a college in Atlanta. Underneath the seal in neat raised letters were the words *George Andrew Hardy, Ph.D., Assistant Professor of Mathematics*. My heart gave a start, for underneath those words were these:

Dear Miss Pugh,

Our arrangement will be for Mondays and Thursdays. Compensation will be five dollars per diem. Employment, of course, is conditional on your fulfillment of the requirements set forth by Mr. Freeman.

There is no expectation that you improve the entire house at once. The challenge, I'm certain, is formidable. Perhaps you can begin with the kitchen and bedroom and tackle the desk if you have time.

You have come highly recommended by Mr. Freeman, so I thank you in advance for your assistance.

Sincerely,
George Hardy

So my stranger wasn't from around Kinship. And he had a name. Hardy. George Hardy. George Andrew Hardy. A name. And an occupation. And handwriting that was firm and bold. Not the handwriting of someone who lolled around in a pigsty.

I had always been a good reader, but some of the words puzzled me. *Formidable. Per diem.* What about *compensation?* Wasn't that just plain *money?* Didn't George Hardy know that people in Kinship didn't talk like that? Was Mr. Hardy a slob and a show-off to boot?

The "Mr. Freeman" business got me too. Didn't he know that "Mr. Freeman" shuffled around town, trading sheets of tin foil for cotton balls, swapping whisk brooms for plastic flowers? Didn't Mr. Hardy know that everybody just called him Zeke? How could an assistant professor of mathematics be so plain-out dumb?

But I had to admit it. There were things I liked about what I had read. I liked being "highly recommended." I had never been highly recommended for anything in my life.

I liked being thanked for my "assistance" too. The best I got from Mama after a hard morning of work was "Well, now, Maggie. You're slow, but your work ain't too shabby."

I liked the green five-dollar bill on the top of the note best of all. It was thanks enough.

I stuffed the money in the pocket of my jeans and tackled the desk. I stacked the opened letters neatly, wrapping them in a rubber band. I laid the unopened bills on top. I made squared-off stacks of the papers with mathematical scribblings. I gathered the legal sheets together with a paper clip. I put the pencils, scattered like Gardenia's pickup sticks, into an empty coffee mug on the corner of the desk.

But the ink bottles were a puzzle. They were a mishmash of greens, blues, reds. Each of them, like ladies who had mixed up their hats, wore different lids, so that a person who wanted red ink would have to find it under the black lid. Or a person who wanted blue would have to look under green. Like the messy stranger with the neat handwriting, it made no sense to me.

Figure it out, Maggie Pugh. Haven't you been highly recommended?

I unscrewed the lids, matching inks and tops. Then I took a pencil, a piece of paper, and wrote a note of my own. It read:

Excuse me, Mr. Hardy, sir, but I put the ink tops on straight. You can find the red ink under the red lid, the blue ink under the blue. Etc. Etc. I hope this doesn't confuse you.
Sincerely,

Magnolia Pugh (Housekeeper)

I brightened at my solution and moved back to the kitchen, taking pencil and paper with me. I laid another note beside the sparkling Coke bottles. *I don't mean to be bold, Mr. Hardy,* I wrote, *but if you wash out your Coke bottles, you won't get ants.*

Then I wrote another note, setting it atop the germ-free dishes on the drainboard. *You could use half a dozen dish towels, Mr. Hardy. Gleason's Hardware has them on sale this month.*

I smiled. I hadn't been highly recommended for nothing.

Then I moved to Mr. George Hardy's bedroom.

It was tucked at the back of the house in full view of the woods. The blinds tilted at an angle. They were coated with dust, but through them I saw yellow pines and loblollies and caught a glimpse of a pond.

A gold terry-cloth robe was flung on the bed. As I hung it up, the length of it fell past my ankles. Mr. George Hardy was a head taller than me, and I was a tall girl.

The bedsheets had been kicked out at the end, and as I tucked in the corners, I saw that my stranger was not just tall like me. He was restless too.

As I began to fold down the top sheet, I saw the open pages of a magazine with a bright yellow cover. It lay at the edge of the pillows, under George Hardy's reading light.

Across the page was spread a picture of an African village, the dusty browns of the desert in the distance, the villagers themselves in the foreground. The women held bowls at their waists and babies at their hips, and the children sat on the ground before gap-toothed men holding spears and shields. The African chieftain in the center of the picture caught my eye. He towered above the villagers. He stood tall and proud, his head held high, his long flowing robe a blaze of royal golds and purples. Something about the way he held his head reminded me of Zeke.

I turned the page, curious and eager. And then I jumped back. Shocked. Horrified. My eye scanned a series of photographs. In one of them naked African women waded in a blue lagoon. Their breasts, floppy and huge, hung down to their belly buttons. In another a white man with a safari hat on his head and a camera around his neck stood with his arms around a whole slew of them. The last one showed a native man, his head thrown back to laugh, his arms outstretched, the muscles in his limbs twisted like roots. And he was standing under the spreading leaves of a tropical tree. Buck naked.

I quickly shut the pages of the *National Geographic*. My heart was thumping in my chest. I yanked up the bedspread, smoothing it down with my hands. I felt for the five-dollar bill in my pocket, anxious to slip quietly out of this stranger's house.

As I quickly plumped the pillows, my mind raced. What kind of a person would take pictures of a naked man like that? What kind of a man would lie in bed looking at them under his reading light? What kind of a girl would clean for a man like that? Sweet Jesus, there was so much dirt in Kinship.

Then I ran to the desk, scrawling a final note, placing it on top of the pillows.

Dear Mr. Hardy,
Thank you for my job. But could you please close up your magazines before I come on Thursday?
Sincerely,
M. Pugh (Housekeeper)

Chapter 3

If you lived in Kinship, you had your place.

If you lolled your head, you got sent to the school for retards in Macon.

If you were colored, you couldn't take a seat on the main floor of the Bijou in town. You had to sit in the balcony.

If you lived in the west end of town like the rest of our kind, you had no money, no talent, no brains, and no ancestors to brag on. You were snubbed by the surely rich people to the north and the nearly rich people to the east. Only the color of your skin kept you on the right side of the tracks.

And if your name was Pugh, you ate jelly every morning of your cotton-picking life.

We had jelly on toast, jelly on bread, jelly in a soupy mess of eggs that Mama called an omelette. Jelly was Mama's way of rescuing us from the ranks of the no-account.

"Come on, Magnolia," Mama'd say. "Why don't you try a little of that marmalade on that end of toast? It's got little bits of real orange peel in it. Makes you think you're on a trip to Florida."

Then she'd turn to Gardenia. "Now, baby," she called her although Gardenia was fully seven her last birthday. "Wouldn't my little precious angel like to spread some jelly on her biscuit?"

Every day of my life I faced a glass jar of Wegman's jellies and preserves. We ate jelly, and Mama collected the colored glasses. That June she nagged Daddy into building shelves in the front parlor window to put her glass collection on display. After he had hammered them up, Mama gave a satisfied sigh, hoping she was finally equal to all the Kinship ladies who had the leisure to collect spoons in racks or thimbles or ceramic owls. Mama had twenty-four jelly glasses that summer. They were lined up like Easter eggs in a carton—pink, purple, yellow, blue. The window squares let the light shine through, and the parlor window in our house sparkled like stained glass.

"Stop lickin' your fingers, Maggie," Mama said, frowning at the way I got the sticky stuff off my hands. "Do like Gardenia does, dippin' her napkin in her water glass and wipin' up like a lady."

I looked across the table at my sister Gardenia. When Mama wasn't looking, she stuck out her tongue at me.

Mama never knew just how hateful Gardenia could be. All Mama saw was a precious little angel.

The worst time was at night. At prayer time. Right

before Gardenia went to sleep. Mama beamed as she listened to her pray. Gardenia always ended with "God Bless Molly, Golly, and Polly, Angel and No-No, Griselda Ortega, Meg and Peg, and Mr. and Mrs. Rowe on their fishing trip to Canada."

Molly, Golly, and Polly were Gardenia's goldfish. Angel and No-No were dolls. One was sweet and obedient, the other ornery as the devil. Griselda Ortega was her Spanish doll, the one with the combs in her thick black hair, and Meg and Peg were doll twins. Mr. and Mrs. Rowe had come back from their fishing trip to Canada at least two years ago, but Mama thought it sweet the way Gardenia still remembered them in her prayers.

For years I refused to pray publicly like Gardenia, promising Mama that I'd pray silently once I got in bed. But Mama didn't know that I never prayed at all anymore. Since what happened last summer, I didn't hold much stock in praying.

"We got work to do this mornin', Maggie," Mama said, patting Gardenia on the head. "Your daddy and I is addin' some touches to the yard. You'd better start clearin' the table."

Mama was vain of her "touches." They included the rosebushes in the back, the mailbox on which she had painted some Georgia peaches, and a pink flamingo stuck on a spike that Daddy brought back from a J & J convention in Tallahassee. This morning those touches would include purple periwinkles set out by the stoop.

As I cleared the dishes, Mama's voice floated through the kitchen window.

36

"No, Henry," she said. "The periwinkles is going in *front,* not the *back.* Don't you know no better? Anybody comin' to visit's gonna come in the front. Ain't nobody but the milkman comin' to the back stoop. You don't waste a good flat of periwinkles on no milkman. You know as good as I do that Miriam Simpson'll be bringin' my application to the UDC any day now, and she'll sure to goodness come in the front."

UDC stood for the United Daughters of the Confederacy. Mama was dying to be a member. To join the UDC it didn't matter whether you were rich. You just had to have a blood relation who fought for the South in the War Between the States, and you had to prove it by sending to Washington for papers. Mama had a great-grandfather, Ermal Vesey Merritt, who she hoped would get her in. I thought it was funny the way a dead person could get you into a club.

I never knew how Daddy stood the nagging, but I knew what Daddy would do. Daddy would quietly lift the packs of flowers, hauling them to the front of the house, silently muttering Scripture. He reminded me of one of those Chinese oxen in my social-studies text, a yoke slung across his back.

"Lordy, Henry Pugh," Mama said, admiring her plans for the flowers. "Won't it be *beautiful!* Now," she said, shifting her gaze to the yard of the Boggs family, who lived next door, "if'n we can just get them ol' lazy Boggs to beautify their lawn like Pughs!"

I wrung out the dishcloth, thinking there was nothing beautiful about Boggses. Never had been and never would be. Nobody knew that better than me. I looked down at my hands and saw that I had twisted the cloth so hard it was nearly dry. Just thinking of the Boggses did something to me.

"Get on out here, Maggie," Mama shouted. "We got a pile of weedin' to do. Bring Gardenia on out with you. And get a paper sack. You can weed, and Gardenia can throw out the stumps."

Gardenia wandered outside, trailing me. She had Angel, golden and delicate, in her tiny fingers. Mama had won the doll for her at the Easter Pageant raffle up at First Baptist Church. There was a big fight about it. Some of the Baptists thought a raffle was a form of gambling. The way Gardenia was brushing Angel's yellow hair, I could see that Gardenia wouldn't be much help with the stumps.

Mama carried on about the Boggses while Daddy bent his back to the hoe. "Just look at the way they let that paint peel, Henry. Makes people think the whole neighborhood's goin' to the dogs. You'd think they'd take some pride in bein' white. And look at that ol' cocklebur patch they call a yard, Henry Pugh," she said. "Boggs can grow only two things. Cockleburs. And babies."

I bent to the ground with my trowel, stabbing at the earth. Earlier, when I'd had the dishcloth in my hand, I had wanted to wring something hard. Now, the point of the trowel under my fingers, I wanted to root it out as well. Cockleburs and babies were bad. So were the drunken rages and the sawed-off shotguns and the prison sentences. But Mama didn't know what I knew about the Boggses: I knew things even worse.

38

Since last summer, I had kept those secrets to myself. Everybody in Kinship knew that Cecil Boggs drank and lost his job. Everybody in Kinship knew that Maxine Boggs brought home unwanted babies. Everybody in Kinship knew that Jim Bob Boggs got ten to twenty in the Reidsville State Pen. But nobody but me knew about the horror that was Virgil Boggs. Mama was afraid of poverty. Daddy was afraid of Hell. Magnolia April Pugh was afraid of Virgil Boggs.

He was seventeen and spiteful. Dropped out of school at twelve. Did the regular bad things like broken windows, slashed tires, shoplifting. But Virgil Boggs wasn't just regular bad. He was a different kind of bad. He was mean.

Once Virgil and his friends tied little Mickey Harris to the tailpipe of the skeeter truck, the big noisy machine that sprayed insecticide in summer, keeping down the mosquitoes that bred out by the swamp. They stuffed Mickey's mouth with his own undershirt to stop the hollering. And when the skeeter truck started up, spraying its great white cloud, Mickey Harris choked on insecticide all afternoon, passed out, and went into a coma. Mickey's mind hasn't ever been the same since.

Of course, Sheriff Keiter tried to get Mickey Harris's folks to press charges, but they never did. His own parents said Mickey was slow to begin with. Inside, I suspected what they feared: that Virgil Boggs and his friends might try something even worse.

Just this summer Virgil and his pals kidnapped Charlie, Martha Leonard's retarded boy. They hooded his head and took him out to the Negro Park in Attica, where they threw him on the tire swing, twisting and turning him, making Charlie crazy with dizziness. They left him, late at night, roped and naked, on top of the statue of General John B. Gordon. Sheriff Keiter had to get a cherry picker to haul Charlie Leonard down, and Martha Leonard's heart was near broke. She would have pressed charges, but Charlie's head was hooded, and he couldn't be sure who had got him. Besides, who would believe a retard? It was almost as bad as being colored.

Mama beamed with pride at her flowers and then hovered over me, inspecting my work. "Comparin' Boggs and Pughs is like comparin' night and day, Maggie Pugh," Mama said, her hands crooked behind her waist like chicken wings. "Or like comparin' black and white."

"Except, Mama," I pointed out, loosening the dirt around another dandelion head, "we're both *white.*"

Mama sniffed at that, and I grabbed the ragged top of the dandelion, giving it a firm, steady pull. The taproot came all the way out. I dusted my hands on my jeans.

"We may both be white, Miss Know-It-All. And we may both be poor," Mama said. "But Pughs ain't trash. You remember that, Miss Smarty. You ain't too dumb to see the difference, is you, Maggie?"

Looking up at Mama, who was glaring down at me, I was smart enough to hold my tongue. If I'd learned anything at all through my whole life, it was that Pughs weren't trash. Pughs amounted to something. Leastways they were hoping they could. It was why Mama had been so proud of Daddy's sample case. It looked like a cross between a doctor's bag and a lawyer's briefcase. She was hoping that sample case meant that Daddy was headed right for the Rotary. She hadn't figured on his getting fired. Mama didn't look on things the way I did. I didn't mind that people didn't take much notice of another family of poor white folks.

I stared up at her, searching her face. Often this summer I caught myself staring at things: the bend in Daddy's back, the delicacy of Gardenia's fingers, the magazines in a stranger's house. And now Mama. I stared at the long horse face with the ears high up and the jaw low down. At the way her mouth made a straight thin line that balanced on the round ball of chin. I stared at the hair pinned up with bobby pins and the scarf wrapped around the head to disguise the fact.

"Stop that starin', Maggie," Mama said. "There you go gettin' that ol' bug-eyed look in your eyes again. A-starin' just like an old mule. You stop that now, you hear?"

Mama folded her arms across her chest and looked over at the house next door. "I got half a mind to march right over there and tell them Boggs what I think of their housekeepin'," she said. As she talked, she gave a little stamp with her foot.

I stood up and faced her. "Mama," I said, "you leave the Boggses alone, you hear? They're mad enough on their own, Mama. You don't give them help with it." As I spoke, I punched at the air with my trowel. "And I do believe one thing, Mama. I truly do. If you go stirring up trouble with Boggses, you really *do* have half a mind!"

Mama raised her arm like a whip. "That's enough of your back talk, girl. There's nothin' I hate worse'n a youngster sassin' an elder."

Daddy came up behind her, putting his hand on Mama's shoulder. "Leave the girl be, Izzy. Ain't gonna make no difference," Daddy said. "Boggs ain't gonna improve their housekeepin' on your say-so."

"Well, Henry Pugh, it sure ain't gonna improve if you never say nothin' about it. Besides, don't you hate all the briars and grasses chokin' up that yard?"

"Don't much like it, I reckon, Izzy."

"And what's the point of my truck tire planted with pretty geraniums, if all you see next door is oceans of chickweed?"

"Well, Izzy, I guess the birds like chickweed well enough."

"Birds? Birds, Henry Pugh? That just means there's more birds to come here and peck at our new-planted seeds. And do you like the way all them birds plop their bird-do all over your windshields? Do you?"

"No, Izzy. I guess I don't." Daddy rarely complained, but one thing he didn't like was bird-do on his windshields. And the Boggses had mulberry bushes. That meant *purple* bird-do.

Daddy shrugged, giving in. Mama always had the last word.

Now she snapped her fingers, calling for me.

"Yes, Mama," I said, rising from a stoop. Gardenia

had smoothed out the earth, making a little stage for her doll. Angel was taking curtsies. Gardenia hadn't bagged a single dandelion stump.

"Your daddy and I is goin' uptown to Gleason's Hardware. We heard they're givin' away free zinnia packets." Mama was pulling the bobby pins from her head and tucking them into her apron pocket. "While we're gone, I want you to go out back with these here clippers and cut back my rosebushes. I don't want a mess of suckers this year. And don't let Gardenia out of your sight. You keep an eye on your baby sister, hear?"

I heard. I took the clippers in one hand and Gardenia in the other. I was glad for the quiet, glad I didn't have to hear any more on the subject of the Boggses.

Gardenia sat at the edge of the lawn where our grass turned into the Boggses' chickweed. I opened the clippers and began the work that I hated. I'd been trimming these prickly bushes since I was small.

While I worked, a line of sweat sprouting on my upper lip, Gardenia flipped Angel in the air, making her dance and spin. While Angel danced, Gardenia sang "Skip to my Lou." Lord knows Gardenia had a pretty voice.

Suddenly I heard Gardenia cry, "Maggie! He's got Angel! He's got Angel!" The sound reminded me of the guinea pigs we once owned, squealing, "Wheek, wheek, wheek," in the middle of the night.

Buster had the doll in his foxlike snout. The dog was part collie, part kitchen sink: like the Boggses themselves. Angel's arms and legs dangled from his slobbering jaw. Buster turned and blinked at us before trotting through the chickweed, up the porch, and into the Boggses' house.

Gardenia was sobbing and pointing. "Get her, Maggie. Please get Angel for me! Don't let that mean ol' dog chew her half to death. Please, Maggie, please!"

I knew I'd be in trouble when Mama got back if Gardenia was still sobbing about her doll. I patted Gardenia's bobbing head, brushing her cheek with the back of my hand. "Don't you worry now, honey," I said. "I'll get Angel for you."

I wiped the sweat from my upper lip, took a deep breath, and plowed through the chickweed, the clippers in my hand. I looked back over my shoulder. Gardenia was sobbing, rubbing her eyes with her fists.

At the bottom of the porch step was a rusty bucket filled with rainwater. At the top of the crumbling porch was a swan planter with its wing busted off. Beside the front windows, shutters swung from loose hinges. The doorbell was broken, its wiring hanging loose. The front door was half open, so I was hopeful. Maybe I could sneak in and grab the doll without being seen.

I could smell bacon frying and heard the noise from a TV. It sounded like some kind of game show.

I stepped into the empty living room. The stuffing was coming out of the sofa, and pillows were scattered across the floor. A baby bottle and a ratty blanket sat on a scuffed coffee table. A riding scooter that said PLAYSKOOL was parked in front of the TV.

Suddenly I felt something behind me, something warm and greasy on the back of my neck. I smelled the sour odor of unbrushed teeth. I jumped when I heard the voice of Virgil Boggs in my ear.

"Don't your Mama teach you to ring the doorbell?" he said.

"Your doorbell's broke, Virgil," I said.

"Well, Maggie," he said, "maybe you can learn to knock, then. Maybe I can teach you. I 'spect, Maggie Pugh, that you got a quiet, tender little-girl-type knock that cain't be heard." He moved closer. When Virgil moved forward, he came hips first. "Maybe," he said, his loose lips close to mine, "I could teach you how to knock like a grown-up woman, Maggie."

Virgil Boggs must have thought he was real funny, because he started laughing. When he laughed, I could see brown stains on his teeth from all those Chesterfields he smoked. I didn't laugh back. I remembered hearing that laugh before. It was evil, ugly. I went stiff as a board.

"So, Miss Pugh," Virgil said, "why you come calling on me?"

I stammered like I used to when the spelling bees got hard. "It's not you I came to see, Virgil. It's your dog."

Virgil sneered. "Buster?" he said. "You come over here to see Buster?"

"He's got Gardenia's doll. She was sitting on the grass playing with it, and Buster snatched it out of her hands and ran off into the house with it. I just come to get it and leave."

He gave a whistle for Buster and moved closer to me. "I'se real disappointed, Maggie," he said. "I thought you might've come to see *me*. You know, wantin' to get to know me better, seein' how we're neighbors."

I blushed pink and backed away against the wall. I could see the grimy handprints on the woodwork and hear the TV droning, "Let's see what our contestant has won now, Johnny."

"Virgil Boggs," I said, reddening, "you're the meanest boy in Kinship, and you'd better stop talking to me like that or I'm gonna tell my daddy."

Virgil backed me to the wall.

He put his left arm on the wall next to my right ear and leaned the weight of his body on it, smiling at me. I caught the stale odor of tobacco as he talked. "Ain't gonna do no good to tell your daddy on me, is it, Maggie? You wants somethin' done about it, honey, you'd best tell your mama."

"Don't *call* me that, Virgil." I spit my words into his left ear.

"Don't call you 'Maggie,' you mean? Ain't that your *name?*"

"No, Virgil. The other one. Don't call me that other name." I could hear the TV announcer. The contestant had just won a Chris-Craft, an outboard motor, and a boat trailer.

"You mean 'honey,' honey? Is that the 'other one'?"

"Yes, that one, Virgil."

"Which one? 'Maggie' or 'honey?' Which one don't you like?" Virgil was baiting me, the way he had baited Mickey Harris and Charlie Leonard. Virgil never picked on someone his own size.

I hated Virgil Boggs with my whole heart. " 'Honey'! 'Honey'! 'Honey'!" I said. *"That's* the one I don't like."

I pushed him away hard. I looked at the rose clippers in my hand and knew I was not afraid to use them. I held the sharp end in my fist by my ear and jabbed at Virgil with them.

Buster wandered in, Angel still locked in his jaw. The clippers grazed Virgil's ear, and I stabbed again and again at his shoulder.

Virgil lunged for the clippers. His skin was slippery as axle grease. As Virgil tried to wrestle the clippers from my hand, I went wild with anger. I could feel my grip on the clippers loosening, so I opened my mouth, bared my teeth, and bit him hard on the wrist.

Virgil winced, then swung his body behind mine, pinning my arms behind my back. He had the clippers now, and his mouth went for the back of my neck, kissing me with his hot wet lips. "I like this, Maggie," he said. "I like a girl wild like you. Wild like an animal."

I kicked back with my heels, gouging him in the shins. Virgil cried out in pain, let go of me, and then lunged for the dog.

Virgil ripped Angel from Buster's mouth, tearing her silky white gown. Something in the way Virgil looked at me then told me that something inside of him had turned. I had seen that same look last summer.

"You want your baby sister's doll, Miss Maggie?" he

said, taunting. He held it high over my head, just out of reach. Angel's arms flailed and twitched.

" 'Course I do, Virgil. You know that." The words came out haltingly. I could scarcely speak.

"Well, Miss Maggie," he said, "here she is for you, now."

Then Virgil Boggs ripped Angel's clothes clean off, tossing them over to me. I clutched them to my waist. Her clothes were shreds and tatters.

Virgil leered.

He ran his grimy index finger the length of Angel's naked body. "She's awful purty, Maggie," he said.

"Purty here, Maggie," he said, running his finger under Angel's chin.

"Purty here," he said, touching the doll's sloping shoulder.

"Purtiest of all, though, right down here." Virgil licked his finger, running it all along Angel's naked private parts.

My hands trembled. I could feel the shame hot and wet behind my eyes.

And then Virgil Boggs began tearing at Angel's arms and legs, ripping them from their sockets, tossing the appendages at me. I caught one arm, then another, then two legs. Angel was now a head on a limbless torso. I cringed, remembering the wheelchaired veterans over at the VA.

Virgil held the doll by her mass of curls. She dangled in the air while Virgil clicked open the clippers.

Virgil was enjoying my terror. "You got most of your baby sister's baby now?" he asked.

48

I nodded my head, unable to speak, sweat pouring down my cheeks and neck.

Virgil took Mama's rose clippers and hacked away at Angel's curls. They dropped to the ground one by one. White. Round. Quiet as snow. Buster moved his snout over them, sniffing.

Angel's head was a field of stubble.

Virgil tossed the head to me.

I tasted metal rising in my throat. I ran through the door and across the yard, the doll's body parts clutched to my chest. I looked back over my shoulder and saw Virgil Boggs framed in the doorway, tossing back his head, laughing like he was crazy.

Gardenia was jumping up and down at the edge of our yard. Her skirt billowed in and out. "Oh, Maggie, thank you. Thank you, Maggie," she said.

Gardenia looked at the bundle clutched to my chest and laid her fingers across my arm. "Let me have her, Maggie," she said. "Let me have my Angel."

"No, Gardenia. Not just yet, honey." I knew I had to keep Angel hidden from her until I could fix her up. "No, Gardenia," I said. "Maggie needs to take care of Angel for a while before you can see her. Give Maggie a little time, Gardenia, okay?"

Gardenia slapped my hand and stomped her foot. "Maggie, you're not fair. You're not being fair. Give me my doll, Maggie. I want my baby doll. She's mine." She thrust out her lower lip, pouting.

Then she began peeling away at my fingers, poking at the bundle I held at my waist. She tugged hard at a

49

stray leg, and Angel's body parts came tumbling to the ground.

First a leg.

Then another.

Then the two arms.

When Gardenia saw Angel's head fall on the ground, she covered her ears with her hands and began to scream, and I heard the car wheels crunching onto our gravel drive.

"Mama, Mama," she called, "Angel's dead. She's dead, Mama." Tears streamed down Gardenia's face. Her cheeks were red and flushed. I heard the car doors slam, saw Mama and Daddy rushing across the lawn.

"There, there, Gardenia," I said, kneeling on the ground, tucking Gardenia's head to my shoulder. I could feel her tiny body heaving against my own. "Maggie'll fix Angel up for you. Just give me a little time. I'll take Angel to the Maggie Pugh Doll Hospital, and I'll make her all better for you. You'll see."

I felt Mama's shadow moving toward me. "It was Virgil Boggs did this, Mama," I said, hoping to explain. "Virgil and that dog of his."

"Didn't I tell you to keep an eye on your sister, Maggie?" she said. Mama's mouth was a thin straight line.

"Now, Izzy," Daddy said. He looked smaller than Mama to me although he was fully a head taller. "I'm sure there's an explanation. Maggie's a good girl."

"You're a fool, Henry Pugh," Mama said.

She turned her eyes on me. She was squinting and they looked like tiny slits. "What kind of a good girl don't look out for her baby sister? What kind of a good girl lets her baby sister's doll get torn limb from limb by them Boggs monsters? You got an answer for that, Henry Pugh?"

Daddy hung his head. "I'm sure there's an explanation, Izzy. Let the girl talk."

Mama moved to the rosebushes I had been trimming. "Seein' what's been done to that baby doll's talk enough."

Mama moved to the front stoop, pulling on a pair of garden gloves. She picked up a rose sucker that I had trimmed from the bush and laid across the paper sack. Then Mama turned to me. She lifted the stem high over her shoulder.

It had happened before. I'd had whippings from the time I was small. Belts. Razor straps. Pussy-willow switches. Never rose stems like this.

But this summer was the first time I had seen it the way I did now, my pupil open wide, my eye a lens. Staring. Snapping.

The gash between Mama's eyes looked like a ditch as she glared at me. *Click. Snap.*

I saw the rose stem raised like a whip. It reminded me of cowboys breaking horses. *Trip the shutter, Maggie. Click.*

I watched the angry green stem flail my face and hands and arms. I saw thin red trails, the color of Kinship dirt, rising up in its wake. *Advance the film, Maggie. Trip the shutter. Click.*

"Get to your room, Maggie," Mama said, flinging the rose stem to the ground. "Get to your room."

I threw myself across my pillow. It wasn't fair. From the time I was small, things had never been fair.

I sobbed, remembering the first of many strappings.

It came at Byer's Drugs. When I was five years old. And I think it was June then too.

It had been hot that year, and I had broken out in prickly heat all over my chest. Mama had taken me to Byer's for medicated powder.

It was before Elmer Byer had put in the lunch counter, and the beauty aids section was to the left where the counter is now. Mama sent me off to get the powder while she complained to Mr. Byer about not having the two-for-one sale this year.

I couldn't read yet, so the letters on the powder cans were just a bunch of wiggly lines to me. I was hot and thirsty, so I went to the fountain in the back of the store by the rest rooms for a drink. I had to stand on tiptoe to reach, my mouth just barely touching the curved spout of the fountain.

I felt the cool wetness of the water on my tongue and then the hot sting of the smack that was the back of Mama's hand. I saw Mama pick up a copy of Life *magazine from the magazine rack, watched her fold it down the middle, and felt her swat again.*

"Don't you know no better than to drink outa that fountain, missy?" she said, swatting still.

I blinked in confusion. "Mama," I said, my back-side smarting, "don't you always let me drink out of Mr. Byer's fountain at the back of the store when I'm thirsty?"

"That *one*," Mama said, pointing to a water fountain that was identical to the one I had been drinking from. "*Not* this *one*," she said, pointing to the fountain I had tiptoed up to reach.

I stared back at Mama, confused still.

"That one says WHITE," she explained. "This one says COLORED. Don't you know what color you is yet?"

I pinched up the skin on my arm, examining it for the first time. "I'se white, Mama," I said.

"That's right, Miss Maggie," Mama said. "Just like the letters says, 'W-H-I-T-E.'" She pointed to the lettering on the other fountain.

I stared at the letters as Mama pointed. They looked like they'd been stenciled on by hand.

"Mama," I said. "Mama," I blubbered. "Don't you know I can't read?"

"Not bein' able to read's no excuse for bein' ignorant," she said, dragging me by the wrist through Elmer Byer's store.

I wiped my eyes on the corner of the pillowcase. My tears made tiny gray puddles on the white cotton. As I drifted into sleep, I caught the corners of something I couldn't name. A wish. A dream. Of a garden. In a land far from Kinship. A place where things could freely grow, beautiful things planted by my own hands. There would be hyacinths and lilies and jasmine and orange blossoms, but there wouldn't be roses. In this land of green and freedom I wouldn't have a single rose.

Chapter 4

When I awoke, the house was quiet. Mama had left a note. They had taken Gardenia out for ice cream, it said. To cheer my baby sister up.

It was fine with me. I knew exactly where I would go: to the top of the pecan tree in the corner of our yard. It was my own private place. From the top of the pecan tree, sometimes I even liked the way Kinship looked.

From high up I could see the cars crawling up and down Fenwick Street and forget that no-accounts like Virgil Boggs drove them. From high up I could look down on Byer's Drugs and feel cherry Cokes tingling in my nose; I could forget Hazel Boggs's dirty looks when she thought I was trying to read from *Photoplay* without paying.

From the top of the pecan tree I could fly from earth. Like those astronauts and cosmonauts fixing to launch themselves into the sky. Huntley-Brinkley was talking about it all the time on TV, and I didn't much care who got up first. I thought it would be nice for anybody to get away for a while. An American could get away from the car payments and taking the dog to the vet. A Russian could get away from the winters and the Communists.

I balanced the sewing kit on a nearby branch, pulling out a length of white thread, resting the torn white piece of chiffon on my knees. Angel's arms and legs had snapped on easily. Good as new. The chiffon of her gown, frayed and fragile, would be more difficult. Especially for someone like me. Someone with big hands.

As I struggled to put the thread through the eye of the needle, I thought about how Daddy and I were lucky, luckier than Mama. We knew how to escape. I escaped by climbing the pecan tree or fiddling with my camera. Daddy escaped to his handyman work or his belt-buckle collection.

When the yelling got too bad, Daddy took on a home-repair project, replacing the faucet washers, applying wet concrete to the front walk, patching the screens. "Ye are to be quiet, and to do your own business, and to work with your own hands," Daddy said. "Thessalonians." Mama did the last part, the working with your own hands. She had trouble with the other two.

Sometimes, though, Daddy would stop his working and get like me. Quiet and still. Dreaming and thinking. That's when he'd sit on the back stoop, rattling his collection of Civil War belt buckles in his hands. He'd sit and swab those brass buckles with an old diaper, polishing carefully in all the cracks.

He had one of J.E.B. Stuart in his plumed hat, another of Lee and Grant at Appomattox. He had one of Jackson and Lee the night before the Battle of Chancellorsville, sitting on hardtack boxes in front of a roaring fire.

Stonewall Jackson was Daddy's favorite. His most treasured buckle showed Stonewall Jackson leaning on his sword at a Presbyterian prayer meeting, his troops on their knees at his feet. When Daddy got sad, he mumbled Stonewall Jackson's last words: "Let us cross over the river, and rest under the trees." It was the only time Daddy ever quoted anything but Scripture.

Daddy got his buckle collection out of a mail order catalog. When it arrived, it included a buckle of General Sherman. Which Daddy threw away right off.

I struggled with the cloth under my fingers. The chiffon of Angel's gown had escaped the point of my needle once again when I heard a familiar voice calling up to me. "Hey, Maggie!" the voice said.

I looked down and saw my friend Pert Wilson. From the top of the tree the back-combed top of her head looked like a tiny bird's nest.

"Hey yourself," I called back. I dabbed at my eyes with the hem of Angel's gown.

"Wanna go for a ride?"

I was tired of stitching. Tired of everything ripped and broken. Tired. Thirteen years old and plain-out tired.

"Lord, yes, Pert!" I said, setting Angel and my sewing things against a thick branch and scrambling down the trunk.

"Whooo-eee!" Pert said, reading my face. "Looks like you got a good case of the weeps."

I rubbed my eyes where it was still damp. "Naw, Pert," I said. "It's just all the pollen out. Makes me itch and sneeze."

"Pollen, my *foot!*" said Pert, stamping hers. "I know a teardrop special when I see one, Maggie Pugh." Then Pert's eyes got round as hubcaps. "And look at those scratches on your face and arms." After Pert's eyes made their long slow way down one of the thin red lines that ran from my wrist to my elbow, she said, "Who did that to you, Maggie?" Then she pointed to a spot on the grass. "You just sit on down here with me right this minute and tell me the truth, Maggie Pugh. You know better'n to try to fool Pert Wilson."

I sat. Under the pecan tree, my legs crossed Indian-style, I told. About Virgil and Gardenia and Angel. I had never breathed a word to a soul this side of the grave about how my mama was, but I now told Pert. About Mama and the rose stem and the tears. About the anger and the injustice and the shame.

When I had finished, Pert hopped up and started pacing. "I can't believe this, Maggie," she said, looking down at me. "I just can't hardly believe this." One deep line ran straight across Pert's forehead. It surprised me. I'd never seen Pert Wilson with a wrinkled brow one day in this world.

"What can't you believe, Pert?" I asked. "You mean you can't believe about what Virgil did to Angel?"

"No, Maggie," Pert said. "I don't have any trouble believing what Virgil did to Angel. Everybody knows he's just a low-down, good-for-nothing deadbeat," she said. "Brains in his pants and mean to boot! Him and that trashy family of his. And that Buster ain't more than a hotel for fleas!"

"So do you mean you can't believe the part about how Virgil tried to scare me too?"

"Shoot, Maggie," Pert said. "Ain't nothin' too hard to believe in that. Only thing Virgil Boggs knows anything about is how to scare people." The grassy place where Pert had been pacing was mashed down. A thin film of green had even begun to stain the soles of her white leather boots.

I stood up to face her, and Pert stopped pacing. "So what's the part you don't believe, Pert?" I asked.

Pert put her index finger across her lips and her thumb under her chin in a way that said she didn't want to tell me. Then she sighed and said, "The part about your mama. The part about what your own mama did to you. That's the part I can't believe, Maggie. Mamas don't act like that."

I kept quiet. I could feel things getting blurry in my mind the way they always did when I didn't understand. I didn't know much about other mamas. I knew Aunt Lolly was a slave to her kids and even cut their own meat for them at every meal. I knew what everybody in Kinship said about Rae Jean Wilson, Pert's mama, whispering how she never made Pert and Jimmy eat regular meals at regular mealtimes. But far as I knew, Rae Jean Wilson never raised her fist or her voice to either Jimmy or Pert.

I couldn't tell Pert that the rose stem wasn't the first time. I couldn't tell her about Grandpa Pugh's razor strap that raised welts on the backs of my thighs or about the telephone Mama ripped from the wall and threw across the room at me or about the time Mama slammed the butcher knife across the cutting board when I was chopping onions, just missing my fingers.

I looked at my friend and stammered about how Mama didn't mean it, how she was just upset about Gardenia and Angel and me and Daddy's being out of work and having to live in Kinship her whole blessed life. "I don't exactly know what to say, Pert," I stammered, the words awkward and halting like someone playing an instrument for the first time. "I know my mama loves me and all, Pert, I surely do." Because I didn't know what else to say, I stopped talking and hung my head.

"Well, *I* sure know what to say, Maggie," Pert said. "And I say it's wrong. Plain wrong. The whole thing's plain out wrong." She was pacing again, and the fringe at the top of her boots began to dance. "It's so wrong that if your mama ever does that again, I am going to come over here personally and shoot her dead my own self." Pert was punching the air with her fists. "And," she went on, punching still, "after your mama's out cold, I'm gonna march on over next door and shoot that Virgil Boggs right between the eyes." Then Pert turned her balled fist into a pistol, took aim, and blasted an imaginary Virgil with her finger.

I couldn't help it. Watching her made me bust out laughing.

"Come on, Maggie," Pert said, puckering up and blowing the smoke from the snout of her imaginary pistol. "It's good to see you laughing again. You've had enough jabberin' for one day." She slipped her imaginary pistol in the imaginary holster at her waist. "Tell you what, Maggie. Your pal Pert thinks it's time for a sneak. How about a trip to the Negro Park?" Pert had hopped on the fender of my Roadmaster bike before I'd even had time to accept. Pert was always raring to go.

I loved heading out of town with Pert Wilson. We'd been doing it for years. Sailing past the chickweed lawns and the sagging porches of our end of town. Skidding across the sidewalks closer in where plastic deer and squirrels decorated the grass. Soaring past the grand homes on Clifton Hill, the boxwood carved into circles and squares. Thumbing our noses at the people we didn't like. Flashing our teeth at the people we did. Pert was the outlaw, and I was the sidekick.

After we'd biked past Clifton Hill, we headed south. This was where coloreds lived. It was like a mirror image of the white part, only cracked and cloudy. Coloreds had their own barber, their own grocer, their own school. But the barber shop didn't have the nice peppermint-striped pole outside and the grocer didn't have the fresh-meat case and the school had orange crates instead of desks. In the middle of colored town were the shops and stores and houses for people who could afford the monthly rent.

But down below that was Attica. It was tar-paper shacks and shanties and smoke floating from the chimneys like a cry for help. Beyond Attica, stretching for miles to the west and east, were the green piney forests, silent and deep. The Negro Park was due east, halfway between the pine forests and Fenwick Acres; it sat close to where the Crooked River emptied into Pearl Lake. Pert and I had always loved it, even though we weren't supposed to go there. The Negro Park was laughter and music and the sour odor of beer. There was nothing like the Negro Park if you needed to get away from Kinship. At least I had felt that way before last summer.

We stopped first at Old Jake's Carry-It, the general store that sat at the edge of Pearl Lake. We dropped the bicycle there, and Pert bought us Dixie cups with the money she made at Byer's. I picked vanilla. Pert took chocolate. Then we walked the short distance to the Negro Park.

I knew the archway of trees that overlooked the park all too well. Before last summer those trees had for years been invitation, entertainment, shelter. Now they loomed threatening and dangerous. Since last summer I had stayed away.

Holding her Dixie cup in her teeth Pert sprinted up the big horse chestnut. She waved to me with her one free hand and called out in a loud whisper, "Come on up, Maggie."

"Can't, Pert," I said. Something like fear was walking up the steps of my spine.

"Why not, Maggie?" she called down. "It's got the best view."

No one knew better than I that the big horse chestnut in the middle of the archway of trees gave the best view of the park. I had been there last summer when it happened. When I'd seen what I wished I hadn't. I forced myself to shake off the memory, reaching for the lowest branch and starting to climb.

Pert was high above me. "Come on, slowpoke," she urged. "What's the matter with you, Maggie?"

I had climbed almost as far as Pert. I opened my eyes slowly, making myself look down. I could see some of the coloreds in the park below me. As I watched them moving and swirling on the ground, I felt dizzy. I tightened my grip on the branch. "Nothing's the matter, Pert," I lied.

"How many down there, Maggie?" Pert had settled herself where one branch forked into two, making a natural seat. She dipped her wooden paddle into her Dixie cup, pulling it through the ice cream like an oar.

When I looked down to count, my vision got blurry. I had been looking down like this last summer, trying to count the people below from this same tree. I steadied myself against the branch, forcing my eyes down again. Through the palm-shaped leaves I could see the coloreds below me, some of them jiggling babies on their knees. "Looks like over a dozen," I said. "Not counting babies."

"I can make out Zeke," said Pert, loading her paddle with chocolate and running it across her tongue. "He's easy 'cause he's the biggest one. But I can't make out anyone else. It's hard telling people by the tops of their heads."

I could make out Zeke, too, fighting off the memory of how easy he had been to see last summer, turning my mind to something else the way you turned your camera away from a difficult shot.

"There's Missy Moses down there, Pert. See her sitting on that bench with her two grandbabies?"

"How'd you know her, Maggie, without her apron?"

Missy Moses stood outside Shriner's Grocery weekday mornings. The big white apron that she held out in front of her and sold fruit from was stained with the juices of peaches and grapes and strawberries, the same colors as Mama's jelly glasses.

"Know her by the way she bends, Pert," I said. "See the way she bends to those grandbabies on her lap? It's the same way she bends to you when she sells you her fruit. Like she's really listening to what you're saying, listening to what you need." I was mooshing up my ice cream, turning it into vanilla soup.

Some of the coloreds were clapping and singing. They had gathered around a group of kids who had started to dance.

"That can't be Stumble Martin down there dancing, can it, Maggie? There's no way Stumble could dance."

"Is so, Pert. That's Stumble. Just because he walks with a limp doesn't mean he can't dance if he wants to. What's wrong with you, Pert?" I had taken a twig and snapped it into tiny wood splinters. I held them in my fingers like a stick bouquet.

"Ain't nothin' wrong with me, Maggie. Just never seen a cripple dance before." Pert was licking a dab of chocolate from her wrist.

"That's the problem with Kinship," I said. "If you live here long enough you start thinking that a person's his apron or his limp or his bankbook or his religion."

"What you mean, Maggie?"

"I mean, doesn't it bother you the way people act so stuck up to you and your family?" Pert, her brother, Jimmy, and her mama, Rae Jean Wilson, were the only three Roman Catholics in Kinship. Now that Frank Alhambra had started the taxi business, Rae Jean took Pert and Jimmy to the Catholic church in Troy every Sunday. Before that she just made them kneel down before the little shrine with a candle and a statue of Mary in a corner of her trailer.

Pert nodded. "I reckon it does bother me some." Although people in Kinship snubbed Pughs indirectly, people in Kinship snubbed the Wilsons straight out. They said Catholics were a stuck-up religion; you could tell by the way they crossed themselves right and left.

"And don't you think they snub you because all they can think of when they see you is that you're an RC?"

"Probably," said Pert. "Sure seems like it."

"Well, they do the same to Pughs too. Just sort of ignore us 'cause they think we're nothin' but poor and not worth the time of day."

"Well, you *is* poor, ain't you?"

"Yes, Pert, but we're not *just* poor. Pughs work

hard and they're Godfearing and Gardenia's downright beautiful. We're more than just poor. When people think you're no more than a limp or an apron or a person with empty pockets, it kind of cramps up what you can do, don't you think?"

"I swear to goodness, Maggie Pugh, you sure got a way of thinkin' 'bout things." Pert's face was so close to mine that I could see the Scotch-tape marks on her cheeks. Pert slept with Scotch tape on her face every night. It kept the spit curls in place.

I threw my stick bouquet at Pert and climbed up to a higher branch. The people below me had stopped dancing. They sat in a circle around Zeke, who had started playing his harmonica. I settled back against the branch and closed my eyes. The music drifted up, slow and mournful. It loosened something inside of me, and I forced myself to look back down again. I fixed my eyes on Zeke, wanting not just to look but also to *see*. Images from last summer flashed back to me like snapshots.

I had been in Byor's Drugs, waiting to pay for Mama's Epsom salts. I saw Boyce Johnson and Russell Simmons drinking coffee at the lunch counter and my cousin Willie thumbing through the comic books. Hazel Boggs, Virgil's big sister, was working the register. Two people were ahead of me. Mae Parsons was paying for a tube of liniment, and Olive Shriner was dropping off the pictures of her niece's wedding for developing.

65

Click. Snapshot 1: A still shot. The checkout counter.

I saw Zeke come in the front door, tucking his head down to get under the frame. Three or four coloreds that I'd never seen in town before were with him. I heard Elmer Byer's bells jingling behind them when they came through the door.

Then Zeke headed to the back of the store by the water fountains and the rest rooms. I heard a commotion back there and the sounds of men shouting. Boyce Johnson and Russell Simmons had jumped from their seats at the lunch counter, and I could hear Elmer Byer's voice.

Step back, Maggie. Try to get all of the figures into the viewfinder. Click. Snapshot 2.

It was my turn. I had just handed Hazel my money, noticing the way the clamps that held the dollar bills looked like the mousetraps Daddy set out. Suddenly I heard the police-car siren, and I knew it was Sheriff Keiter. He burst through the door, his keys and handcuffs jangling at his thigh, his nightstick in his upraised hand. He rushed to the back of the store. "Come on out of that rest room, Zeke," he said. "The rest of you niggers too. You know that door says WHITE, don't you?"

Elmer Byer had on the green eyeshade he always wore when he sat in the back counting his money. He started kicking at the rest-room door and shouting, "Rules is rules." When Elmer started kicking the door, the coloreds I'd never seen before came out one by one.

They folded their hands in front of them and kept their heads bowed down.

"You, too, Zeke," Sheriff Keiter called. He stood at the door, shouting into the rest room, his keys dangling from the belt on his waist. "You come on out of that rest room, Zeke Freeman, or I'm gonna have to arrest you."

I thought Sheriff Keiter and Elmer Byer looked like a couple of morons, the way they shouted into that rest room and kicked at the door. What was wrong with them? Didn't they know Zeke couldn't read the difference between WHITE *and* COLORED*? Couldn't they just let Zeke pee in peace? What harm was Zeke doing, anyway? Why did they need to arrest him for an innocent mistake?*

All of a sudden I heard Zeke's voice. I knew it was Zeke because it had that deep brassy sound like the instruments in the horn section. The voice was loud and clear. It didn't sound one bit scared. "I've got as much right as any man to be in here, Sheriff," Zeke said. "I've got rights, too, same as whites."

I had moved to the back of the store for a closer look, and I saw that Elmer Byer was hopping mad. His ears were bright red. He kicked on the door some more and then threw up his hands and shouted, "I own this store, Zeke Freeman, and you better get out of there before you ruin my business. We got laws in this state to keep things separate, and you and your friends here better learn to respect them."

Then Sheriff Keiter shouted into the rest room,

"You're going to have to come out of there, Zeke. You're under arrest."

The other coloreds stood around fidgety as all get out. And then I heard Zeke's voice clear and strong. "I'll come out, Sheriff Keiter," it said. "But I want you to know that if you decide to arrest me, Sheriff, you're taking away a man's natural rights."

Then I saw Zeke's long body come out from behind the bathroom door. He held his head proud as a king.

Snap quickly, Maggie. Things are moving fast. Advance the film. Click. Advance. Click again. Snapshot 3.

I held on to the branches against a sense of dizziness. I would force myself to remember.

Although Zeke came out quietly, before you knew it, Russell Simmons had Zeke in a grip. He pinned Zeke's hands behind his back as if he was the outlaw on a TV western.

Then Boyce Johnson began slugging Zeke in the stomach, blow after blow, and Sheriff Keiter cracked his nightstick across Zeke's head. Russell Simmons was still holding Zeke so he couldn't move, and a pool of blood spurted from Zeke's forehead.

Boyce Johnson was yelling as he threw his blows. "Don't you know no better'n to use that rest room, Zeke?" Now he began kicking Zeke in the shins while Russell Simmons kept Zeke's hands pinned. Over the sounds of the blows and kicks Elmer Byer was shouting, "There's a law about that, you know," he said. "It says WHITE over there and COLORED over here. Over there is ours. Over here is yours. Ain't you nothin' but ignorant, Zeke Freeman?"

The other coloreds were shaking in their shoes as they watched Zeke, but Boyce and Russell and Elmer and Sheriff Keiter ignored them; they only seemed interested in Zeke.

Move quickly, Maggie. Try to get this down. Snapshot 4. Focus. Snap. Advance. Focus. Snap. Advance.

Zeke tried to hold his head high. He didn't even struggle to free himself or to cover his head with his hands.

My mind raced. Zeke had come out as they had asked. Why, then, did they have to beat him? The sound of the blows echoed in my head even after they had stopped, even when the only sound was of Sheriff Keiter's handcuffs snapping around Zeke's hands. I watched them drag Zeke by his wrists, shoving him into the cruiser. I surely knew what Zeke was asking himself. What had he done wrong? What could be expected of him if he didn't know how to read? Why, if he came out as they had asked, did they have to beat him? I thought of Mama and the sting from the Life *magazine when I was small. I knew what it was for an innocent mistake to have a terrible consequence.*

Advance the film, Maggie. Turn your camera on the town, to Kinship. Snap the groups of gossipers huddled at gates, on doorsteps. Advance to the wagging tongues on the street corners. Snapshots 5, 6, 7.

They talked about nothing else for a week. Zeke's arrest was explained one way if you were colored, another way if you were white. But although the accounts of the details of Zeke's arrest depended on who was telling them, everything else was clear as day. Zeke was

69

sprung from jail after only a day and a half. Zeke got an attorney, poor as he was. Zeke filed a lawsuit. It was for legal things I didn't understand. Battery. False imprisonment. I swear to goodness I'd never seen anyone stand up to hurt like Zeke.

The coloreds down below were singing now, a mournful chorus of "My Lord, What a Morning." Zeke had reached the part where the song goes, ". . . when the sun refused to shine."

My camera eye snapped shut. Inside my mind something had gone black, the sun shut out, the light vanished. I knew that there were other memories inside the camera that was me, other undeveloped snapshots. I had looked at some of them, but I couldn't look at all of them just now. Even here in this tree, from the branch that had allowed me to witness what I wished I had never seen, I couldn't fully look. Maggie Pugh was still short on nerve.

While Zeke played on his harmonica, Pert motioned to me. "Psst, Maggie!" she whispered. "Let's get out of here! I've had 'bout enough of this weeping for one day."

I reckon I had too. I'd had enough weeping for a lifetime. "Okay, Pert," I said. "But where we going?"

"Just a minute and I'll tell you, Maggie." She pulled a comb from the back pocket of her jeans and started teasing her hair. "Did I get my pouf back, Maggie?" There's nothing Pert Wilson hates worse than having her hair go flat.

"Yes, Pert," I said, laughing, marveling at my friend.

Pert wore nail polish, plucked her eyebrows, and worried about her pouf. I was happy with just a bath.

Pert flashed a smile at me. The freckles that dotted her cheeks looked lighter. She'd been putting lemon juice on them and bleaching them in the sun. "Okay, then, Maggie," she said, returning her comb to her pocket. "How 'bout the TV shop?"

Pert didn't wait for my answer. She was already scrambling down the trunk of the tree. To tell the truth, that was one of the reasons why I liked Pert Wilson so much. She hurried through things. I lingered too long. Our friendship worked like a seesaw. It kept each of us from crashing down too hard either way.

Pert had already hopped on my fender, and we biked all the way to the new shopping center sprung up at the edges of Fenwick Acres.

The TV shop was called Stay Tuned. They had radios and hi-fis all over the place, but the best thing about it was the TVs. Mr. Beezle, who owned the store, had dozens of TV sets going at the same time, all tuned in to different channels.

We loved to watch the soap operas. *Love of Life. Search for Tomorrow. The Edge of Night.*

The news was on all the sets when we got there. Pert Wilson hated the news. I liked it. News was about the troubles in the world that went on and on and never got solved. It reminded me of the soaps.

But there was one problem with TV news. They kept telling the same story over and over again. Like today the big story was still about how Kennedy was going to get the nomination for President. Either him or Lyndon Johnson. I didn't trust Lyndon Johnson for one doggone minute. I'd heard how he was so swell-headed he even named his dog with his own initials: Little Beagle Junior. But mostly I wouldn't have voted for him if I could. All those Texas relatives like Lady Bird and Lynda Bird. They sounded just like dumbbells from Kinship.

Plus the news was still making a big deal about how Floyd Patterson KO'd Ingemar Johansson even though they had made just as big a deal about it last year when Ingemar knocked out Floyd. They were trying to make it like coloreds were on top of the world now with the bus station sit-ins and the church kneel-ins and now Floyd Patterson busting open a white man. I didn't believe all those claims about change for a minute. I knew Zeke.

"Hey, Maggie," Pert said, pulling on my sleeve, "it's starting." We put our heads close together and stood in front of the biggest-screen Motorola in the store. Lord knows I'd give anything for a TV at home. Gardenia could watch *Lassie*. Mama could watch *Lawrence Welk*. Daddy and Uncle Taps could watch *Make That Spare*. And Pert Wilson and I could watch the soaps like this every day of the week. I felt a catch in my throat as the music started. Organ music on a soap opera gets to me quicker than the organ music in church. It gave me goose bumps when the announcer said, "And now . . . *As the World Turns*."

We didn't notice how Mr. Beezle was watching us. We were just staring at the picture of the black sky of space and the Earth madly spinning like a giant washer tub.

Then we saw fingers drumming on the top of the set and Mr. Alvin Beezle's body blocking half the picture.

"Is there something I can interest you young ladies in?" he asked, his Adam's apple bobbing above his red bow tie.

"No, sir, Mr. Beezle," Pert said, smoothing the front of her blouse. "We're just looking." She said it in that high-and-mighty way she sometimes had. Then she strolled down the aisle of TVs, running her fingers across the tops of the sets, flipping the channel selectors, fiddling with the horizontal and vertical buttons. Pert held her head high. Like someone who had more than one bank account.

"You like that Magnavox over there, Maggie, or do you like this here Zenith better?" she said.

Suddenly Mr. Beezle grabbed Pert by the collar of her blouse, pulling her up to his chin.

"Listen, you," he said, his eyes big behind the thick black glasses. "You keep your cotton-picking hands off of those dials. You and your friend here just keep out of my store unless you're accompanied by either an adult or real money."

Pert shook him off her collar and went nose to nose with him. "Listen yourself, buster," she said. Her face was right up in his. "You keep your cotton-picking hands off of my shirt collar or I'm gonna ram one of your rabbit ears up your you-know-what." Then she brushed her hands together, turned on her heels, and sashayed out of the store.

I tagged quietly behind, watching my friend. She was hopping mad. Her nostrils flared, and she gave a toss of her head. Although the pouf had gone out of her hair again, she still looked pretty. When Pert was born, her daddy said she was the prettiest baby in Georgia. He wrote *Perty* on her birth certificate before he disappeared to Tennessee.

Pert Wilson and I were different. When trouble raised its head, she gave it her fist, and I ducked. I watched my friend stride on ahead of me and felt ashamed. By God, Pert Wilson was long on nerve. And Maggie Pugh was still short on it.

Chapter 5

The morning after my strapping with the rose stem, Mama reminded us all that she was long on nerve too.

"Get up, girl," she said, poking me in the ribs. "Don't you remember we got serious shopping to do?"

I remembered. Today was the day of the First Presbyterian Church Rummage Sale. And Gardenia needed a dress for the pageant.

The presence of the First Presbyterian Church was felt in every corner of our Baptist household. In the bathroom we had the crocheted hat with the spray of flowers that hid the spare roll of toilet paper on the top of the tank. In the kitchen we had the plastic corn holders that you stuck on the end of your corncobs to keep your fingers from burning while you chomped. In the living room we had Daddy's rocker, one of our best rummage-sale finds. When we brought it home four summers ago, one of Tommy Lumpkin's baby rattles was still stuck up under the yellow cushion.

Mama knew that the few rich women in Kinship belonged to First Presbyterian. The congregation included Ida Perls, Margaret Matlack, and Orma Jean Philby. They had family jewelry, rich husbands, and pets that came with papers. Our end of town just had Poppit beads, husbands out of work, and strays.

To my surprise, although the morning was gray and dreary, the weather seemed to cheer Mama up. As we smeared marmalade on our toast, Mama even whistled to the tunes on the radio.

"What's gotten into you, Izzy?" Daddy asked her, washing down the sticky-sweet orange flavors with hot tea. "You're just a-whistlin' and a-singin' like a teakettle this morning, Izabelle Nelly Pugh. I thought you'd be down in the dumps what with these rain clouds hanging over your rummage sale."

"Lands, no, Henry," she went on. "This is the best thing that could of *happened* on a sale day. Especially on a sale day as important as this one. You see, Henry, the clouds is gonna keep folks away. Then there's not nearly so much competition for the *good* stuff."

Smiling in the face of the good fortune of bad weather, Mama put on an old plastic slicker and pulled a pair of heavy black rain boots on over her shoes. She stuck the plastic rain hat that folded like an accordion into her pocketbook.

"I see the rain as a good sign," she said, sticking her umbrella under her arm. "The Good Lord is lookin' out for me and my baby. Rain means He wants Gardenia to have a good dress. It means the Lord God Himself wants my baby to win that beauty contest."

We marched out to the car, rain clouds marking our sign of favor from the Lord.

When the church doors opened, Mama headed straight for the children's clothing section in the southeast corner of the basement. She quickly bypassed the table of baby blankets, bottle sterilizers, and bumper pads, rushing to a table identified by a rough handmade cardboard sign. GIRLS: 6x, it said. Clothing went flying behind Mama like sand behind a child digging to China. Behind her she flung pleated skirts, sweater vests, and winter leggings.

I drifted off into another corner of the basement, eyeing the cameras. I picked them up, one by one, looking through viewfinders, composing imaginary photographs. There were a couple of vest-pocket Kodaks: I recognized one model as the kind made just for Boy Scouts. I looked at a Leica Model A, running my fingers across the J-shaped bar that hooked onto the lens and looked like a hockey stick. I peered through the viewfinder of a Retina I and sighed, putting it down. Lord knows it would be swell to have money. I looked across the basement and saw that Mama had found what she was looking for. She had put two fingers between her teeth, giving a whistle that brought Daddy, Gardenia, and me toward her from the corners of the room like iron filings to a magnet.

It was then that the fight began. Mama had hold of the skirt end of a white ruffled organdy gown. Sarah Deems, whose daughter Dawn was entered into the Hayes County Little Miss Pageant just like Gardenia, had hold of the top end of the same gown, at the part where the scooped neck met the puffed sleeves.

"It ain't fair, Sarah Deems," Mama wailed, tugging to beat the band. "You got you a husband with a steady income, your own job in Simmons's pecan factory, and a sister with a rich husband and nice hand-me-downs over in Warm Springs. So you just let go of that dress." It was true. Sarah Deems took care of the billing at Simmons's Georgia Pecans. She didn't have to take in rich ladies' laundry for fifty cents a basket like Mama did now.

Sarah Deems replied, "Fair is fair, Izabelle Pugh. I got here first. I'm first come, and I'll be first served."

"What you don't know, Sarah Deems," Mama said, "is that the Lord is on the Pughs' side today."

I couldn't believe my eyes. With that, Mama seemed to take her courage from either the Lord or the Devil. She lifted her rain boot, hoisted the pointed end of her umbrella like a sword, took a deep breath, and then stomped and thrust.

Later that afternoon as I pedaled into the open country on the way to my stranger's house, I played over the scene in my mind. After Mama stabbed her with the umbrella, Sarah Deems finally let go of the frilly white gown, falling back into a pile of long johns. Mama left the church pleased as punch, waving the white dress over her head like a flag.

That made *two* people I knew who were long on nerve.

When I reached George Hardy's, I hid my bike under the trees, remembering to keep my presence secret. Quietly I entered George Hardy's house by the side door.

I took the chain from around my neck, turned the key in the lock, entered the mudroom, and took a quick look around. The newspapers had been stacked neatly and tied up with string. The ashtrays had been emptied. The soup cans had been put in the trash. Praise be! Mr. George Hardy had tidied up a bit.

I had brought towels from home and an apron. I thought wearing the apron might make me look professional. It was a bright red apron with a big Santa Claus appliquéd on the front. Aunt Ella, Uncle Taps's wife, had given it to Mama for Christmas. Mama refused to wear it. She thought it looked ridiculous. She gave it to me with a few "welcome-to-its" and "good riddances."

I walked into the kitchen, tying the apron behind me at the waist. The kitchen was neat and tidy. The Coke bottles had been put in a paper sack. The countertops had been wiped down. A thick stack of blue-and-white gingham dish-towels was lying beside the drainboard. They were still in their plastic packages. On top of them was a note written in black ink. It said, *Dear Miss Pugh. You do splendid work. You are right about the need for dish towels. Unfortunately, they are not on sale until August. Sincerely, G. Hardy.* The note was written on that same fancy letterhead, the kind that said *George Andrew Hardy, Ph.D., Assistant Professor of Mathematics.*

My heart turned a somersault. I looked over the note. Especially at the word *splendid.* Somebody thought I did "splendid work." *Splendid.* It was a wonderful word. One of those fancy British words to drop from the lips of a knight or a duke. And someone had used it on *me!* I longed for my own fancy letterhead. I'd have it printed in Charleston or Atlanta, and it would read, *Magnolia April Pugh, Housekeeper, Splendid Work, Kinship.*

I moved to the living room and scanned the desk. Bottles remained in order. Mr. Hardy had even collected stray mechanical compasses and protractors, gathering them up neatly into a cigar box. The mail had piled up again. There was a circular from Pearl Lake Memorial Gardens over by Troy. Daddy had got one too. "Can't they let me die first?" he said when he tossed it into the trash. There were some official-looking envelopes from organizations in Montgomery and Atlanta, and a couple of letters in a light feminine hand from a Miss Ida Mae Thatcher.

Over in the corner of the desk lay a swatch of green, a five-dollar bill, and another note. *Dear Miss Pugh,* the note said. *Thank you for retrieving the trading stamps. Although I do not collect them myself, I understand many people do. I will try to remember to leave them out for you. If I forget, please feel free to help yourself to them at any time. Consider them a bonus for your good work. Sincerely, George Hardy.*

I felt like tap-dancing, and Baptists don't dance. When I brought the trading stamps home, Mama'd be proud of the daughter who worked for the folks in Fenwick Acres, earning money and trading stamps too. I determined to keep up my "good work." I wanted to justify my employer's faith in me. Mr. Hardy was not going to be dissatisfied with my work. Not if I had anything to do with it.

The kitchen was tidy and neat, so I began with the living room. Except for the desk it remained a disaster.

Splendid, I thought, running my rag across the old-fashioned buffet, thinking on that wonderful word. I imagined George Hardy with gold braids at his shoulder, medals on his chest.

I cleared the dining-room table, wiping across the smooth mahogany surface. The wood gleamed, and I imagined his monocle. Glinting. Catching the light as he bent to greet the queen. He would smile under his neatly clipped moustache. His bow would be modest but strong. I dusted the lampshade, making a mental note to stitch the fabric where it was worn. It was the least I could do for someone who gave me trading stamps straight out. *A bonus for your good work,* he had said. He'd let his servants have things too. The silver teapot that had begun to leak. The satin pillowcase with the torn hem. He'd send home leftovers with the ladies-in-waiting. Sides of beef. Plum puddings.

I saw that I liked housekeeping. I could control things when I cleaned: the angle of a picture frame, the edge of a paper, the placement of an ashtray. I liked the repetition of the motions in sweeping, dusting, polishing. It was soothing.

I began to tackle the pile of books that lined the room at its borders. Some of the books were old, some new. Some of them were thick, some thin. Some of them were familiar. There were Bibles in several versions. I knew *Walden* by Henry David Thoreau. Mrs. Parello had made us read it last year. Some of the books had titles by authors I'd never heard of. Somebody named Kierkegaard. Someone else named Goethe. Many of them looked like law books; they were thick and heavy and worn.

I decided to straighten the piles to keep them from toppling. When I moved the piles at the far end of the room, the end where the window looked out onto a thick grove of red oaks, I discovered a glass screen and a pair of rabbit ears. Mr. George Hardy had a TV!

I turned the knob and watched the picture fill the screen. A TV program came on that I had never seen before, and I pulled up a chair to watch.

A man with a ringmaster's moustache was interviewing all kinds of ladies. Some of them were weeping, and some of them were angry, and some of them were hugging the ringmaster, whose name was announced as Mr. Jack Bailey. While the women turned on the waterworks, Mr. Jack Bailey held a microphone to their lips and offered them Kleenex.

The ladies were telling him things like this: that the only thing in the world they wanted was an electric washing machine so they could do laundry for their ten kids; or that they had to have a wheelchair for their husband who was diabetic and got first his leg and now his fingers amputated because of it; or that they wanted to take their mother-in-law to Florida to see her only grandbaby before she died of cancer in a couple of months.

Something about the set to their jaw and the tears

welling in their eyes reminded me of Mama. Jack Bailey's ladies dreamed of the same things Mama did. They wished for a world like Fenwick Acres, a world with boys on shiny bikes and girls twirling batons and Frigidaire repairmen pulling up to houses and mothers bringing sacks of groceries into homes where they'd be stored in freezers charged by a secure electric hum. I felt like I was going to bawl. It was the way I felt whenever I heard the story of Judas betraying Jesus. Lord knows that's no way to treat a friend. There was something about betrayal in those ladies' voices, something that reminded me of Mama.

I heard the applause meter on the TV and saw Jack Bailey put a white robe and golden crown on the lady that wanted her dying mother-in-law to see her grandbaby in Florida rather than the wife of the amputee. The arrow on the applause meter was bending like mad. You couldn't argue with the applause meter. It was clearer every day what people wanted.

I wiped the tears away from my own eyes. Why was I crying? Was it for the lady who had lost out on the wheelchair? Was it the idea of happy people in places like Fenwick Acres? Was it the thought of my mama having to take in rich ladies' laundry? Was it the image of my own future, which lay on my heart soggy as a dish towel?

I flipped off the TV and went into the bedroom.

Shoes were scattered across the floor. The gold bathrobe was sprawled across the bed. The bedclothes had been thrown back and the sheets kicked out again.

But on the top of the pillow was a pile of half a

dozen *National Geographics,* tied up neatly with string, a message written on that same raised letterhead. It read:

Dear Miss Pugh,

    I am sorry if I offended. These are first-rate magazines. They will show you there is a whole world outside of Kinship. I have taken the liberty to place asterisks by the articles that you might enjoy most. Feel free to keep them. I'd like them to be yours.

Sincerely,
G. Hardy

Hesitantly, I picked up the pile of bright yellow covers. Then I sat down on the edge of the bed and untied the string. As I pulled at the knots, something inside of me felt like it was opening up.

Mr. George Hardy had placed asterisks by many articles. "Arctic Buffalo: Beast of Burden." "Something Old in New Patagonia." "Reykjavik: Iceland Comes into the Modern Age." "The Greening of New Zealand."

I lay on the bed and turned page after page, my senses flooded like rivers in spring.

Peruvian women bending over basketwork.

Llamas prancing in Paraguay, children on their backs.

A Chinese panda climbing the steps to a shrine.

An African boatman steering a raft down a rapids.

The images were foreign and strange. The pictures

froze time. I felt my blood rush the way it did whenever I put a camera to my eye.

I retied the magazines neatly, setting them carefully on the bedside table. Then I rose to make the bed and straighten up.

When I had finished, I was tired. And thirsty.

I went to the refrigerator and opened it. Inside was a bottle of cream soda and an opened can of tomato juice. When I saw the open can, I was horrified. Mama had taught me that juice cans contained lead and that the acid in the juice caused the lead to leak out of the can, seeping back into the juice. If you drank it, your brain could swell up and you could become a retard. It was even possible for you to die.

I rummaged in the cupboard for a juice pitcher, pouring in the thick red liquid, tossing out the can. I headed for a pencil and paper from the desk in the living room and quickly scribbled this note: *Your tomato juice is in the big white pitcher. Didn't you know about lead poisoning from cans?* I thought for a moment, and then I added, *Please take better care of yourself. Sincerely, M. A. Pugh, Housekeeper.* I didn't want George Hardy to turn into a retard.

I turned off the lights and walked through the mudroom, the stack of *National Geographics* tucked under my arm. I locked the back door with my key and then turned the key over in my hand. It was gold and bright and shining. I smiled and slipped it around my neck. As I pedaled home, I could feel it bouncing lightly next to my heart.

After I dropped my bike in the backyard under the

pecan tree, I slipped into my tiny room and lay across the bed, carefully turning the pages of the *National Geographics*. I saw the way the photographers worked to suggest the size of a Mayan temple or the color of a New Zealand valley. Maybe, someday, I could do that too. That kind of splendid work.

I picked up my own camera. It felt good in my hands. I moved to the lamp on the dresser and removed the lampshade. I turned the lamp on its side, aiming it toward my bed. I slipped off my sandals and stretched my legs the full length of the bed, propping my back with pillows and peering down into the viewfinder. Through it I could see my toes spreading out from my feet like tiny peninsulas. I tripped the shutter, smiling.

Then I stood up, holding the camera in front of my face as I stood before my cracked mirror, legs apart. In the mirror my body looked like a tripod mounted with a square eye. I saw how tall and strong I was. How splendid.

I took a brush from the dresser, stroking my long auburn hair. I examined my face: the rounded eyebrows over my deep brown eyes, the wide upper lip jutting out over the lower like a cliff.

I steadied the camera in my hands and tripped the shutter. Then, startled, I jumped. I thought I had heard a twig snap in the grass near the window, and I rushed to the screen to look. I cocked my head, listening. It was quiet and still.

I returned to the mirror and unbuttoned my blouse,

letting it slide from my shoulders. I stared at my body, naked from the jeans up. I pulled my thick hair to one side, letting it rush down my left shoulder like a water-fall. I saw the way my neck sloped into my shoulders, curving like a river into a gentle bend. I stared at my breasts, tender as new-laid eggs.

I picked up the camera. Through its lens I could see my image in the mirror: the camera at my waist, the long flowing fall of hair, George Hardy's key dangling between my naked breasts. I tripped the shutter. Splendid.

It was then that I heard him. It was unmistakable. The laugh was ugly and mocking. Like a whinny. "I always did like a big strong girl, Maggie, honey," it said.

I dropped the camera on the spread, covered my chest with my blouse, and ran to the window. I saw where he must have stood: at the far corner where the screen was torn, where the sheet that served as a cur-tain came up too short.

I watched his back moving away to his house, and he stopped and looked across the lawn at me. Then he stood in the middle of the chickweed, threw back his head, opened his mouth, and laughed.

The laughter caught somewhere behind my eyes, stinging and pricking like tiny knives. I had heard him laugh like that before, that terrible time when I saw with my own eyes what I wished I had never seen. I laid my fingers on the windowsill and saw that they were trembling.

I looked down at the golden key dangling at my neck, dancing against my heaving chest, and saw that there was nothing splendid in Kinship, Georgia. Nothing splendid at all.

Chapter 6

The first time I met Zeke in secret I was scared.

My breath caught and my stomach dropped when I heard his steps moving across the wood floor as I waited by Pearl Lake behind Old Jake's Carry-It. But when I saw his head ducking under the back door and the laundry sack where he kept his trading things slung over his shoulder, I relaxed. In spite of everything that had happened, he was still Zeke.

"Hey, Zeke," I said, "come on and sit." He walked down the back steps and across the sand toward me. Together we moved to the edge of the dock overlooking the green water, sitting quietly for a long time. Stray pieces of popcorn floated in the water. A child's broken plastic boat, its stern bashed in, bobbed on the surface.

Finally, Zeke spoke. "I'm wonderin' why you wanted to see me, Maggie," Zeke said.

"Missed you, Zeke," I said. It was true. I missed

seeing him in town something awful. "Wanted to thank you too."

"Thank me?" Zeke's forehead wrinkled into two wavy lines. "What for, Maggie?"

"Lots of things, Zeke. For Daddy's shaving mug. For that radio we listen to every day." Those things were easy to say. But I was more thankful for Zeke's friendship, his many kindnesses, his example of courage. Those things were harder to say, so I kept quiet.

"Well, you're welcome, Maggie," Zeke said.

I wasn't sure how to go on. I picked up some pine needles from the dock and began to braid them. After a while I stopped and looked at Zeke. "But I don't want to just thank you in words, Zeke. I want to thank you in a better way."

Zeke's lips stretched into a grin. "You bring money, Maggie Pugh?" he said. His shoulders were shaking gently as he laughed.

"No, Zeke," I said, grinning back. This first secret meeting with Zeke took place last summer, and even though Daddy still had his job with Johnson & Johnson back then, Pughs didn't have much extra money. "I want to thank you by teaching you something, Zeke. I want to teach you to read."

Zeke looked away from me and started fiddling with the drawstring on his trading sack. I glimpsed a length of rope, a feather duster, and a copy of *Spiderman* peeking out of the canvas. I didn't know what Zeke was thinking. When he turned to me, the whites of his eyes were runny looking, like soft-boiled eggs. He said, "Well, now, I'd really 'preciate that, Maggie. You reckon we could start today?"

We'd started right then.

"Zeke," I said, "we'll need a pencil and some paper." He fetched a notepad from his sack and the stubbed end of a pencil that had been broken in half. He passed them to me.

"Now," I began, "I figure there are two words you're most needing to read, Zeke, so I think we'll start with them." I began writing the words on the notepad. "The first word is *white*," I said, pointing to my letters. "The second one is *colored.*"

I felt Zeke's hand across my own. It told me to put down the pencil.

"Hold on a minute there, Maggie," Zeke said. "I need to tell you something." Zeke paused before he went on; he kept his hand across mine. "You're right about one thing. I can't read a lick, and I want to learn. But I been livin' in Kinship long enough to know the white door from the colored. There's all kinds of things for a man to read in this world. They's not all made out of letters."

I stared into the pond; the scummy green water was lapping gently at the pilings of the dock. I was concentrating hard. "You mean you went into that white rest room on *purpose?*"

Zeke was quiet. He simply nodded.

"Let's get this straight, Zeke," I said. It felt like trying to fine-tune a radio when the station wouldn't come in. "You got yourself arrested on *purpose?*"

He nodded again.

"You mean you walked on into that white rest room in Elmer Byer's store on purpose, knowing full well that you'd get arrested, beat up, or both?"

He nodded. He was waiting for me to take everything in. This was hard for me. I knew what it was to get beat. I'd do anything to avoid a beating.

"Why, Zeke?" I said. "Why would you do that?"

"Wanted to get Elmer Byer to think about his policy. Wanted him to see how wrong it was to keep my people and your people separate. Wanted him to change his rules. If he wasn't willing to do that, I wanted to get arrested, Maggie. If Elmer wouldn't change his policy, I wanted to go to court about it. I was hoping the court would make it clear that there was something powerful wrong about separate rest rooms, separate lunch counters, separate parks."

"But didn't you know Elmer Byer never changed a rule one day in his life? And didn't you know that if you went to court you'd *lose?*" Coloreds weren't ever believed in court.

"Knew I likely *would* lose, Maggie," Zeke said with a shrug of his shoulders. "But I was hopin' to get an appeal and push it on up to a higher court. Thought I might get 'em to work justice that way. Wanted to get 'em to face the truth."

Zeke's words reached way down inside me. They reminded me of that story about Jesus walking smack dab into the middle of the temple and turning over the tables of the money lenders. I was thinking that Zeke Freeman and Jesus Christ were about the two bravest people in this world.

"Why do you care so much about getting folks to face the truth? Seems to me like facing the truth's about the last thing Kinship has on its list of things to care about."

"I'm not sure why, Maggie. Seems like in every life there's a time when a person's got to face up to the truth. To say out loud about what he sees with his own eyes."

"And what was it that you saw with your own eyes, Zeke?"

"Just about everything in Kinship. From my tradin' cart."

I knew it was true. Zeke was in the center of things. Just like the bank.

"I can tell you a story about the kinds of things I saw, Maggie," Zeke said. "One thing happened just this spring. Priscilla Adkins, that fine white lady, came runnin' over to my cart last April, crying out to see my third shelf."

I knew Zeke's third shelf. It was like a miniature pharmacy stocked with Fletcher's Castoria, headache powders, bunion pads, and Listerine. Priscilla Adkins's Timmy had broke out in chicken pox right in the middle of Fenwick Street, right before time for his afternoon nap.

Zeke smiled, remembering. "Poppin' out like corn from a skillet. One right after the other. One spot busted out right on the tip of Timmy Adkins's nose," Zeke said. "And Miss Priscilla was half crazy with fright. She had shouted for me, and I came runnin' with

my cart and rubbed her boy's spots down with calamine lotion from my bottle."

"So what's Timmy Adkins's chicken pox got to do
with telling the truth about Kinship, Zeke?" I drew up
my knees and hugged them with my arms.

"Thing is, Maggie, that the same thing happened
that very morning to Pearl Jackson, over on the black
side. Her Corinthia popped out in spots too. She was
yelling for me and cryin' and runnin' around and callin'
for Zeke's cart. She was needing my calamine lotion
too."

I didn't understand and I said so. "What's that got to
do with anything, Zeke?"

"Maggie," he said, putting his face right next to
mine, "don't you *see? We's both dippin' from the same
bottle,* Maggie. White or black."

I thought about what he said, listening hard.

"Let me ask you somethin' else," Zeke said, rubbing his chin. "Don't we breathe the same air, black
and white?"

I thought about it and nodded my head.

"Don't we get the same red dirt in the cracks of our
toes?"

"Uh-huh."

"Don't we be sweatin' under the same sun?" It was
nearly noon. The sun was rising high in the sky. I
could feel it hot against my back.

"Yes, Zeke," I said, "we do."

I saw the beads of sweat gathering into a pool on
Zeke's forehead. "If we do all that stuff the same, Maggie," he said, "how come they make us eat separate,

marry separate, be buried separate? Ain't we all in the same family?"

Zeke had me cold. I couldn't think of an answer. All I could think of was how smart Zeke was to see these things and how brave he was to say them.

Zeke turned away and began rooting around in his sack. "Didn't you want to be givin' me a reading lesson today, Maggie?" he said.

"Sure, Zeke," I said. Although Zeke couldn't read, I was beginning to see that he knew more than folks who had written whole books, and I was starting to wonder which one I was going to be: the teacher or the learner.

He pulled a Bible from the laundry sack. "I'd like to learn to read from *my* book, if it's all the same to you, Maggie."

"*Your* book?"

"Yep, Maggie. I want to learn to read my book. Ezekiel. You didn't know that *Zeke* stood for *Ezekiel,* Maggie?"

"Guess I never thought about it, Zeke."

"My mama named me Ezekiel Jeremiah Freeman. After two prophets in the Bible. Before she died, she told me to live my name. 'Be a prophet, Zeke,' she said. 'Offer out some hope.' I guess that's what I want to be doin'.''

He held the Bible in his hands and stared at the white leather cover. "My favorite part's Chapter Thirty-seven," Zeke said. "Know it by heart. Want to be able to read it. Can you find it for me, Maggie?"

I flipped through the pages of Zeke's Bible for him.

My hands were shaking. Zeke couldn't read. He couldn't even find the chapter numbers that he needed. Yet he could stand up to Sheriff Keiter and Elmer Byer and everybody in Kinship. Lordy, but Maggie Pugh was lucky in her friends.

When I found Chapter Thirty-seven, I began to read. It was the story about how the Lord brought Ezekiel into the valley of the bones and about how the bones were dead and dry. Zeke's eyes were closed. He was listening to the words as if they were music.

"Here it comes, Maggie," Zeke said, interrupting me. "The best part." He raised both hands in the air like a conductor. "Here comes the question the Lord asks ol' Zeke." From the way he said it, I didn't know if "ol' Zeke" meant the Zeke in the Bible or the Zeke sitting by me on the dock.

I decided that I had done enough reading. I put the Bible into his hands and ran my finger across the text. "Here, Zeke. If this is the best part, I want you to learn to read it yourself."

I jabbed at the words for him as I read. "Son. Of. Man," I said. "Can. These. Bones. Live?"

When I had finished reading the question, Zeke clapped his hands together. "Yessirree, Maggie," he said, "those is my favorite words in the holy Bible."

Before we finished our first reading lesson, I listed every word on the notepad for Zeke. "Son. Of. Man. Can. These. Bones. Live." I told Zeke to study those words for next time. Zeke's face was shining when he turned to leave.

We met lots of times after that. Zeke learned

quickly. At our second lesson I taught Zeke the alphabet. We practiced with our same word list, only this time we put the words in alphabetical order: "Bones. Can. Live. Man. Of. Son. These." I saw that Chapter Thirty-seven was better than the readers Gardenia had in school. The words were simple, and they gave you a lot to talk about.

Every time we met, I had questions for Zeke.

After one lesson I asked, "So why's Chapter Thirty-seven your favorite, Zeke?" There were a lot of chapters in the Bible. I didn't see how you could pick just one.

The sun was stretching toward late afternoon, and as he talked I could see Zeke's shadow jumping excitedly across the boards of the dock. "In Chapter Thirty-seven Ezekiel's talkin' about his people, Maggie," he said. "The Israelites. Been banished from their land. Hopeless. All dried up. Nothin' but a pile of dry bones."

The arms of Zeke's shadow were moving in and out, a kind of background chorus to his words. "Ezekiel's speakin' 'bout my people, Maggie. About the black folks here in Kinship, here in Georgia, here all over these United States. Been so bad, my brothers and sisters been askin' the same question as ol' Ezekiel, the same question you've been teaching me to read. 'Son of man,' they've been asking, 'can these bones live?' "

"So what's the answer, Zeke? What's the answer to the question? *Can* those bones live?"

Zeke studied my face real hard. Like there was something written there that he wanted to read. "Don't know, Maggie. Don't rightly know. In the Bible, when Ezekiel spoke his prophecy, a great wind raised up. And the bones, they start a-rattlin' and a-shakin' and then they all come together with flesh on 'em now and everything. And they start breathing, breathing like they was *alive* again."

The word *alive* hung in the air. I saw the way the shadows of Zeke's arms were moving, the fingers moving the wristbones and the wrists moving the lower arm bones all the way to the elbows and the elbows moving the upper arm bones all the way to the shoulders.

Then he turned away and frowned. "But whether new life can happen in a place like Kinship's something else. My people have been given hope for new life in Montgomery, in Nashville, in Atlanta. Whether they can have a new life in a place like Kinship is what I'm trying to find out the truth about."

It looked to me like Zeke had found out plenty. He had found out that a place like Kinship beat you up and threw you in jail. It did other things too. Things I couldn't bear to look at. There were things that everybody in Kinship knew. That they'd brought the lawyers in and the people from Atlanta. That the trial was all ready to start. That all of a sudden Zeke dropped the suit and the city folks slammed their briefcases shut and went on back home and then Zeke stayed off the street more and more and Kinship just went back to the way it always was. Not everybody in Kinship knew why. But I did.

"Zeke," I asked him another time, kicking off my

shoes and running my feet through the water, "what was it like in jail?" Sometimes I could be like Mama. Plain nosy.

"It wasn't too awful bad, Maggie. Jail's mostly nobody talkin' to you, food that ain't fit for a crow, and doors slammin' all the time."

I smiled at that. Jail sounded familiar. Like living with Pughs.

"But I wasn't in jail too long, you know. Got out in only a day and a half."

"How'd you manage that, Zeke?"

"I got friends, Maggie. Reverend Potter passed the plate at church on Sunday, and Frank Alhambra took out a loan from the bank."

"And did they raise money to pay for your court trial, Zeke?"

"I was lucky, Maggie. I had a lady lawyer from Atlanta who was going to represent me for free."

"Why'd she want to be doing that, Zeke?" I found it hard to believe that anybody'd want to take on all the whole pile of ignorant Kinship for nothing.

"Because she's black like me. Because she knows the way my people are treated is wrong. Because she believes that Boyce Johnson and Sheriff Keiter and Russell Simmons and Elmer Byer shouldn't be allowed to do what they did to me. Because she's needin' to be free, too, Maggie."

I thought about what Zeke said. It was   colored that needed to be free from things.

After just a few reading lessons I was even teaching Zeke to write. I loved seeing the way his big hand held the stub of a pencil and the way he hunched over the paper, concentrating. He was pleased as punch the day he first wrote his name. He was delighted with the letter Z. "If you turn it on its side, it makes the letter *N*, Maggie," he said, turning his paper around and around, making the *Z*'s turn into *N*'s and back again.

Then Zeke put down his pencil and reached deep into his trading sack.

"I got something for you today, Maggie," he said. "A present." He pulled out the camera and passed it to me.

I couldn't believe my eyes. I'd never held anything this expensive in my hands in my whole life. Cameras were right up there with silver teapots and real pearls. I pushed the camera back over to Zeke. "I can't take this, Zeke. I'm sure it cost a bundle."

He pushed it back. "It's yours, Maggie. I won't take nothin' for it." The look on his face said it was mine.

"Thank you, Zeke," I said, holding the camera awkwardly. I had never held a camera one day in my life. I felt like a new mother, afraid she'd drop the baby.

"Here, Maggie," Zeke said. "You don't have to be afraid of it. It's well made and strong. Let me show you what I can about how it works." He showed me how you raised the cover on the viewfinder, how you held it at your waist, how you looked down into the glass, how you tripped the shutter.

I danced across the dock, framing pictures. The line of evergreens at the far end of the lake. An egret poised on the sand. A Baby Ruth wrapper floating on the water. My heart gave a skip every time I snapped the shutter, and my feet felt light.

"Thank you, Zeke," I said, plopping down next to him, studying his smiling face through the lens. "This is surely the finest present a girl could have in this world. Now why would you think of such a gift for me?" I tripped the shutter just as his smile began to fade.

"Remember what I told you when you were small? When you stole those two dimes for your daddy's birthday mug?"

I reddened at the memory. I hated being caught in a lie, even an old one. "I remember the mug, Zeke, and how you gave it to me for free. Don't rightly remember what you said."

"I said, 'Never be afraid of the truth.' Remember now?"

I nodded my head, remembering. Problem was, I was still afraid. Of lots of things. Especially the truth. "But what's that got to do with this camera, Zeke?"

"I thought it might help you. I've been studying you for a good while now, Maggie Pugh. Every time you come up here to give me a lesson. Sometimes I see the look in your eyes that says you're worried or scared. Sometimes I see your shoulders holdin' up the weight of the world. Sometimes I see bruises or welts. I know the hurt in that, Maggie. Just don't know the truth behind it."

I remembered all the whacks for sassing and the slaps for the looks on my face. In my mind they were all mixed up with the blows from Boyce Johnson and the sound of Sheriff Keiter's nightstick as it cracked across Zeke's head. I remembered other things too. Things I couldn't tell the truth about just yet. One thing was plain as day: Zeke and I both knew about hurt.

I was grateful that Zeke didn't try to make me talk about any of it.

A dragonfly, bottle-green, circled Zeke's head and then darted away. Zeke pointed to the camera. "So I got you this camera, Maggie, to help you with the truth. So you'll first trust your eyes to see it and then trust your own voice to tell it."

I held the camera firmly in my hands. In the short space of a morning this little black box had become important to me. "I'm afraid, Zeke," I said. "Most of the time I don't rightly know what the truth is. Sometimes I feel I'm getting close to it, but then things go blurry and the truth slips away. How could I ever come to speak it, Zeke, if I can't even see it yet?"

"Maybe the camera will help you with that. You can trust the camera's eye for a while; then maybe it will help you trust your own. Besides, Maggie, telling the truth doesn't mean not being afraid." The dragonfly returned, darting and buzzing around Zeke's head.

As I continued to teach Zeke and as Zeke continued to teach me, I began to wonder. Zeke wasn't in town at all now, but more and more our reading lessons led to the messages he had to write and the letters he asked me to deliver to people in town or to the post office. As Zeke got busier, our lessons became less frequent, and I had to make the most of them when they came.

More and more Zeke was putting the Bible aside and pulling out pencils or envelopes. More and more we'd have lessons in which he'd ask me to look over his writing.

One day it was hot as blue blazes. The noon sun was a golden circle in the sky. "I want you to check my writin', Maggie," Zeke said. "Here's an envelope from Reverend Potter to Mr. Hardy that I'm needin' you to deliver. Want to get the words *Mr. Hardy* wrote down right." When he stuck a pencil behind his left ear, Zeke looked like an overgrown schoolboy.

"Sure, Zeke," I said, watching him begin. He took the pencil in his hand and struggled with the lines. Beads of sweat glistened on his forehead, and he mopped his brow on his white cotton shirt.

While Zeke worked, I turned curious. Lately I was never sure how soon I would see Zeke again. I had to make the most of the time I had. I had to work fast.

"Why you think Mr. Hardy's so sloppy, Zeke? There's nothing but piles of tobacco and clothes dropped all over that house."

Zeke was working on the two humps of the letter *M*.

"Sloppy 'bout some things, Miss Maggie. Not so sloppy 'bout others," he said. His front teeth were clamped over his bottom lip as he strained after the letters. "Mr. Hardy got more important things on his mind than hangin' up clothes."

"Like what, Zeke?" I asked. "If he's got such important things on his mind, what's he doing in Kinship?"

Nothing important ever happened in Kinship. Never had and never would.

Zeke was working on the *R* now. The pencil was swallowed up in his giant fingers. "Mr. Hardy got some unfinished business here, Maggie, I reckon."

"How do you know George Hardy, Zeke?"

"Came to town last summer with all them lawyers." He had mastered the *M* and the *R*. He was on to the *H* and the *A*.

"And he's back again? Why, Zeke?"

" 'Unfinished business,' I said."

I looked over at the letters Zeke had written on the envelope. I pointed out the place where he forgot to put the period after the *Mr.,* and he added a big black dot. When he finished, he smiled, hooking the pencil behind his ear.

I knew better than to be so nosy. I knew I should just have been plain grateful for the job and left it at that. I knew Zeke had come for me special at Edmonia Jennings's tomato stand and that Mr. Hardy never forgot to pay me. I knew enough not to pry. But I also remembered Mama's words: "Curiosity killed the cat, but satisfaction brought him back." I guess I was just bent on satisfaction.

"What kind of 'unfinished business,' is it, Zeke?" I said.

He looked straight at me. "No more questions, Maggie, hear? You know that's why I got you your job. I know you're good at keepin' secrets. Remember what I told you, Maggie. About 'Don't ask.' "

When Zeke rose to leave, his black head moved for a moment in front of the sun. It reminded me of that picture of a solar eclipse in my science book, and I could see there would be no more satisfaction today.

Chapter 7

It felt good to be back in the stranger's house. It felt good to be on the outskirts of Kinship. Far from our family's shame. Far from Virgil Boggs. Far from everything. I liked the aloneness, the TV, the electric fans. I flipped on the TV right away. A game show came on with bells ringing and lights flashing and showgirls in tight dresses pointing to prizes.

I turned the TV way up so I could hear it in the kitchen while I swept. I stepped over the pile of laundry dropped in a heap on the living-room floor, tying my Santa Claus apron around my waist. As I picked up the balding broom, I realized I'd have to leave another note for George Hardy. His broom was an old stick of a woman whose hair had fallen out; he needed a new one.

I swept, washed dishes, straightened cupboards, the TV making chattering noises in the background like birds. Then I heard a sound at the door to the mudroom and peeked around the corner to look.

A man was standing at the threshold. A colored man. What was he doing here? I knew almost every person in Kinship, colored or white. Who was he? I took in the brown skin and the black hair, wondering what he wanted.

He paused for a moment at the doorway and smiled at me. His teeth were even and white.

The television set blared. A gong sounded, and the studio audience was giving a great big round of applause. It was so loud that the man cupped his hands and shouted, "So you're the young woman who's been fiddling with my TV," he said. "And taking me to task for my housekeeping," he added. "And trying to protect me from lead poisoning."

Buzzers and gongs exploded from the TV. A giant roulette wheel made grinding noises as it turned on its axle. "If you don't mind, Miss Pugh," he continued, his hands around his mouth like my Uncle Taps when he called birds, "you could turn down the television, and then we could have a proper introduction."

My jaw dropped open. I could feel my cheeks flushing red. This was Mr. Hardy. George Hardy. My stranger. And he was a *colored* man!

I tripped over the broom and the rug in my rush to the living room, clicking off the TV. I knocked over an ashtray on the way back to the kitchen. I felt embarrassed, ashamed. White girls didn't clean for colored. In Kinship it was the other way around. Colored waited on white people, didn't they? Hadn't I been shown that since the day I was born? Dear God and Jesus Christ Himself! If you were a Pugh, was there never an end to the shame that showed up on your doorstep?

As I watched him cross the floor, my eye opened: wide as a lens.

Load your camera, Maggie. A colored man. Your secret stranger is a colored man. Get a picture.

I focused in on the easy swing to his walk, all limber legs and arms. *Click. You need these pictures, Maggie.*

I saw the way he walked on the balls of his feet as he moved across the room. Lightly. Like a panther. *Focus for the middle distance, Maggie.* I saw the way the hem of his jeans brushed the laces of his sneakers and the way his white cotton shirt billowed out behind him. *Click.* I saw that only his shoulders showed any hint of tension. They were hunched and rounded. Like those of a person who spent his time over a desk or a book. *Trip the shutter, Maggie.*

He had crossed the kitchen floor and stood right next to me. His dark face looked down at mine. I saw the beard outlining his mouth and jaw, the round tortoiseshell glasses glinting against the light. *Adjust the lens, Maggie. Focus for a close-up.*

His skin filled my lens, so close it blinded me. *Trip the shutter, Maggie. Advance the film.*

I wondered what George Hardy felt as he moved across the kitchen and looked at me. Was he taking his own kinds of pictures?

He extended his hand. "I'm pleased to meet you,

Miss Pugh," he said. "You are efficient in all things. And I am George Hardy, your employer."

I wiped my hands nervously on the white Santa beard of my Christmas apron, thinking how ridiculous I must have looked. "I'm very happy to meet you, too, Mr. Hardy, sir," I stammered, putting my hand in his. "Thank you for the job." His hand felt dry and warm. Mine felt damp and clammy.

He held my right hand in his for another moment, studying it. He turned it over, appraising it the way I'd seen Zeke appraising something for a trade.

"You have strong hands," he said. "I've always admired people with good, strong hands. That's why you do such splendid work."

I felt surprised but happy. Splendid, in fact. Like someone whose name had been drawn out of a jackpot. "Thank you," I said. "But you should see my *sister's* hands. They're all white and delicate and look so fine crooked around a cup."

George Hardy smiled down at me and stroked his beard. There were thin strands of gray in it. They looked like the curling bits of thread after Mama ripped out hems. As he ran his fingers through his beard, I saw that George Hardy's hands were deep pink on the bottom and brown on the top. Where they met, they were like the places beyond Attica where the pink sunset meets the brown hills.

"So you have a sister, Miss Pugh?" he said, moving to the living room, motioning for me to take a seat at the end of the couch. He took a seat for himself at the other end, his long body folding up like the ruler

Daddy used to measure things. "Does your sister do housework too?"

"Well, sir, Mr. Hardy," I said, unsure of what to do with my hands, however much George Hardy had admired them, "her name's Gardenia. But no, sir. She doesn't do housework. Not unless Mama says she *has* to." I smiled, remembering the pout on Gardenia's face when she bent to pick up her toys. I stuffed my hands in my pockets.

"Actually, I've never been any good with my hands myself," George Hardy said. "I always wanted to be the kind of person who could make things with his hands from scratch. The way my mama made cakes. As you can see by the state of this house," George Hardy said, sending his finger in a circle around the living room, "mostly I've had to labor with my mind. Sometimes it's been a kind of sentence."

I didn't understand what he meant by *sentence,* but there was a pick-on-rock sound to the word that rang on something inside of me.

"So your strong hands," George Hardy said, "are something I respect."

Something jumped inside of me. Something that took off like a tiny jackrabbit when I heard that word. *Respect.* It was the same way I felt when I heard the word *splendid.* I pulled my hands out of my apron pockets, resting them in my lap.

"My mama had hands like yours," he said. "Quiet and strong. We lived over in Attica," he went on. "Got our heat from wood. My pap had left us long ago, and it was my older brother who was like you, the strong

110

one. He used to split wood first thing every morning, grunting with every stroke of the ax. I did all the mental things. Tutoring a neighbor boy in arithmetic. Figuring out how best to divide our nickels."

George Hardy drew a pipe out of the back pocket of his jeans and took a pouch of tobacco out of the pocket of his shirt. I watched as he carefully stuffed the tobacco in the bowl. When he lit the match, the spark struck something inside of me. Then he lifted the cover of the matchbook up and down over the bowl like someone lifting the lid off a pot of dumplings.

"I'm not sure how my mama bore it," he went on, drawing on the pipe. "She never complained about us, though. Seemed to accept Nathan's body and my mind as equal parts of an equation. Her hands worked all the time. Like yours. She was the midwife round about Attica. Our color was a kind of cholera. No doctor wanted to treat the infection of us. I used to run back and forth carrying messages about impending births in the village. Nathan and I came to the deliveries with her. Nathan would haul over wood in the cart, and I would mind any other kids about."

There was something slow and easy about the way he talked, all patient and unhurried. He wasn't in a rush the way Mama always was, jumping into judgments. As he spoke, time seemed to stop for me the way it did when you concentrated on the hands of a clock.

"I remember," he went on, the indraft from his pipe making a quiet sucking sound, "watching Mama heaving heavy kettles of water from the fire and wringing out sheets dipped in boiling water, her muscles twisted as tight as ropes, steam rising off the sheets, sweat on her brow and sweat on the body in front of her lying on an old mattress or sometimes lying on nothing more than a bed of hay. I learned early on that both living and birthing were equally labored undertakings. You learn those things young when you're poor," he said.

I felt quiet inside, the way I did before I fell asleep at night, all sober and wondering.

"So what about you, Miss Pugh?" he asked, curling his knees up on the couch, facing me directly. As he rearranged his limbs, his jeans hiked up his calf. He had on thick white socks with stripes at the top, the kind that basketball players wore. His legs were limber as fishing poles. "Tell me the story of your young life," he said.

I kept my hands stuffed tight in my apron pockets and stammered, "I don't know exactly what to say."

"Well, then," he went on, soft and easy, "what about your name? Why don't you start by telling me about your name?"

"My name, George Hardy?" George Hardy, I was discovering, had a way of surprising me, tipping me off balance. "Why would you want to know about my name?"

"I think," he said, "that names are important. I'd like you to tell me about yours."

I pulled my hands from my pockets, wiping a loose brown strand of hair from my forehead with my arm. The gesture gave me time to think. "Well," I began, "my whole full entire name—the one they put on the birth certificate—is Magnolia April Pugh. The *Magnolia* is because it's my daddy's favorite tree. The *April* is for the month when they begin to blossom. But I never really liked it much."

"That's too bad," he said. George Hardy rubbed his beard with his thumb and index finger in the area where the beard wrapped around the corners of his mouth. "A person should like her name, don't you think?"

I pulled on the fluff of the Santa Claus beard, wondering if there were colored Santa Clauses and whether their beards would be white or black. "I guess I never liked my name because I felt it just didn't fit me. I mean, I think a person's name should fit her just right. Like a glove or a shoe. And mine didn't."

"That's an interesting observation, Magnolia April Pugh. A name fitting like a glove." He was smiling at me. He was cleaning his glasses on his shirttail now and smiling from his eyes. They were large and round and set back deep in their sockets. The shaggy black eyebrows protected them like a canopy.

"But Gardenia," I said, clapping my hands together, finding a good example. "Gardenia June's just perfect as a name. Fits like a glass slipper."

George Hardy pushed his eyebrows close together. When he did that, he looked like he was thinking hard. "Why is that?"

"Well," I said, remembering the golden curls and the white skin and the structure underneath it all as delicate as chicken bones, "she's fragile and white like gardenia petals, and she was born in June. The gardenia bushes had stopped blooming by then, but Mama said her newborn baby smelled just like their perfume."

"We had gardenia bushes too," George Hardy said. "They grew beside the shacks and shanties and helped disguise the stink of everything else that was there. I never liked them much. In strong sun they brown and wither. Gardenias are too fragile for my taste."

He rose from the sofa, unfolding himself and striding to the desk. He looked over the pile of handwritten letters lying there, picked out four or five, and stuffed them in the back pocket of his jeans. He worked with his back to me, concentrating. It was clear that he was finished with our conversation.

Then he tapped out his pipe tobacco, spilling half the bowl onto the floor. He grabbed a large manila envelope as he moved to leave. The tail of his shirt swept across the edge of the desk, and letters and bills floated to the carpet. He left them there. I saw that when George Hardy put his mind to one thing, he forgot about everything else.

"I just stopped by for some papers," he said, feeling in his pockets for them and then passing me the manila envelope. "Can you see that this gets to the post office for me as soon as possible?"

I nodded. "Sure."

"I'm happy to have met you, Miss Pugh," he said, heading for the landing.

"It's okay if you want to call me Maggie," I said.

"Maggie it is, then," he said, smiling. I liked the way his white teeth gleamed. He turned to leave. "Oh—

there is one thing more," he said, balancing lightly on the balls of his sneakers. He looked me straight in the eye. "Do you have any trouble with the idea of working for a black man?"

I laced the fingers of my hands, squeezing the knuckles together. George Hardy had asked me a hard question, and I remembered what Zeke had said: about never being afraid of the truth. "Yes, I do," I said. "And also no, I don't. I mean I don't personally have any trouble with working for you. For you your own self." I groped for words like a light switch. "It's just that if anybody knew. My mama or anyone—"

George Hardy interrupted. "If your mama or anyone knew you were working for a black man? Isn't that it? Isn't that what you mean to say?"

I nodded. What he said was true.

"They have names for us, Maggie. Ugly names. You probably know them. Like I said, names are important. I just wondered if you had any trouble with the notion of working for a black man. There was something about the way you stared at me when I came in. Almost like you were taking a picture. Because you couldn't believe your eyes."

"I'm sorry if I stared," I said, happy to have the manila envelope in my hand to worry over. "I do that all the time. Mama's always getting on me about that. And I can't say I wasn't surprised. It's not every day that white cleans for colored. Usually it's the other way round." I felt like George Hardy had been scolding me.

I laid the envelope on the desk and bent to pick up the papers he had scattered. I was grateful for the mess. It gave me something to do. I stacked the papers neatly, separating letters from bills and clamping the stacks together with a paper clip. Then I turned to George Hardy. "Mama says I'm plain stubborn. Like a donkey. I hold on to things. So I'd like to hold on to this job, if it's all the same to you."

"I'd like you to, Maggie," he said. "Just let me know if a white girl decides she's too uncomfortable working for a black man."

I nodded, setting to work. I wondered why he kept calling himself "black." Didn't he know that people in Kinship said "colored"?

He hovered at the door frame a minute, watching me. I pulled a dustcloth from my apron and dusted the ink bottles. Then I squared off the papers on the desk, scooping the rubber bands and paper clips into the desk drawer.

"By the way," he said, turning to leave, "about magnolias." I liked the way he balanced lightly on the balls of his feet. "They take forever to mature. Sometimes as long as twenty years. But once they do, there's not anything you can do to destroy them."

Then George Hardy felt in the pockets of his pants again, brushed off his jeans, and disappeared down the steps with that easy, swinging walk.

I let out a long full breath and turned to the laundry piled up on the floor. I began to sort the clothes. The dark pile, the light. Jeans in this pile, Maggie. Undershirts in the other. Towels with the jeans. White socks with the undershirts. Work, Maggie, I told myself. It's what you do best. Enter by the side door. Keep a secret. Clean.

I carried the clothes to the washer. I would have to do two loads. One for the darks, one for the whites. It was a rule about laundry. Laundry, like dishes, had rules. You kept things separate, Maggie. You kept them apart, like Mama said. You didn't want them bleeding into each other.

I put in detergent, shaking it carefully around the clothes in the bin. Mama'd kill me if she knew I was working for a colored man. She'd plain out kill me.

Well, then, Maggie Pugh, I thought, dropping the lid, hearing it thump: *Mama isn't going to know.*

Chapter 8

I shouldn't have worried. My secret was safe. Mama wasn't interested in me. Her every thought was focused on Gardenia. Especially today, the day of the Hayes County Little Miss Pageant.

She made Daddy and me get up to finish our chores early, shushing us all morning, scolding us for talking too loud or tripping over pails or banging our dishes in the sink. "Can't you fools be quiet for one mornin'?" she said. "Don't you know Gardenia needs her beauty rest?"

Mama had risen even earlier herself. She wanted to set the ironing board up and start her pressing, and she was nervous as a sitting hen. As she struggled with the folds of white organdy, she kept scorching her fingers, dropping the sprinkling can, and muttering, "Sweet Jesus," under her breath.

It went like that all morning. I was even able to slip away to the post office to mail George Hardy's enve-

lope. It was going to some organization in Atlanta. Elsie Fish was postmistress and looked like Annie Oakley
minus the rifle in a building that looked like a fort.
After the War the Kinship post office became a symbol
of Yankees. People threw their garbage up on the roof
and covered the floor with tobacco juice. You could
still see the stains today. The only other sign of Yankees in Kinship was the name of the county. It was
originally called Lafayette County after the famous
French general who came down on a visit. But after
Reconstruction, when the new President Rutherford B.
Hayes withdrew the hateful federal troops, the county
fathers, in a burst of gratitude, changed the county
name to Hayes.

I watched Elsie Fish toss the envelope into a bin
and then I headed home. It was ten o'clock when I got
there, and I was told to go wake Gardenia. "Gently
now, Maggie. We don't want to upset Gardenia on the
day of her show," Mama said.

Quietly I crept into her room. I had always envied
Gardenia because her room was larger than mine and
it was filled with special treasures. Gardenia had her
own Parcheesi set and two fans, and Daddy had set up
the radio so that Gardenia could sleep with quiet string
music from the longhair music station in Atlanta playing all night long.

Beside Gardenia's sleeping head was Angel, her
stubbled hair the same color as Gardenia's curls. I
watched my sister's pulse beating in her neck and
traced the delicate blue streams of veins with my fin-

gers. "Wake up, Gardenia," I said quietly. "It's your big day."

She stirred, her lips making a pout. "Oh, go *way*, Maggie, and let me sleep," she said, turning over, pulling the quilt up over her shoulders.

"Hey, Gardenia," I cautioned. "You'd better get going. You don't want to make Mama mad. She's all nervous as a cat already, and we haven't even started getting dressed yet."

"Oh, pooey on Mama," she spit.

So I reached over, changed the radio dial, and turned up the volume. "You Ain't Nothin' But a Hound Dog" came blasting out over the airwaves. Gardenia grabbed a pillow, threw it hard at me, and stood up.

It seemed she was purposely slow that morning. I always figured that Gardenia dawdled then, as she often did, to get attention. But inside I wondered if Gardenia wasn't awful nervous.

Daddy had escaped to the out-of-doors chore of washing the car. It was that kind of morning. I helped him sweep the seats and polish the grille while my long auburn hair air-dried in the sunshine.

Finally we were ready to go.

Mama had on her black linen funeral dress with the antique brass brooch tacked to the bodice. She had coiled her graying hair with bobby pins all night and now had brushed it out fiercely, sweeping it up at the sides and anchoring it with combs. For all her efforts she looked worried and suspicious. Like a black crow scanning a dry field for grain.

Daddy had slicked his hair down with Vitalis, using

the excess to polish his shoes. I had caught him smiling at himself in the mirror, and then he winked at me over the top of his red clip-on bow tie. I had braided my hair, winding the braid with a white ribbon. The braid made a fine heavy brown rope down my back, and with my crisply pressed white cotton blouse and my clean navy skirt, I felt I looked presentable.

But Gardenia was the one. Looking at her then, it struck me that the world was divided into two types of women: those who lived by their hands and those who lived by their beauty. Gardenia was the second type, and for the first time in my life I understood her special kind of pull.

"Get your camera, Maggie," Mama ordered. "And hurry up about it. We don't want to be late."

Mama couldn't make up her mind about the picture. First she wanted a family shot, the three of them standing in front of the car. Then she thought she might like a mother-daughter picture, just Mama and Gardenia arm in arm under the pecan tree. Finally she decided a picture of Gardenia all by herself would be best. Mama sat her on the front stoop, the purple periwinkles spread out around Gardenia's feet, her patent leather shoes crossed at the ankles.

I focused for a midrange shot. Through the lens I saw that Gardenia looked as white and fragile as her name. Mama had wound a strand of pink satin around the waist of the organdy dress; it was starched so stiff it spread out from Gardenia's hips like a fan. The pale pink color of the ribbon made me sad. It reminded me of baby bottoms and talcum powder and the fact that

Daddy had lost his job. *Click. Advance the film, Maggie.*

I focused on a close-up next. Gardenia's hair had been treated to a fresh lemon-juice rinse. It glistened with a platinum shine like the angel hair we used to drape around the Christmas tree. Mama had bought some styling gel special, and Gardenia's curls lay in neat ringlets around her face, bouncing gently with each step in her shining shoes. *Focus. Click.* Even from behind the lens Gardenia's beauty made my breath catch.

But just as Mama was pushing us into the car and the engine had finally kicked over, Gardenia stood stock-still in the gravel drive.

"Let me go back inside with Maggie for a minute, Mama. I forgot Angel." She stamped her tiny foot.

Mama scowled. "Well, all right, honey. Only, you got to leave Angel in the car when we get there. We don't want that ol' banged-up doll ruinin' all the pictures they'll be takin'."

Gardenia grabbed me by the hand, pulling me through the doorway. Once we were inside, she threw her arms around my neck, choking me hard.

"Oh, Maggie," she said, starting to sob. I could feel her body shaking next to mine.

"Shush, now, Gardenia," I said. "What's the matter, honey? Don't cry. You'll get your ringlets all damp."

"I can't go, Maggie. Mama'll kill me." Her voice was whiny and shrill.

"Why not, Gardenia?" I asked. "What's the matter?"

122

"Promise you won't tell, Maggie?" She gripped my neck in hopes of a promise.

"Okay," I said. "I won't."

Gardenia took a deep breath, lifting her starched skirt. "I wet my pants, Maggie. The ones Mama got me with the lace instead of the plain kind like you got. They's all wet and soggy, Maggie."

"All right, Gardenia," I said. "It's okay. You can wear a pair of mine. Here, honey, I'll go get them."

She slipped the panties around her ankles and handed them to me. They were sure wet, and they stunk like diapers. I ran to the bedroom and fetched her a pair of plain ones from my drawer. Gardenia tried to hike them up, but they kept slipping down. I ran to the sewing basket for safety pins.

"Thanks, Maggie," she said, giving me a soft peck on the cheek. Then she wiped her eyes and ran to the bedroom for her doll.

"What took you so long, Maggie?" Mama said as we headed back to the car, Gardenia trailing Angel in her hand.

"Nothing, Mama," I said, remembering my promise.

Then Mama looked at Gardenia, who was bending to climb in the car. "Don't you look like an *angel,*" Mama said, "in that white organdy dress and that big pink bow and them golden curls and big blue eyes. Lord, Lord, but you look like an *angel.*"

I slid in next to Gardenia, thinking about Mama's angel and her plain white panties held up with safety pins. And of all the secrets I was holding this summer from Mama.

Chapter 9

I shifted the heavy weight of the wicker basket onto my right hip. Inside the basket were Peter Matlack's clean white handkerchiefs and Margaret Matlack's white linen blouses and Skippy Matlack's undershorts and the Matlack family's sheets and towels, pressed and ironed under the weight of Mama's will. I would cross the fields and climb the hill to the Matlacks' house, delivering them, as I did so many mornings, into the hands of Georgia, the Matlacks' maid. Then I would go back down the hill with the basket filled with dirty clothes, the money Mama earned each day resting in the pockets of my jeans.

That laundry held secrets. I had watched Mama struggle when she thought I was asleep. I spied her working at night, stringing rich folks' laundry across the line Daddy rigged up between the house and the trunk of the pecan tree. By morning the sheets would be dry, and I spied Mama rising before dawn, darting out of bed, slipping off the sheets that flapped like ghosts on the line. For Mama the secret was the shame of taking in laundry like a colored girl.

But this morning there was less shame than there had been in weeks. I caught myself whistling as I thought back to yesterday and the Hayes County Little Miss Pageant.

Mama had looked worried when Sarah Deems came out, setting fire to the ends of her daughter Dawn's baton, watching Dawn twirl and circle to John Philip Sousa. Mama looked even more worried when it was Gardenia's turn. I saw Mama taking a deep gulp of air when Gardenia began, looking like she did when she tried to swim underwater at the YMCA in Troy. But she shouldn't have worried. I saw Gardenia putting the judges in her corner one by one. There was nothing sweeter than Gardenia when she sang.

> Amazing Grace, how sweet the sound
> That saved a wretch like me.
> I once was lost but now am found,
> Was blind but now I see.

By the time she reached the last verse, she had her arms spread before her, her palms open wide, and the audience had joined in, the gym throbbing to the familiar words. Mrs. Russell Simmons sat in the row in front of us, dabbing at her eyes with a hanky.

> Through many dangers, toils, and snares
> I have already come.

'Tis grace has brought me safe thus far
And grace will lead me home.

Mama fainted when Mayor Cherry announced how Gardenia had won fifty dollars, an all-day shopping spree in Savannah, and the chance to compete in the state pageant. Mr. Russell Simmons revived Mama by splashing his cup of 7-Up in her face.

Although the memory of the pageant made my heart light, the basket at my waist was heavy. I sat down on a rock to rest when I reached the Dancing Trees. Looking up, I saw the way the branches fanned out like fingers. I felt the breeze gathering high up in the leaves and then dipping down to cool the back of my neck.

There were dozens of Kinship legends about the Dancing Trees. Some said these live oaks had heard more romantic confessions than a priest. Others said that lovers who kissed three times under these branches would happily marry. Still others believed that Hattie Mae Withers, the sorceress over by the swamp, made up her potions from the bark, the sap, and the leaves of the Dancing Trees.

I didn't put much stock in those stories, but I did understand how the Dancing Trees got their name. They swung toward each other at midpoint. Their branches met at waists and shoulders. The Spanish moss draping their limbs looked like shirts and shawls. When the wind moved high in the treetops, their garments rustled and swirled.

Suddenly the silence was broken.

I heard a whinny, a rough, full-throated snort. Like a horse tossing back its head.

It startled me, for I had thought I was alone.

"Mornin', Miss Maggie," the voice said.

The voice was low and the words were slurred together like someone on a drunk. "I'se hopin' that you might be in mind to do some dancin' like them trees here."

I froze in my tracks. The voice played hide-and-seek with me. It seemed now to come from over here, then to come from over yonder, flitting between the branches like a frisky ghost. I was terrified.

"Where are you?" I called, cocking my ear. The voice appeared to be coming from behind the Dancing Trees, but the moss and the thick veil of leaves made it hard to see.

"I'se over here, Miss Maggie," the voice replied. "In the trees. About where the lady's belly button begins. About even with the fella's balls." Then the voice whinnied and snorted again, a laugh that I recognized.

"Virgil Boggs! I should have known it was you right off. What you doin' tryin' to scare me in the middle of the morning?"

"Well, Maggie, honey," he said—I could see the shadowy outline of his body between the Dancing Trees—"you know how I've been gettin' to know you real good. Watchin' you prance before that mirror of yours. Threadin' that long brown hair across your shoulder. Admirin' them pretty naked breasts, ripe as peaches. Figured it's time, Maggie, to get to know you up close."

I saw Virgil's long, skinny body emerge from the trees. I could see the pattern of his ribs under his tight white undershirt. My heart sank.

"You just stay away from me, Virgil, you hear? You're the nastiest boy in Hayes County. And you should be ashamed of yourself for spying on me like that. You're just lucky I didn't call Sheriff Keiter."

"Shoot, Maggie. I'se a *man,* not a boy. And I know a purdy young body when I sees one. You don't know what a big girl like you does to a man, Maggie. Cain't blame a man for lookin', now, can you? Lookin' ain't no crime."

I saw him lick his thick pink lips, his tongue running across his upper lip. Then he threw back his head and laughed. I had seen him throw his head back and laugh like that before. Last summer, when I saw what I wished I hadn't. The images came back. I shut my eyes tight, refusing to look at them. Instead, I picked up the basket, which had fallen to the ground, and heaved it ahead of me, marching on, determined to ignore Virgil Boggs.

He stood straight in front of me, blocking my path.

"Didn't you hear me, Miss Maggie? I said I thought you might be in the mood for a little dancin'." He grabbed my arm, jerking the basket from my grip. The clean white garments spilled out over the ground. I was paralyzed with fear. Fear for what Mama would do when I got home. Fear for what Virgil would do to me now.

"I don't know as whether you noticed or not," he said, wrenching my wrist behind my back, "but that man waltzing that lady over there has got his hand like *so.*"

With that he grabbed me around the waist, pulling me so tight I could feel his breath on my cheek. It smelled like medicine. I knew that smell. It was the way Uncle Taps smelled when he was on a drunk.

"And that lady over there has got her arm up real high on his shoulder. Like *so.*" He took my arm and placed it high on his own shoulder. My teeth began to chatter. I could feel the golden key banging against my chest.

"I don't know as to whether you've heard too much about this, but *men*—not *boys*—knows somethin' about dancin' with *women,* not *girls.* Only, the best kind of dancin' is done lying *down,* not standing *up.* Know what I mean, Miss Maggie?"

His wet mouth was against my ear. "The kind of dancin' where you lay down and get real close and you move back and forth and up and down in time with the music you're makin' together and 'fore you know it you've worked up a sweat. It's kind of like at the sock hops over in Troy at the Legion Hall." Then Virgil Boggs laughed. An ugly, dirty laugh.

My heart was thudding against my chest. I could feel it pounding against the bright golden key at my neck. The thought of George Hardy's key, the thought of escaping from everything hateful in Kinship, gave me courage. I began to beat on Virgil's chest with my fists, and I kicked with my sandals at his shins.

He still held me by one wrist, twisting it so hard that the pain shot all the way to my shoulder. I wrenched my head, opened my jaw, and sank my teeth into his shoulder.

He threw me around to face him before he let go. Then he folded his arms across his chest and sneered. "Know what, Maggie? That's good. That's real good. I really like that, Miss Maggie. I like a girl with your kind of fire. I liked it the other day when you bit me on the wrist. I gotta confess I do. I like it when you gets wild like this, Maggie," he said.

Then he lunged at me, throwing me to the ground.

"Spread out one of them sheets, Maggie," he ordered.

I crawled over to the basket and took a deep breath, sucking at the air. I pulled a clean white bedsheet from the basket and shook it open across the grass.

I saw him wipe his greasy brow with his T-shirt. Then Virgil pointed with his finger. "Lie down," he said.

I was crying now. The tears were streaking my cheeks as I kneeled on the sheet. As I stretched out, I felt the golden key knock against my chest, and courage returned. Virgil hovered over me, and I kicked him hard in the ribs.

I rolled out of his way, preparing to run. As I sprang for the open field, my sandal caught on the corner of the sheet, tripping me up.

In an instant Virgil had recovered and was on me. He was pushed against me so close that I could feel him hard against my hips. Suddenly he was ripping at my shirt, his wet tongue licking my breasts, his hand pushed down into my jeans. I could feel his groping fingers, and I heard him rip his zipper open, watching in horror as he pulled it from his pants, hard as a weapon.

The sheets churned and thrashed as Virgil moved over me. My mind filled with the image of Virgil and Gardenia's doll. Virgil and Angel and something else. Virgil and Angel and Zeke. It was all mixed up in my mind, the sound of tearing fabric, the cries and groans, and Virgil's ugly laugh before he did what he did.

I clamped my knees shut tight and tried to hunch them against Virgil. He lifted me by the hair, his mouth by my ear. "You best be opening yourself up for me, Miss Maggie. Sweet as a box of candy, now. Or I got something to tell you. Something important." I could feel the golden key dancing against its chain as he jerked my head while he talked. "You give me a little of your sugar today, honey, or I'll be after your sweet baby sister. She won't look so pretty for her high-'n-mighty beauty contest after I gets through with her, you know?"

I knew what it was like when Virgil got through with things. I remembered what Angel was like when he was through with her.

He pulled at the chain on my neck, choking me. "Why don't you use this gold key for me, Maggie?" He had his dirty fingers around George Hardy's key. "Use it to unlock your pretty secrets for Virgil, Maggie. Use it to give Virgil the key to your heart."

Something like courage shot up my spine. Virgil had soiled George Hardy's key with his touch. When

131

Virgil put his hand on George Hardy's key, he unlocked something inside of me, something strong.

Quickly I raised my knee, heaving with all my might against the hardness that was Virgil Boggs. He fell back against the sheets, his arms doubled across his crotch in pain.

I stumbled onto the grass, dragging my shin across a rock that lay nearby. My sandal caught on loose twigs, ripping at the buckle, shattering into splinters in my foot. As I ran, I groped for the basket, knowing that Mama needed her money as desperately as I needed to escape. But in my fear I tipped it over, undershorts and handkerchiefs spilling across the open fields, scattered by the breeze across brambles and dirt.

Virgil had dragged himself to his knees. He was shouting after me. "You can't escape me, Maggie. You can't escape Virgil Boggs."

I ran, his words haunting me, following me across the field like ghosts. My sandals flapped behind me, tripping me up at every bend and tree trunk along the way back home. My mind whirled. I knew that Virgil Boggs didn't make idle threats. I knew he carried them out.

I burst in our door. Daddy was just stretching his suspenders across his chest, Mama was ladling gravy on biscuits, and Gardenia was lounging at the kitchen table, coloring in a coloring book, the diamond tiara she had won last night atop her ruffled curls.

Mama's fist tightened around the gravy ladle. Her eyes widened as they took in my scratched cheeks and torn feet, the bruises at my wrist and neck, the blood staining my blouse. "You get the basket to Matlacks', Maggie?" she asked, suspicious.

"No, ma'am," I said, hanging my head. My pulse was racing in my throat.

I felt the swat of the ladle across my cheeks before I heard her words. "What you mean, child?" she continued. "You mean you didn't get the laundry to Matlacks'?"

"No, ma'am," I repeated.

"Then I guess you owe me an explanation."

I stood and stared, silent and ashamed.

"Looka here, now, Izzy," Daddy said. "Can't you see the girl's all banged up? Just hold your horses for a minute. Seems to me she needs a doctor before she needs your angry hands or the third degree." He was studying my face with his fingers, tracing them across all the swollen places.

"Where'd you leave your mind today, Henry?" Mama had whirled on him. "Don't you think Doc Jackson'll ask her a few things, Henry Pugh? Her family leastaways got a right to hear about it first."

Mama turned on me, making an effort to keep her voice calm. "I've only got one thing to say, Maggie Pugh," Mama said. "You owe me an explanation."

I stood and stared, numb with shame.

Then Mama raised the gravy ladle and whacked me across the side of my head. "Don't you be pulling that silent act with me, Miss Magnolia Pugh. *I* demand an explanation, Magnolia Pugh," she raged, wagging her finger under my nose. "No basket, no laundry, and no money. And a lost contract for this family, I reckon."

I fell in a heap into the chair at the kitchen table and told it all, blubbering, spilling out the words all at once, my arms heaving, my tears slipping down my cheeks and onto Mama's checkered tablecloth.

Mama went wild. She stormed into the kitchen, banging on the Formica, kicking the metal cabinets. She raged, vowing revenge. She paced in front of the sink, swatting an imaginary Virgil with her ladle, whacking the air with her pot holders.

"Dear God in Heaven," she shrieked. "What'll those monsters do next? We's no better off if we'd be livin' in a jungle, wild animals runnin' loose next door!" She picked up the silverware draining on the dishboard and heaved it all in the sink.

"I'm gonna get those wild Boggs, Henry Pugh," she screamed, "if it's the last thing I do. You just watch, Henry Pugh, I'll get 'em back one of these days, and you won't have to wait too long."

"I think, Izzy," Daddy said, quiet and calm, "that we'd best be calling Sheriff Keiter."

"Sheriff Keiter? Sheriff Keiter?" Mama was heating up like a stove. "Call Sheriff Keiter and have everyone in Kinship talkin' about our girl like she was nothin' more'n a common tramp? Havin' her stand up in court and tell the whole dern county what that monster done to her? Havin' them make up lies like maybe she invited his company because what can you expect from a tramp on the west.end?" Mama was steaming now.

Gardenia piped up. "Maggie ain't no tramp, Mama." She slipped her arm around my waist. Her tiara poked at my cheek, and she took it off, setting it on the table. Her soft yellow curls at my neck felt like feathers.

Daddy moved to Mama by the sink. He tried to put his arm around her, but she swatted him with the dish towel. Every time something bad happened to our family, Mama blamed Daddy. Or me.

"Maybe you're right, Izzy," Daddy said. "Maybe they would say those lies. Even so, I reckon our Maggie here needs a doctor."

Mama looked up like she was talking to heaven. "Lord God Almighty and Sweet Jesus both, bless any woman what has a helpless husband." Then she stopped talking to God and talked to Daddy, Gardenia, and me. "You go'n tell Doc Jackson, and you've gone and told the world. He's got folks in his waiting room. He's got Nurse Davis part time. Ain't those folks got eyes and ears? Better yet, ain't those folks got mouths? We go'n talk to Doc Jackson, we may as well call up Lucy Tibbs and tell her to announce it over the switchboard."

Daddy sighed, stroked my head, and shuffled back into the bedroom. When he returned, he had the Johnson & Johnson sample case that looked like a doctor's bag in his hand. He opened it up, picking out the bottle of Merthiolate.

"I'll take it real easy, Maggie, honey," he said, coming up close with the applicator, swabbing my scratched cheeks. "I'll try not to hurt you."

It stung like fire, and I cringed. "Hold on, Maggie," Daddy said. After each application he blew on the scratches, cooling the flames.

Mama paced while Daddy worked, holding her tongue.

When he had finished with his cleaning and bandaging, he brushed my hair back off of my forehead and closed the sample case. Then Daddy put my head to his chest, stroking my hair as if I were a kitten, wiping my tears with his red bandana.

"You done with the girl now, Henry?" Mama said.

Daddy didn't answer. He kept right on stroking.

"If'n you're done with the girl now, Henry, we got a basket of laundry that's missing and some money too. What're you goin' to do 'bout that?"

Daddy spoke to me, not to Mama. He whispered in my ear as if Mama weren't even there. "It'll be all right, baby," he said, crooning the word that Mama always used for Gardenia. "It'll be all right. I'll go back for the basket, Maggie, baby, and we'll fix up the laundry. It'll be all right, baby. It'll be all right. You'll see."

Daddy went back alone across the fields, his Bible tucked under his arm. While he was gone, I ran the water in the tub and washed, trying to scrub away everything of Virgil Boggs that had touched me.

Mama paced, and Gardenia's crayons moved faster.

Finally Daddy came in the door, Mama right on his heels.

"Did you get the laundry basket, Henry Pugh?"

"No, Izzy. No."

"Well, did you bother to look for it carefully?"

"Of course, Izzy. Looked everywhere."

"Like *where?*"

"Like everywhere Maggie said she was. By the

Dancing Trees. Near the rocks. Behind all the bushes. I retraced the whole route, Izzy. All the way to Matlacks' and back."

Mama fanned the fires that burned inside her with another deep breath of air. She marched out the back door, hovering at the edge of lawn before it turned into chickweed at the Boggses'. She raised her fist, shouting at her enemy.

"You lazy, good-for-nothin' spiteful Boggs. You come out here and hear me out. Tryin' to ruin my daughter, ruin the neighborhood, ruin everything decent in Kinship. I'm vowing revenge on every last one of you. Maxine and all your kids. Even the baby. Gram. Jim Bob. Cecil. Hazel. But specially you, Virgil Boggs. You ain't gonna wait long to hear from Izabelle Pugh."

There wasn't a sound from the Boggses' house.

Buster lifted his head for a moment, hearing Mama out. Then he bent to lap from the bucket.

I could have told Mama to save her breath. Boggses wouldn't listen. Boggses wouldn't change. Like the chickweed strangling their yard, they choked out everything splendid in Kinship. Everything splendid that struggled to grow.

Chapter 10

I'll never know why, but it didn't seem to matter to Mama that we found the basket the next morning. It had been set beside the back stoop, and the clothes had been folded neatly into white squares and rectangles. A penciled note in a hand I recognized but didn't let on about lay atop the crisp white garments. *"Georgia say the close never got there,"* it said. *"New you needed them."* I felt happiness creeping up alongside of guilt. I had never taught Zeke about homonyms. I swore I'd get to *clothes* and *close* and *knew* and *new* next time.

But the basket didn't seem to matter to Mama. None of it mattered. What mattered now was that Mama had made a promise. Because of that promise she forgot her anger at me, and I escaped the back of her hand for the moment. When it came to promises, Mama was like Virgil. She always made good on them.

She had promised the Boggses that they wouldn't wait long to hear from her.

I didn't know she meant the very next day.

In the morning Mama went on a spree of closing things out and shutting things in.

"Get inside here now," she called to Gardenia, who had run outside to pick stalks of dandelion fluff.

"Keep those drapes drawn," she ordered me when she saw me peeking out the kitchen window.

"Don't you dare go up that tree no more," she demanded when I protested. I felt like a prisoner in my own house. "We got to stay inside. Away from them animals next door."

She sent Daddy to Gleason's for dead bolts. Then she looked them over, dissatisfied. "Take back these old dead-bolt locks, Henry Pugh," she complained. "Go get double dead bolts. I wants this house *secure* from them delinquents next door."

Daddy protested. "What you doin' with this madness, Izzy? Tryin' to play God? Don't you remember that 'vengeance is mine, saith the Lord'? " He tried to caution her, but her rage burned on.

"Maybe so, Henry," she admitted. "But the Lord don't have to live next door to the Devil every day. If'n He did, He'd want double dead bolts too."

The double dead bolts were followed by locks for the windows. The locks for the windows were followed by tacks, nails, and sealing tape for the screens. We would live in a four-walled coffin of Mama's making with the windows locked, the drapes drawn, the doors double-bolted against the world. I felt like I was preparing to be buried alive.

"But what if there's a fire, Mama?" I was worried. "Maybe Boggses won't be able to get in. But, Mama, maybe Pughs won't be able to get *out.*"

"Hush, you donkey," she said, swatting me with her words. "Don't you know we's been burned almost to death already by those careless hotheads? No fire can be no hotter than what we's walked through already."

Mama scurried between the doors and the windows, peering out. It had begun to seem like the source of her fear was more than just Virgil Boggs: it was the entire world around her.

Then Mama lit on the idea of a fence.

"Start up the car, Henry Pugh," she ordered. "We's all goin' for a ride. Call that lazy brother of yours. He oughta be free. Turkey season's over and squirrel season's yet to come. And we's gonna need his help."

We were mighty grateful to get out of the house. We had been sweating like pop bottles hauled from a cooler. After we picked up Uncle Taps, Daddy, Gardenia, and I, desperate for air, hung out the car windows like dogs.

"Where we going, Mama?" I asked.

"We's going to pick out fences, Maggie Pugh. Your daddy here is going to build us one."

Daddy almost swerved into the hay wagon ahead of us, and Uncle Taps slapped his knee and laughed. "Hey, Henry Pugh," Uncle Taps said, "we'd been wonderin' what we'd be doin' the rest of the summer. And now we knows."

We rode all over Kinship, noticing fences as if for the first time. We saw tall fences, short fences, sturdy fences, flimsy fences. Split rail. Picket. Chain link. I liked the kind with the boards shaped like dog ears. Gardenia liked the Fenwicks' fence. Mr. and Mrs. Fenwick's daughters had a playhouse that was an exact replica of their own home, right on down to the tiny white picket fence around it. Gardenia begged Daddy to make her a playhouse that was a copy of our house, but I kept quiet. I couldn't see the fun in a playhouse with drawn drapes and double dead-bolt locks.

Mama's favorite fence was Ida Perls's. It was made of black wrought iron and was nearly seven feet high. There were spikes that looked like the points of lances at the top of each of the iron posts. The fence was completely covered by purple bougainvillea vines.

"Oh, laws, Henry Pugh," Mama said. "That's just the purdiest fence I ever *saw!*" She made Daddy drive by it slowly one more time. "That's the best kind of fence in the world. It'll keep the neighbors out and the sweet flower smells in."

"Looks like a cell door with funeral sprays on it to me," harrumphed Uncle Taps. I always loved the look to Uncle Taps. He was all joints and angles like a grasshopper.

"And look, Henry," Mama said, ignoring him. "In back they've got that fountain with that little naked boy tipping that jug streamin' real water."

"That ain't no jug, Izzy," Uncle Taps said. "That stream's him pissing."

Mama slugged him with a look and then said, "You just proved your own ignorance, Wilbur Pugh. Fine people don't put up fountains in gardens with people pissin'."

"And why not, Miss Izzy?" You could tell Uncle Taps was having a grand time baiting Mama. His joints were a-working quickly: a bass player when the beat picks up. "Seems to me the best place to piss is in the middle of all them bushes."

"Oh, shut up, Wilbur," Mama shot back. "That's probably pure spring-fed water piped in from Carson Springs, I reckon."

"Water, hell." Uncle Taps laughed. "That's probably wine that kid's pissing. All them people back in those ancient times drank wine. Even the kids."

"Well, I guess that drinkin' wine's something you *do* know about, Wilbur Pugh," said Mama, finishing him off.

We drove through all the streets in town and then out into the countryside where they had split rail fences like Abe Lincoln built. "Split rail's no good for us," Mama sniffed. "It might mark a fella's property line okay, but it can't keep all the animals out. And animals is what we got next door."

When we drove through Fenwick Acres, Mama was taken by the chain-link fences the people had put up to keep their kids and pets in the yard.

"Them chain links looks solid," Mama said, impressed. "I like a fence like that. Like a bulldog what would grab on to your pants and rip if you tried to climb over it."

"But there's a big problem with chain link, Henry," Mama complained. "You can see clear through all them links." Mama wanted isolation, privacy.

"Yeah, but you can see what all the neighbors is up to," Uncle Taps said. "That'd be more fun than a checker game."

"Huh." Mama snorted. "We already *knows* what our neighbors is up to. That's just the problem, Wilbur Pugh."

We drove to Gleason's to check out the price of building materials. Mama's jaw dropped a mile when Bucky Gleason told her chain link was two dollars a square yard.

It was clear that our fence wouldn't be chain link.

Or wrought iron.

Or even split rail.

Mama looked like she was about to bawl.

Daddy scratched his balding head whenever he couldn't think of what to do. After he scratched, the hairs looked like long, sparse grasses raked by his fingers.

"There, there, Izzy," Daddy said, putting his big arm around her, passing her his red bandana. "We'll get you your fence. We'll get pine planks from Bucky right now. Pine is cheap. But it's solid. And it's strong."

"Can you build it as high as a castle wall, Henry?" she asked. There was a tiny pleading sound in Mama's voice.

"Yes, Izzy," Daddy agreed. "As high as a castle wall."

"And can you build it all the way around the property like a fortress?" she asked.

"Yes, Izzy," he replied. "All the way around the property like a fortress."

"And can you put in a special gate that only we can open? With one of them peepholes in it so we can see who's there before we open it?"

"Yes, Izzy," Daddy agreed once more.

Mama's face cracked into a smile. It looked like a mirror that's been dropped.

Daddy turned serious. "But if we build this fence, Izzy," he said, his mouth turned down in a frown, "you gotta promise me that it's the end to all this vengeance."

Mama threw her arms around Daddy and gave his cheek a wet kiss. "I promise, Henry," she said, sweet as pie.

We drove home with a loaded car buoyed up by Mama's high spirits. The pine boards stuck out the trunk, and Uncle Taps had wrapped Daddy's red bandana around the wood for a flag.

They called up all our relations. Aunt Lolly and Uncle Bunny. Cousins Willie, Sally, and Lester. Aunt Ella, who plopped down in Mama's kitchen and started cooking. Newell Puckett, who was only a third cousin; Mama claimed him into the family because of his air conditioner. The Puckett kids came and brought their dog. They started up right away and worked until dark. Measuring. Hammering. Sawing. Pounding. Mama ran back and forth between Daddy and Uncle Taps, giving instructions, her apron strings flying out behind her. Ruff, the Puckett cousins' fox terrier, yapped whenever someone started hammering.

I slept fitfully that night, the bedsheets stuck to my sweaty bottom, and I tossed in and out of a nightmare till dawn. It was about being holed up in a place surrounded by high wood fencing like a stockade. It was a place somewhere deep in the South, a place like the Alamo, a place where I was doomed to be stuck for the rest of my blessed life.

Chapter 11

Tired as I was, the next morning I knew I had to talk to Pert. And I knew I'd find her working the lunch counter up at Byer's Drugs. I was having trouble sorting out everything that had happened to me, and I knew that Pert could help.

The lunch counter was to the left as you came through the door. It was one of my favorite places in Kinship. I liked the metal basket they used for french fries and the vat bubbling with grease. I liked the refrigerated glass case where they showed off slices of Cinda Samples's pies and cakes. I liked the special machine they had for cooking hot dogs. The hot dogs lay on metal rollers, turning like pink logs all day long.

I saw Pert at the counter, dishing up ice cream from the ice cream chest. I watched her add a squirt of whipped cream and a cherry. She was always adding extras for the customers. She never charged for them. Then she sailed the dish down the counter to Lenny

Tubbs, Kinship's only midget. A long line of coloreds was standing at their special section of the counter. They were waiting for Cinda to dish up their orders of corn bread and collard greens to take home. Coloreds weren't allowed to sit.

"Whooo-eee!" Pert said when she saw me, touching my bruised cheeks with her fingers. She had a pearl-colored polish on her nails, and the tips of her fingers felt cool. Mama didn't believe in white nail polish. "You've been in a royal knuckle-buster, Maggie. Come here and sit down."

She took me to a booth, stacking the dirty plates of the last customer at one end of the table, making enough room for our elbows. She called to Cinda that she'd be on break, and then she turned to me. "You look awful, Maggie," she said. "Was it your mama done this to you?"

"No, Pert." I hung my head. "Not my mama."

"Good thing," said Pert. "I swore I'd kill her if she laid a finger on you again, and I mean it, Maggie. So who done this to you?" Pert squinted her eyes together for a minute, thinking. Then they got as big as one of her sunny side eggs, and she slammed her fist on the Formica. "VIRGIL!" she said. "Virgil Boggs did this to you!"

Two identical pools of water formed in the pockets of my eyes, and as I talked, they began to trickle onto my face. I told her about Virgil's hot breath, my terror, the spilled sheets, my daddy's tenderness, my mama's fury, and now the fence.

Pert kept pulling napkins from the dispenser and

passing them to me. In between she banged on the tabletop. "That low-down mean pile of trash."

In between bangs she made her hands into fists, slugging the air. "I'll get him back for you, Maggie. You just wait," she said, one of her slugs toppling the salt-shaker. "He ain't gonna do that to you. I ain't gonna let him." Pert sounded a lot like Mama.

Pert got up from the table. "Be right back," she said. When she returned, she set a plastic package in front of me. "Open it up," she said, pointing to the package. It said, GOODY HAIR FASHIONS. "It's for you," she said. "To cheer you up."

A rainbow of hair ribbons spilled onto the speckled Formica.

"That's to help you start fixin' yourself up more," Pert said. "Once those scratches heal, Maggie, you're gonna want to feel pretty again. 'Course, I couldn't give you no nail polish, seein' as how you bit all yours down to the quick." Nail polish was a fancy notion of Pert's. She wanted to get a big job like a receptionist in a big company like Coca-Cola in a big place like Atlanta. She wanted to be rich enough to buy all the nail polish she could ever want. The job at the lunch counter after school and summers was just temporary.

"Thanks, Pert," I said. Fixing myself up was something Pert was always encouraging me to do. She fixed herself up all the time. Pert even fixed up her toenails.

"See," she said, "you can take that thick brown hair and tie it in a ponytail and then wrap a pretty ribbon round the rubber band. Just don't use the blue or purple right now. They'll highlight them bruises."

"Pert, thank you," I said again, slipping the ribbons through my fingers, grateful for my friend. "You didn't steal these, now, did you?"

" 'Course not, Maggie. Got 'em from the half-off table and paid every penny my own self." She gave me a proud and satisfied look. "Hey, Maggie," she said. "Cinda's giving me the evil eye. I gotta get back to work. Why don'tcha sit up by the counter and talk to me?"

The lunch counter was filling up. Olive Shriner took a stool, her fat bottom hanging off the sides. Boyce Johnson took a stool close to me and nodded, which was his way of saying hi. I reckon he had forgotten how I didn't care to speak to him.

I loved to hear Pert sending orders to Cinda. Listening to her chatter reminded me of Craddock Hooch, the auctioneer in Troy. When you listened, he drowned your troubles in a flood of words.

"That'll be one moo, a stack, and two eggs. Wreck 'em." Boyce Johnson had ordered a glass of milk, a stack of hotcakes, and two scrambled eggs.

"One tuna down," Pert called. Olive Shriner had ordered a tuna sandwich. *Down* meant she wanted it toasted.

Pert started on a malted, sliding the stainless-steel cup under the rotating blades of the milk-shake machine. While it whirred, she fiddled with her hairnet. That hairnet was one thing Pert Wilson hated about her job. The hairnet ruined her pouf. But it was a rule of Elmer Byer and a county health law to boot. Anybody that worked a lunch counter in Hayes County had to wear a hairnet. Lord knows there's nothing worse than eating a mess of grits with hair in it. When Hannah Bean was working the counter last year, she never wore a net. Mr. Byer came in one afternoon and fired her on the spot. "Rules is rules," he said.

Pert poured the malted into a soda glass, sliding the glass down the counter to Olive. She drank it down in one long gulp without a straw.

Then Pert got started on another order. She dropped two pieces of bread into the toaster, dipped a brush into a tub of melted butter, and greased up the grill. Then she cracked an egg into the butter. While it sizzled, Pert turned to me, serious.

"You better watch yourself, Maggie. Virgil's real dangerous. You already know that. And your mama's fence is gonna make him madder than he usually is. You just watch out for yourself, hear?"

I heard. I was worried.

I realized that Pert was making a fried egg sand-wich when I saw her pop the yolk. She popped it right at the last minute so it could cook a bit but still stay runny.

She slid the sandwich on a plate and set it down in front of me. When I looked surprised, she said, "Don't thank me. Thank Elmer Byer."

I didn't know how Elmer Byer could afford all this free food. And I couldn't figure out how to thank him for something I wasn't supposed to have in the first place, so I just said, "Thanks, Pert," and took a bite. "If I ever get thrown in prison over at Reidsville and sen-tenced to die in the electric chair," I said, licking the yolk from the corners of my mouth, "I'm gonna ask for one of these for my last meal. A Pert Wilson fried egg sandwich is my favorite thing in the world."

Pert leaned her elbows on the counter and grinned at me. "And if you ever get throwed in prison up in Reidsville and sentenced to die in the electric chair, I hope it's for cuttin' Virgil Boggs's *thing* off."

There's nothing that cheers me up better than a talk with Pert Wilson.

While I ate, I watched Cinda Samples. Watching Cinda work was satisfying as a square meal. She planted her heavy feet wide apart and worked behind the counter with her arms, slapping chicken pieces in a plastic tub of flour, shaking the fries in the fryer, ripping open cardboard boxes of napkins and straws. Cinda Samples was heavy as a side of beef, and when she breathed, her chest heaved in and out. She was big, but she was sweet too. The deep hollow in the middle of her chin reminded me of the well she made in the mashed potatoes before she slipped gravy in. The pin she thrust through the gray ball of hair at the nape of her neck put me in mind of Grandma Pugh's crochet hooks.

I thought Stumble Martin was soft on Cinda, for whenever he came in, he sweet-talked her. "Queenie," he'd say, "you're lookin' right fat and sassy today." Cinda would smile at his compliment. Fact was, everybody in Kinship liked Cinda Samples.

Cinda Samples never missed a trick or a day of work. Everybody in town knew she was the reason why Elmer Byer's lunch counter was a success. She spent every noon hour dishing up her food to the coloreds that stood in line. Bigger Baby Goolsby always ordered Cinda's corn bread and collards. Stumble Martin took corn fritters and poured maple syrup on them. Reverend Potter took two slices of pecan pie with whipped cream on top. Old Jake came all the way from Attica on Wednesdays to stock up on Cinda's fried chicken and sweet-potato pie for his Carry-It. Missy Moses ordered a quart of vegetable soup and a pint of bread pudding. Rocker left his post in front of the First National Bank every noon to stand in line for Cinda's dumplings. Rocker's real name was Eby Craddock but everybody called him Rocker because they said he was off his. Rocker always paced in front of the First National Bank of Kinship, giving out religious pamphlets. He wore a white robe even when it was hot, and his uncombed black hair fanned out from his face like the halo of a crazy angel. Most days he'd pull the shirttails of people going into the bank and whisper, "Is You Prepared to Meet Your Maker Today?" Every so often Sheriff Keiter would threaten to arrest Rocker for disturbing the peace, but most folks felt like my daddy: "Ain't no crime, Maggie, in having a few buttons missing."

I watched Pert pour a cup of coffee into a clean white cup and set it in front of me. Then she poured one for herself.

"What's this for?" I asked. "You know I don't drink coffee."

"That's just the problem," Pert said, wiping her greasy hands on her apron. "You gotta learn. It's what all grown-ups do when they're down in the dumps and want to feel better. They get a cup of coffee and then they sit and talk. Besides, there's only two things a girl's ever gotta learn in this world. How to drink coffee. And how to get her a man." She took a big gulp from her cup, set it back in the saucer, and smiled at me.

"But Mama won't let me drink it, Pert."

"Does she let you mess with boys either?"

"No, you know she doesn't."

"Ever wonder why parents got such a fear of boys and coffee?"

I stirred my coffee with the tip of the spoon, wondering.

"Same reason for both," said Pert. "Stunt your growth."

I laughed, and the coffee slopped over the rim and into the saucer. "You're a card, Pert," I said, dumping the spilled coffee in the saucer back into the cup. "A regular card." I felt better already.

I stared as Pert dumped some sugar from the sugar dispenser into her coffee. The dispenser had a tiny chute in the top, and the sugar poured out like grain sliding down the chute at the feed mill. I stared into my cup, taking in the color of the liquid. It was the same color of the bittersweet chips Mama put in cookies.

"Take a picture, Maggie," Pert said. "It lasts longer." She always noticed when I stared.

"Sorry, Pert," I said. "I guess I was just thinking."

"About Virgil?" she asked.

I nodded.

"Well, Maggie," Pert said, putting her cup down on her saucer, "what *about* Virgil?"

"Whadda you mean, 'What *about* Virgil,' Pert?" I asked.

"You know, Maggie. What about *it?* His *thing?*"

"Lord, Pert, it was moving so fast, I could hardly tell." I sipped again, thinking. "But it was stiff and hard, and the color was a pasty pink. Something like the color of bacon 'fore it's cooked."

Pert and I looked at each other hard for a minute, and then she choked on her coffee, laughing. I choked on mine, sending a spray of coffee across the table at her.

After a while, Pert and I were hooting to beat the band, and the other customers had turned to stare. Boyce Johnson moved himself two stools down from me. I had been laughing so long that the ribs on my right side were beginning to hurt.

"Hey, Pert," I said, "I better get going before I get you in trouble." I slid off the stool. "Thanks for the sandwich. And the coffee."

Pert shot me a smile and wrung out a washcloth from a tub filled with bleach water. As I turned to leave, I heard Bigger Baby Goolsby grumbling from the colored line, "How come they can take my money, but they can't give me no seat?" It was odd. I could take a seat. But I didn't have any money.

Bigger Baby kept it up. "Get me the manager," Bigger said, slamming his fist at the colored counter. "I want to see the manager." Bigger Baby's chin jutted out like someone itching for a fight, and his arm muscles bulged like sponges filled with water. Bigger Baby got his name because he was the baby in a family of thirteen kids. Plus he weighed fourteen pounds, nine ounces when he was born. They wrote it up in the *Troy Tribune*. To my mind Bigger's been pushing his weight around ever since.

Hazel Boggs left the register to go get Elmer Byer. He came out of his office in the back, his green eyeshade on his forehead.

"What seems to be your problem, Bigger?" Elmer Byer asked.

"Ain't my problem, Elmer Byer," Bigger said, talking right up into his face. "It's your problem. You got a separate line for coloreds at your lunch counter, Mr. Byer. It ain't right. We pay our money, same as white. I figure you owe me a seat."

"The law don't say I owe you any more than what you pay for, Bigger Baby," Elmer Byer said. You could tell Elmer was hopping mad because the back of his neck had turned red. "You order a quart of Cinda's collards, it's seventy-nine cents. You want a milk shake, it's forty-nine. The law don't say nothin' about no seat."

"Well, we'll just see about that, Mr. Byer," Bigger said. He waved his fist in Elmer Byer's face, then turned on his heels and stomped out. Funny thing of it was, Missy Moses, Stumble, Reverend Potter, and Rocker stomped out too. Only Old Jake stayed in line, waiting for his carryout.

I stopped by the magazine rack on my way out. I

had always loved magazines. I never could resist the pictures.

This month's *Modern Screen* had a photo spread of Kim Novak's house. It was all done in lavender, her favorite color. I thought taking pictures of movie stars' houses would be the most wonderful job in the world. *Look* had a layout of the last veteran of the War Between the States, who had died last year. They showed him wrapped in the Stars and Bars and leaning on a rifle. I even liked the pictures in the ads. Swanson TV dinners, the aluminum triangles filled with turkey, corn, mashed potatoes. Thom McAn shoes. Gold Medal flour. The Chesterfield ad with a man and a lady in bathing suits, lighting each other's smokes.

But I liked *Life* magazine best. The pictures told stories. One of the features in *Life* this month had pictures of people and their dogs and showed the way they looked alike. My favorite was a peroxide blonde with a bouffant holding a little white poodle. The photographer had snapped them with their heads close together, looking like best friends. I hoped Hazel Boggs wouldn't see me when I ripped a tiny corner out of the magazine. It was an announcement for the *Life* amateur photographers' contest that they had every year. Maybe some of my pictures of Gardenia might turn out nice and I could send them in to the address they gave.

I stuffed the announcement in my pocket and flipped through the rest of the pages. I was fixing to close the magazine up when a series of black-and-white images caught my eye. Like the pictures in

George Hardy's magazines, they captured the jumble and swirl of life. They showed a group of coloreds, the men with their pants hiked up, the women lifting their skirts, splashing and wading in a public beach. They showed a picture from South Carolina with white people pointing fire hoses at colored people, spraying tear gas and throwing eggs. They showed burning crosses from Marietta and Savannah, their white flames glowing eerily against the black night. They showed a picture of a white professor from Montgomery who was fined one hundred and seventy-three dollars just for eating lunch with coloreds. It looked like there were a lot of towns like Kinship.

Hazel Boggs was giving me dirty looks from the register. I slapped the *Life* back on the shelf and wondered: Now, how was a schoolteacher supposed to come up with that kind of money?

Chapter   12

I was learning lots of things about George Hardy, and he was learning lots of things about me. Regular things about him like how he hated to watch people chew with their mouths open. Regular things about me like how I hated when people talked in the movies.

But the things I liked learning were the special things. Like how George Hardy said it was okay to look at things up close, even if it was painful. He said it was the only way you could expect to understand. He said other things too. Like how you could understand people by figuring out the things they were afraid of.

"What do you mean by things people are afraid of? You mean like snakes, George Hardy?"

"No, Maggie. I don't mean things like snakes. Or spiders or bugs either."

"Well, what then? You mean like flying on an airplane?"

"No, Maggie. Don't mean that exactly."

"Well, what?" While we talked, I was stitching up the torn fabric on the lampshade.

"Let's take you, for instance. Why don't you tell me, Maggie, something that you're afraid of?"

I thought for a long time. "Lots of things, George Hardy," I said. "I'm afraid of lots of things."

"Like what?" He was circling things on math papers while we talked.

"Well, my mama, for one," I said, tightening a stitch.

"And what scares you about your mama? Is it the whippings?"

"Yes, it's the whippings, sort of. But it's more than that. It's more than just the whippings."

"Like what? What else besides the whippings?" When he stopped and looked over at me, he ducked his head a little, and his glasses glinted in the light. It reminded me of a monocle, catching the light as a duke bowed to the queen.

"Well, it's the meanness in her, the meanness in her that's not her fault. It's the meanness and the spite that I'm afraid of. I don't know where she got it from." I cut a strand of thread with my teeth.

I could tell he was listening closely. His pencil had stopped moving. "And what about the spite, Maggie? What is it about the spite that scares you?"

George Hardy asked the hardest questions. It was what I liked about him the most. I was quiet a long time. "I think it scares me, George Hardy, because I'm afraid I might catch it too."

"And what makes you think you're in danger of

catching all that meanness, all that spite, Maggie Pugh?" With George Hardy it was questions inside of questions. They lay inside your mind like nesting boxes. I put down the lampshade to look at him.

"I think I'm in danger just like everyone else in Kinship. Mama. Daddy. Pert Wilson. I think the meanness comes from living here, from living in Kinship day by day." Something inside me lifted when I said these words. I had never told anyone anything like this before.

George Hardy put down his math papers. He took his glasses off his nose and rubbed his eyes. Then he set his glasses on top of his head and turned to me. "You see, Maggie Pugh? I learned that you're afraid of your mama, your mama's spankings, and your mama's meanness. You're also afraid of catching that meanness from living in Kinship day after day. Is that right?"

I nodded.

"See?" George Hardy said, picking up his glasses and then blowing on them. "See all you can learn about a person by understanding what she's afraid of?" He rubbed at the lenses with the tail of his shirt.

I wanted to tell him more. That there were more things I was afraid of. That I was afraid of the poverty that haunted our family like a ghost. That I was afraid of the fence my mama and daddy were building. That I was afraid of Virgil Boggs. Of all the things that he had done. Of all the things that he might do. Some things I was still too afraid to tell.

"Now, George Hardy," I said, "let's be fair. Now

you're going to have to tell *me* something *you're* afraid of. It's only right."

"That's easy," George Hardy said. "I'm afraid of getting up and talking in public at that Independence Day speech over by Attica." George Hardy's talk wasn't on the July Fourth Independence Day for white people. George Hardy's talk was on the Independence Day a few days after. They had it every year just for coloreds. This year it fell on my birthday.

I was glad to hear him admit to being scared. He'd been trying to write that speech all week. There were papers balled up all over the living room. George Hardy was having terrible trouble getting started.

"And what about talking in public scares you, George Hardy?" I asked.

"That's easy, too, Maggie," he said, laughing. "I'm shy, so getting up and talking's hard for me. I'm also scared because I want the words to come out just right and I'm not sure if I can make them do that. I can do numbers, Maggie. Numbers are easy. Words are hard. Plus I'm afraid I'll make a damn fool out of myself and ruin everything."

I understood what he meant about being shy and what he meant about working to make the words come out right. I had been working hard to see things clear and knew the next step was to say them with the words coming out just right. But I couldn't imagine George Hardy as a damn fool, and I knew he wouldn't ruin a thing. Especially on a day that was the same as my birthday.

I could hear the wind outside the windows, gathering up air like somebody fixing to whistle. A few drops of rain spit on the roof. I watched George Hardy stuff tobacco into the bowl of his pipe. His hands moved easily, patiently. The sky outside was darkening.

George Hardy set the pipe in the ashtray and stood up and stretched. "It's going to pour, Maggie. You'd best be getting on home before your mama worries."

He walked me to the mudroom and then looked at me, firm and serious. "When you were talking about the things you were afraid of, Maggie, why didn't you tell me about what happened to you?"

"What happened, George Hardy?" I wasn't sure what he meant.

"Didn't you think I'd notice? The bruises? The scratches on your arms? I noticed them as soon as you came in today."

I hung my head, wondering how much George Hardy knew. I wondered why he was here in Kinship. I wondered how much I could ask without losing his friendship.

"Why are you here in Kinship, George Hardy? I don't see how Kinship has anything to do with math." I had broken my promise. *Clean. Don't ask.*

"It doesn't have anything to do with math, Maggie. It's more about words. The words on bathroom doors that say COLORED and WHITE. The ugly words they use when they talk about my people. They're thrown up everywhere in Kinship. Like fences."

His eyes were the warm brown color of the mahogany pews we sat on in church. "But you didn't answer my question, Maggie," he said. "You changed the subject." The rain was splattering now, and a gray look clouded George Hardy's eyes. He lifted the umbrella from where it hung on a nail and pressed it into my hand. Then he turned to me and said, "Where did you get those bruises, Maggie?"

I remembered how some of my teachers responded whenever we asked them a question they didn't want to answer. Usually they just asked another question. "Do you know who lives next door to me, George Hardy?"

He shook his head, looking puzzled.

"Virgil Boggs," I said.

I looked him straight in the eye. When he looked straight back, he nodded.

Chapter 13

The next morning, just before noon, they were finished with the fence. They worked all morning long, right through the drizzling rain. Daddy held nails in his teeth the way women held sewing pins in their mouths. Uncle Taps came right behind him with the hammer. Aunt Ella urged them on with promises of sponge cakes and meat loaves. Uncle Bunny wore a pair of old hunting boots that sopped up mud and water, leaving tracks like bear prints on Mama's kitchen floor. Uncle Taps went barefoot, his trail leading back and forth from the fence to the beer bottles in the refrigerator. Mama and Aunt Lolly followed behind their kitchen trails with their mops.

Gardenia and I and cousins Willie, Sally, and Lester played with the string Daddy had used to mark the property line. We were like kittens with a ball of twine. Willie would toss the ball to me and it would unravel some, and then I'd toss it to Sally and it would unravel some more, and then Sally would toss it to Lester. When Gardenia got it caught in the branches of the pecan tree, Daddy came out and swatted her with the newspaper and told her to stop fooling around. You had to be careful with Daddy anymore. Since he'd been working on the fence, you had to tiptoe around, avoiding him. He wasn't happy about the fence one bit.

And then they were finally done. They'd hoisted up the last pine plank. They'd put the peephole at the top of the front gate and the heavy slide-bolt lock at its side. Mama was delighted. She jumped up and down on the kitchen floor. Her wet shoes made squeaking mouse sounds on the linoleum. "Get your camera, Maggie," she said. "This is something for the Pugh family album."

Through the screen of rain the fence loomed shadowy and threatening. It traveled all around our property line, closing us off completely. There were two gates: one on the west side to let the car in; another at the front walk to keep the Boggses out. When I looked at it closely, I saw that the fence was higher than I had expected it to be. It was at least six feet high. A short man would have to get up on his tiptoes to see over it. When I put out my fingers to touch it, it felt like the long, thin emery boards Mama used to file Gardenia's nails. It must have been the cheapest kind of pine, for there were many knots in it, some big, some small. The knots spread out into rings the way water did after you skipped the surface with a stone.

I arranged my family before the fence outside the

front gate and held my camera to my waist. Mama tried to put her arm around Daddy's shoulder, and he moved away and stood by Uncle Taps. While I tried to focus, my cousins kept squirming, and Uncle Taps and Uncle Bunny started horsing around. Uncle Taps held up his bare toes and wiggled them, and Uncle Bunny made devil's horns with his fingers in back of Aunt Lolly's head. *Aim. Focus. Trip the shutter. Advance.*

"Just one more," I called. "Now hold still, Gardenia," I said. Gardenia would never learn about pictures. She had moved just as I tripped the shutter on the last one.

It was then that the Boggses came out to look. All of them. Cleotis and Virgil and Cecil and Maxine and her baby, Patsy, who was walking now, and Jim Bob and Gram and Aunt Irene. Their cousin Horace, who had once done time over in Reidsville, was barefoot like Uncle Taps. Betty, who wrote bad checks all over town, came out in heels spiked like weapons. They kept coming and coming, like those painted boxes shaped like eggs with egg after tinier egg spilling out. They stared at the fence.

Cecil was the one to speak. He stood a few feet from the front gate, his scraggly family huddled around him. "Mornin', Izabelle, Henry," he said. "We's jest out admirin' your fence here." He knocked hard on the wood boards. "We're wonderin' if we might come on over to git a better look."

Mama got right up in Cecil's face. "Now, you just stay over to your side, Cecil Boggs," Mama said.

"That's the whole point. Boggs over there. Pughs over here."

"So that's the point, eh?" Cecil said, turning to his family and sneering. "Well, Miz Pugh, Boggs got points to make, too, if'n you don't none of you mind. Ain't that right?"

The Boggses all nodded. Even baby Patsy.

Mama raised her fists at them and cried, "You ol' lazy, no-account, good-for-nothing-but-trouble Boggs. You just stay right over there on your property line. We don't want to see your ugly faces another day in this world. Don't you step one more step further, you hear?" Mama was steamed. Daddy moved to her and put his hands on her fists, pushing them down, trying to settle her. "Come on, now, Izzy. You promised."

It was then that Cecil Boggs gave a big deep harch, spitting a wad of snot smack dab in the middle of the gate. It left a dark green stain on the plywood. They followed after him one by one, harching and spitting to beat the band. Virgil. Maxine. Cleotis. All of them. Gram had a plug of tobacco in one cheek and left a thin brown trail of tobacco juice on the gate.

Mama gaped in horror. Even Daddy's jaw dropped to the ground. Mama raised her fists at them again. "I'll get you for this. I swear on a stack of Holy Bibles. I'll get you for this, every one."

I could see Uncle Taps wasn't going to take it. His chest puffed out, and he threw his shoulders back and then Uncle Taps harched up a big one and spit right in Cecil Boggs's face.

That was all it took. Virgil grabbed Mama by the

shoulders, ramming her against the fence. "You better get out your Bible and pray to Jesus the Boggses don't do nothin' worse to you than this, Izabelle Pugh," he said.

Meanwhile Uncle Taps had crashed a bottle of beer over Jim Bob's head. Gardenia's eyes were bugged out like marbles, watching, and she shouted, "Watch out, Maggie! Betty's right behind you."

I turned and saw Betty Boggs heading for me. She lunged for my camera and tore it from my hands. Then she threw it on the ground, jamming her high heels through both of the lenses.

Finally Daddy gained some control, picking up a shovel and breaking up the fight. He took the point of it and pushed the Boggses back onto their property and then shoved the Pughs through the gate and back into their house.

When Daddy shut the door behind us, his brow was wrinkled deep as a furrow. Everybody stared at him, wondering what he would do. Aunt Lolly. Uncle Bunny. The cousins. Uncle Taps and Aunt Ella. Then Mama threw her arms around Daddy, sobbing, and I saw him do something I had never seen before. He stared as if right through her and began to peel her arms off him, the way you peel bandages from a healing wound.

"You didn't make good on your promise, Izabelle," Daddy said.

Then he took her by the shoulders and sat her down in his rocker. Uncle Bunny coughed nervously.

Aunt Lolly worried with a fold in her apron. The Holy Bible sat on the coffee table in front of Mama.

Over her sobs I heard Daddy say, "You sit still, Izabelle Nelly Pugh. You sit still and stop your bawling. Remember Acts. 'Ye ought to be quiet, and to do nothing rashly.' To my mind, Izzy, you is done plenty already with that there fence idea of yours. And now insulting Boggs by callin' 'em names, eggin' on their hateful behavior even more."

Mama jumped up from the rocker. It rocked madly behind her, powered as if by an invisible force. *"My* fence! *My* fence, Henry Pugh! Who bought all that pine and did all that hammerin' and poundin' and God knows what-all work, Henry Pugh? That fence is yours, as God is my witness!" Mama's anger had a way of drying her tears.

All of us watched Daddy wipe the sweat from his forehead with the sleeve of his shirt before he said, "Izzy. Remember Proverbs. 'He that is slow to wrath is of great understanding.' "

She turned to Daddy, fury in her eyes. "No, Henry," she said firmly. " 'My wrath shall wax hot, and I will kill you with the *sword.'* Exodus, for your information, Henry Pugh." Then Mama kicked Daddy in the shin. He grabbed his shin and hopped around the room.

Mama stormed around the living room. Daddy followed, hopping still.

Then she snuck up behind him, slugging Daddy in the ear. Uncle Taps rushed over and tried to pull her away from him. Aunt Lolly cried, "Stop that, Izzy! Stop this nonsense!"

But Mama wouldn't be stopped. Her arms were now pinned behind her back by Uncle Taps, but Mama kept shouting in the direction of Daddy's ears. " 'In flaming fire,' Henry Pugh, 'take vengeance on *them that know not God.'* And if them no-good Boggses ain't 'them that know not God,' then I ain't the wife of a fool."

Daddy had his hand to his ear. It had turned fiery red. Uncle Bunny stood beside him looking helpless. My cousins' eyes were big as saucers.

Then Mama wrestled free of Uncle Taps and ran to the couch, heaving the cushions right and left, knocking over a vase of plastic flowers and the figurine of the sad-eyed clown she had got with trading stamps. Then she ripped a lampshade from a lamp, holding it before her in two hands.

Daddy tried to talk again, rubbing his ear with one hand. "Izzy, listen to reason," he was bellowing. " 'Vengeance is *mine,* saith the Lord.' "

I could stand it no longer. "Stop it, you two," I screamed. "Stop it!"

Then I bent to the coffee table and picked up the Pugh family Bible, heavy as a sack of potatoes. I looked around at the open mouths of my family before I heard the sound of the Bible's angry thud as I hurled it against the wall and scrambled out the door.

I hopped on my bicycle, pedaling for all I was worth. George Hardy's umbrella hung from my handle-bars and knocked against my thigh. When I got to George Hardy's house, I was bone tired. It was work pedaling through all those muddy puddles. But it was even harder work being a Pugh. Especially in a place like Kinship. I thought of my camera. Smashed, broken. Of everything in Kinship. Smashed and broken to bits.

I didn't know if he would be there or not, but I knew that George Hardy's house was the only place in the world where I could feel safe.

I took the key from my pocket, turning it in the lock. The house was quiet as snow. I stood at the threshold, scraping my muddy shoes on the mat and hanging George Hardy's umbrella on a nail. As I walked in, my footsteps echoed in the silence.

I threw myself across the sofa and pounded my fists on the cushions.

I heard a stirring from the bedroom. "George?" a voice called. It was a sweet voice, a cotton-candy voice, sugary and melting. "You forget something, George?"

Quickly I straightened the cushions, wiping my eyes with the back of my hand. "No," I said, my heart racing. "It's me. Maggie Pugh."

A face peered around the corner from the hall. It was round and soft, the light-brown color of peanuts.

"Who are you?" I asked, looking into the dark-brown eyes.

She came toward me. She was wearing George Hardy's gold bathrobe. She wrapped it all the way around her as she came nearer, tying it closed in the front. When she walked, George Hardy's robe dragged the floor.

She gave a quiet laugh. "Excuse me," she said. "I

hope I didn't scare you. I've heard a lot about you, even though we've never formally met. I'm Ida Mae Thatcher."

I thought of those envelopes on his desk. They had been there nearly every time shoved in with the Hayes County Electric & Light bills and the notices from Pearl Lake Memorial Gardens. I remembered the thin, lilting letters and the light feminine hand.

When she put out her hand to shake mine, the gold robe slipped from her shoulders, and I caught the white lace of a slip.

"Is this a workday, Maggie?" she asked.

"No'm," I said. "No, not exactly. I'm just here because I needed to return George Hardy's umbrella," I mumbled. "He let me borrow it last night."

I rose from the sofa, searching for an excuse for being here. "I'll just straighten up real quick," I said. "No charge, of course."

I headed toward the bedroom and took a look around. The bedsheets had been kicked and thrashed: George Hardy had spent another restless night. I picked up a shirt from the bedroom floor and hung it in the closet. I put a fallen tie back on the tie rack. I straightened a pile of books toppled on the nightstand. Then I bent to the sheets, tucking in the corners at the bottom where they had been pulled out.

Ida Mae Thatcher watched from the doorway and said, "Don't you trouble yourself, Maggie. George wouldn't expect this." I saw how thick and long her eyelashes were. They gave her a dreamy, sleepy look. *"George,"* I thought to myself. *She calls him "George."*

How long did you have to know a person before you called him by his first name all by itself?

"Well," I said, brushing off my hands and heading for the door, "you might want to remember how George Hardy likes things. I usually straighten the desk. George Hardy has an awful way with pens and pencils. And you've got to run the sweeper. Every place he goes he leaves a trail of pipe tobacco. And since he's been so worried about his speech at the Independence Day celebration on Friday, the mess is worse than ever."

Ida Mae Thatcher gave a little laugh. I could smell her perfume as I passed by. "Yes, I know," she said. "Thank you, Maggie."

Now, how do you know all this, Miss Ida Mae Thatcher? I asked myself. *If you know so all-fired much about George Hardy, how come you let him slave on a messy desk and live on chicken-with-rice?*

"Well, ma'am," I said, "nice to meet you, Miss Thatcher. The umbrella's on the nail by the door."

"Nice to meet you, too, Maggie," she said, slipping her hands into the pockets of George Hardy's gold robe. Her hands were thin and small. They weren't near as big and strong as mine.

"Oh," I said, turning to her one last time, "by the way." I hesitated. "Aren't you a lawyer from Atlanta?"

"Yes, I am," she said, nodding in my direction.

"And weren't you here last summer fixing to represent Zeke in court?"

"I was, Maggie," she said.

"And weren't you working for him for free?"

"Yes, Maggie. Why?"

I turned on my heels and headed out the door. "Don't ask," I said with my back.

Chapter 14

Nearly every sneak we ever went on was an idea straight from Pert Wilson. But today was different. Today was my birthday and the Independence Day celebration to boot, and I wanted it to be special. It was plain as day that two white girls weren't going to be invited to a colored picnic, but I was aching to hear George Hardy's speech. So I got Pert Wilson to sneak in the back side of the Negro Park with me, and I knew we'd have to climb into the big horse chestnut, where we could hide behind the thick branches and get the best view. I knew this sneak was going to be better than a picture show and wouldn't cost a cent.

Even though the rain had stopped, the grounds of the Negro Park were still soggy and damp. The south side of town was worse for everything, even weather. When it rained, most of the hilly north side only got damp; the south was a pile of mud. But wet or dry I had always loved the Negro Park. The red oak and gum, the sycamore and dogwood grew wild and natural. I loved the colors most of all. In the spring the park was pink with the flower spikes on the horse chestnuts. In the fall it flamed red with blossoms from the pimentos. In the summer it was dotted with splashes of orange from the honeysuckle vines.

But the park itself looked like the cast-offs from one of Mama's white-elephant sales. After Zeke dropped his suit last summer, Mayor Cherry and a pack of white folks made a big fuss about how they were giving the Negro Park to the coloreds now. The park business reminded me of Mama's Santa Claus apron. How could you pawn off something you didn't want and call it a gift? In addition to the land itself the present that was the Negro Park included some battered picnic tables, a tire swing hung from a tree, a few blackened grill stoves, and a performing platform thrown together with Coca-Cola crates. I didn't understand how the white folks had managed to make a gift of the Negro Park when it didn't belong to them in the first place.

Pert and I shared the same thick branch. She was ahead of me, farther out, her legs wrapped tightly around the branch. I was on a thicker, sturdier part of the branch, closer in to the trunk. Both of us could see real good. Below us the picnic table sagged under the weight of food. People were loading up plates with servings of okra and pickled beets and fried chicken legs and corn bread and pink slabs of ham. What we couldn't see we could smell, for under our noses floated the scents of mustard and cabbage and vinegar and brown sugar.

We could see everybody below. Cinda Samples looked right pretty with her hair out of a net, and Stumble Martin was stuck to her like glue. Every once in a while he took his cane and poked her affectionately with it. Missy Moses carried two grandbabies, one on each hip. Bigger Baby was comparing biceps with Clarence Ringleman. Georgia, the Matlacks' maid, looked more relaxed than she did from the Matlacks' veranda, where she worried over my basket of laundry. There were a few people I didn't recognize gathered around a tall man below, and then I saw that the tall man was George Hardy. He was motioning to a young woman lingering by a stand of loblollies, and I saw Ida Mae Thatcher come closer to him. George Hardy put his arm around her, introducing her to the strangers and to Reverend Potter, who was standing near the group. I saw her smile, tipping her face in Reverend Potter's direction like a pretty hat. I thought, *He's got to come to a picnic to get a plate of decent food. Sho won't fix him anything better than soup from a can.* I thought that maybe the group of strangers might be friends from Atlanta.

The band had started playing. They were beating rhythms out of washtubs, out of empty beer bottles and cans. Under it all ran the switching sound of someone playing a broom. They clattered spoons, the women beating them against their hips or swinging them high in the air like tambourines. The Coca-Cola crates on which the players were perched soon overflowed, makeshift musicians spilling out into the crowd, everyone singing and scatting to frenzied tunes.

All of a sudden Reverend Potter jumped on the platform, shushing the music and the chatter with a wide wave of his arms. Reverend Potter had a face shaped like a triangle that was broad at the forehead and narrow at the chin and was intersected about half-way down by a pencil moustache that jumped when he talked. He wore a straw hat when he went outdoors and looked at his pocket watch often as if he had a great deal to do and a very little time to do it in. He was light on his feet as a boxer and full of that same kind of stored energy. Lord knows you forgot how little he was whenever Reverend Potter talked. His people settled down when he shushed them, and after he cleared his throat to speak, the only sound was an occasional whimper from a baby or the scraping of a washtub as it was shifted. From where we were seated, Pert and I had a perfect view of the platform.

"This is an anniversary of sorts," he said, clearing his throat one more time. "A crazy kind of anniversary. A different one. Most of you will remember just how crazy and just how different because you have been celebrating it here for many years. It's our Indepen-dence Anniversary." While he talked, Reverend Potter rolled up his sleeves. I remember what Zeke had said about him: "Reverend Potter's a man who's always got both sleeves rolled up, Maggie."

Scattered applause broke from the crowd. People answered him with "Hear him, now, brother." Their responses came in short, jerky bursts. "You all know, of course, that this is not a *white* folks kind of celebration, but a celebration for those of us that are *black.*" There was more applause. I thought it was strange. George Hardy and Zeke and Reverend Potter always said "black." They never said "colored."

"But this year's a special year, and this day's a special day," he went on. "Your brother George Hardy and your sister Ida Mae Thatcher and a lot of others have come all the way from Atlanta this summer because we and you and a lot of other folks think it's time we stopped doing so much celebrating and used our energy for *working.* Especially now. It ought to be clear to every last one of us, to every last mother and father and son and daughter of us by now, that Kinship's never going to change unless we *make* it change."

The crowd leaned forward, resting on his words as he went on. "What we need is a miracle, brothers and sisters." He paused, scanning the crowd with his bright black eyes. "And the Bible is full of miracles. The Old Testament miracles of Moses, of Joshua, of Samuel, of Daniel in the den of the mighty lions." When Reverend Potter talked, I noticed the way his voice moved up and down like waves of music. "The New Testament miracles of the man with the crippled hand, the man born blind, the feeding of the five thousand, the wedding in Cana. And yes, brothers and sisters, a miracle can come to Kinship too. But we don't need to wait patiently for it to happen. We've waited patiently. Patience isn't enough. But if, like Jesus, we can link our faith to action, we, too, can make miracles happen. Even in Kinship."

The crowd was cheering wildly now. It was too bad Reverend Potter didn't have a plate to pass. He'd make a haul today.

Reverend Potter's chin was tilted up and his arms were outstretched. He checked his watch while he waited for them to calm down. "So," he said, quieting the crowd, turning his outstretched palms over and pressing them down, "let me introduce you to our Independence Day speaker today, a man and a *brother*, a man who believes that change can come to Kinship, a miracle worker in his own right, your friend and mine, George Hardy."

I settled myself carefully on my branch and remembered how this was the same branch of the tree where I had been last summer.

"How you doin', Pert?" I called over to her.

Pert gave me the okay sign with her fingers. "Fine, Maggie," she said.

They were clapping hard now, welcoming George Hardy to the platform. He leapt onto it with that long, easy stride he had, the stride that knocked over pencil holders and stacks of paper at home. I saw Bigger Baby put two fingers between his front teeth and give a loud whistle. I knew George Hardy was nervous by the way he ran his index finger under the front of his collar before he began to speak.

"Thank you, Brother Potter," he said. "Thank you, brothers and sisters." When he talked, his walnut eyes scanned the crowd. "Reverend Potter here is right. There's not much good in celebrating today, celebrating 'independence,' that is, because there's not much 'independence' in Kinship." The crowd was completely silent. Even the leaves on the trees seemed bent to him, listening.

"Do you call it 'independence' when there's a law that says a black man can't even sit down and play *checkers* with a white man?"

The crowd began to mumble. "Naw, sir," I heard, and "No, that truly ain't."

"Do you call it 'independence' when a black man buys a bus ticket same as a white man and isn't allowed to take any seat that he wants?" I could tell George Hardy was nervous. Sweat was beading up on his forehead. He took a white handkerchief from his back pocket and patted his forehead with it.

The mumbling in the crowd grew louder. Faces turned to each other, nodding up and down.

"Do you call it 'independence' when you have to take the balcony seats at the movie theater, face an all-white jury, and answer stupid questions like 'How many bubbles in a bar of soap?' when you line up to register to vote?"

They were clapping and shouting now. Bigger Baby Goolsby had his fists in the air. He was yelling, "Tell 'em like it *is*, brother."

"Do you call it 'independence' when a black man can't sit down at a lunch counter in the middle of Kinship when he pays his bill same as white?"

His people were really with him now. They were clapping and whistling and bouncing their babies and stabbing the air with their fisted hands.

"And do you call it 'independence' when they did

what they did to Zeke Freeman, our brother here, ar-
resting him, jailing him, beating him to a pulp, when
Zeke was trying to take care of his own business in a
rest room no more than a year ago?"

Zeke was near the platform at the edge of the
crowd. The way he held his head high as a king trig-
gered the images inside of me: the purple robes of the
African king in George Hardy's magazine, Boyce Johnson's knuckled fists, the slant of Sheriff Keiter's nightstick poised to strike. The images were all mixed up
with my own: a magazine against my backside, a ladle
against my cheek, the thorns from a rose stem slicing
my skin. They were images inside me that I wanted to
forget, but they were things, in truth, that I needed to
remember. They were the undeveloped pictures in the
camera of my mind.

"We don't call that 'independence,' do we, brothers
and sisters?" More applause. A group of women was
clanging Coke bottles with spoons.

The voice of my friend George Hardy unleashed
something inside of me. Something laced up, something tied tight. His words pulled and tugged at the
knots that were inside of me, untying them, unbinding
me.

I hovered above the crowd, nestled in that very
same branch where I had been hidden last summer.
The images floated up to me, dark and light all mixed
up together, and I willed the blurred borders and
smudged edges away, permitting myself to witness
what I had seen.

I had come to the Negro Park all by myself and climbed into this very tree, escaping from home. Mama and Daddy had been fighting again.

It was dusk. The sky was clear and about to settle into night. I had rested myself high in the horse chestnut and had just opened my book when I heard the pickup truck grinding to a halt below and the men getting out, slamming doors.

I looked down on the tops of heads and wondered what a gang of white men was doing at the Negro Park. I began to count. Five men. No, six. Through the large palm-shaped leaves I thought I could make out Boyce Johnson, and I recognized Russell Simmons's voice, but I wasn't sure of the others.

And then I saw Zeke. I was sure about that. Everybody else was shorter than him. Everybody else was white.

George Hardy loosened his collar. His voice grew surer, stronger. "We don't call that 'independence.' We call it *shame.*"

Zeke's hands were tied around his back with rope. The men were shoving him up against a tree, pushing him around. The crash of his body against the tree made a dull thudding sound. I saw Zeke tucking his head into his neck, trying to protect his face. I covered my mouth with my hands.

And then I saw a skinny body step out of the crowd. I'd have known that skinny body anywhere. Virgil Boggs. He was baiting Zeke. The way I knew he'd baited Charlie Leonard and Mickey Harris. The way he baited me.

"So you hired all them big-shot Atlanta lawyers and civil rights workers to come down here to little ol' Kinship and tell us white folks what to do, didn't you, Zeke?"

"Didn't hire 'em, Mr. Boggs, sir. They came of their own free will."

"And their own free will, Zeke," Virgil said, moving closer to Zeke, "includes givin' orders to us white folks, don't it?"

Virgil was up in Zeke's face. He had grabbed hold of Zeke's white shirt, knotting it at Zeke's neck.

"No, sir, Mr. Virgil," Zeke said. Zeke was raised up on the fists at his throat, but I could see the way his shoulders and neck were working to keep his head held up proud. He looked straight into Virgil's eyes when he talked. "Ain't wantin' to give orders to anybody. Just wantin' my rights, is all. My rights and my people's."

Virgil gave a quick downward jerk with his fisted hands. I heard a sharp tearing sound. It reminded me of the sound Mama made when she ripped up sheets for rags. I saw Zeke's shirt in tatters, his strong black chest exposed.

Then Virgil let go of the cloth and slapped Zeke across the face. I stuffed my knuckles in my mouth. I felt the sting in that slap across my own face, and I bit my knuckles hard. Zeke groaned, and his shoulders buckled.

"Niggers ain't got no rights, Zeke," Virgil said, look-

ing for support to the men behind him. They nodded and grunted as a group, moving closer, circling Zeke.

Virgil pulled his belt from his jeans and pressed the point of the buckle into Zeke's chest. "You gonna drop that suit, Zeke," Virgil seethed. "Ain't you?" The metal point dug into Zeke's flesh.

"No, sir, Mr. Virgil," Zeke said. "Can't do that."

"And why not?"

"I got my rights, Mr. Boggs. Same as whites. The law is wrong. And it's wrong to beat a man that's not resisting arrest." Zeke wasn't giving in. He was looking square at Virgil.

"I'll teach you about the kind of rights niggers has," said Virgil. "Niggers and gorillas." He had raised the belt like a whip and now brought it down, flailing it across Zeke's chest. I heard it crack and snap, remembering the way the leather of Grandpa Pugh's razor strap burned the backs of my own knees.

"Come on, fellas," Virgil said, "help me out here."

Boyce Johnson stepped in front of Zeke. He had his chin thrust out and his words cocked like weapons. "Look at you," Boyce Johnson said, "your big black body lookin' like an ape, a gorilla. Apes and monkeys ain't got no rights. You, Monkey Zeke," Boyce Johnson called him, jabbing his index finger in Zeke's direction, "ain't gonna see no evil." With that Boyce pummeled Zeke around his eyes. Zeke tried to kick him away with his free legs, but Russell Simmons and Bubba Ziegler stepped up and held Zeke down. Zeke kept ducking his head down to his chest, trying to fend

185

off the blows, but his hands were bound and his legs were pinned. He was completely defenseless.

When Boyce had finished, he said, "Here, Russ. Your turn." It was getting darker. The sky was red as blood. I had to squint harder to see.

Russell Simmons was built like a sack of flour and most of the flour hung over his belt. "You, Monkey Zeke," Russell said, "ain't gonna hear no evil neither." Russell Simmons's fists were as meaty as chops from Mr. Shriner's case. His hands and arms were loaded with black hair. He used them to beat Zeke around the ears.

My teeth bit into the flesh of my own knuckles. Zeke's face was a swollen pulp, and at a final blow to his left ear Zeke slumped to the ground. I thought Zeke was either unconscious or dead. Terrible as it was, I was grateful that he had passed out. I couldn't bear him to endure any more pain.

Then Lem Patterson stepped up to Zeke. "Shoot, fellas," he said. "I was just goin' to get me my turn." His voice had a whine to it that made me sick. Lem Patterson spent more energy on beating his wife than on tending his farm.

Boyce Johnson said, "Don't matter none that he's gone and passed out, Lem. You can still get you your turn." Then all the men laughed.

Lem Patterson reached down and pulled some of the tatters off Zeke's shirt. As he ripped, Zeke's body raised up and down like a rag doll, and he never opened his eyes. Then Lem forced Zeke's swollen mouth open and stuffed the pieces of rag inside, saying,

"Here, Monkey Zeke. You ain't gonna speak no evil in no court of law neither."

George Hardy picked up a soggy American flag that had been stuck in the mud, twirling it in his fingers as he talked. "We don't call that 'independence.' We call it *'ignorance.'*" His words were followed by a loud chorus of Amens.

I listened quietly, my heart thundering. I was seated in the same spot I had been in last summer, looking down. My eyes roamed over the crowd, panning like a camera, and I caught the figure of Zeke below me. He was surrounded by his people, listening too. I could feel the tears smarting behind my eyes at the sight of his proud head. The sight of Zeke and the sound of George Hardy's words were freeing something inside of me. I knew you could tell a lot about a person by what they were afraid of. I opened my eyes wide, taking a deep breath. I was ready. It was time. I willed the images into my mind. I would look at them all. Every last one.

And then something in Virgil turned. He had given an order, and the men were on Zeke.

They stripped Zeke. Ragged shirt, pants, socks, shoes, underwear. His naked body was slung at the base of the tree like his trading sack when it was empty. Then they loosened their own belts, and I heard zippers ripping, and then, one at a time, they took turns. Peeing on him like dogs. Wetting all over his swollen face, his private parts. Laughing while they did it. I held on to the tree branch, gripping with all my might, unable to look away. I had never imagined so much ugliness, so much spite. And when Virgil Boggs began jerking his hand up and down over the thing that was hard, the men fell silent. When the stream from Virgil had run down Zeke's chest like a milky thread of spit, I saw Virgil pause for a moment while he looked at the men around him. Then he threw back his head, opened his mouth, and laughed. The men looked at Virgil and at each other, and then they all began laughing and slapping each other across the back, the thick ugly laughter of Virgil Boggs drowning out the others.

From my perch in the tree I felt the salt rising behind my eyes at my secret, my own terrible secret. And I stopped praying from that night on.

George Hardy continued, shifting his weight easily on the balls of his feet, using his eyes to scan the crowd below him like a conductor claiming the attention of an orchestra. "We don't call that 'independence,' " he said. "We call that *injustice.*

"We know words like *shame, ignorance, injustice.*" George Hardy's voice was swelling, rising to his message. "But we're not going to study those words anymore, are we? We're going to study words that are fit to read. Words like *equality, mercy, justice.*"

George Hardy looked at Reverend Potter as he continued. "We have people here today, brothers and sisters, who can help us study the right words, who can help us learn. We have people here today whom we can thank for their teaching. Reverend Potter's one of

them. We can thank him for the money he's raised to support our work. The money from the collection plate, from the lunch boxes, from the pockets of your work pants. Even more we can thank him for the way he's raised our spirits. He started this work long ago. He's been laboring at it for a lifetime. Remember the way he turned Memorial Day into something for our people? As a remembrance to the brothers and sisters who were victims of lynching and mob violence throughout the history of this state, the hundreds of brothers and sisters strung up without trial, without the right to face their accusers? We owe a debt of gratitude to Brother Potter here."

George Hardy raised his hands high, clapping them together over his head. The crowd joined in, hundreds of pairs of burnt-sienna hands following his lead. Reverend Potter joined George Hardy on the platform, and they took each other's hands, raising their arms high, forming two letter *V*s.

Then George Hardy quieted the crowd and said, "We owe another debt of gratitude to Zeke here. He's faced the Devil for sure, and he's been scared to the point of death, but Zeke hasn't made fear a way of life. In spite of all that's happened to him, he's been working long and hard in our cause. We're all learning courage from Zeke. Me. Reverend Potter. Sister Ida Mae and the good workers from Atlanta." He paused, pointing out Zeke and the strangers in the crowd, and George Hardy's people cheered for them.

"And we pledge," George Hardy said, "on this Independence Day, on all that is holy, that we will never

tolerate anything like what happened to Zeke last summer! We will never tolerate a black man being beaten like that without fighting back in some way—in some way, great or small—fighting back against the shame and the ignorance and the injustice and working to learn the lessons of equality, mercy, justice! Let me hear you, brothers and sisters!" George Hardy said. "Do I have your *word?*"

The crowd went wild, breaking into a frenzy of cheering and shouting. George Hardy tossed the soggy American flag into the crowd as he left the platform. Bigger Baby caught it, waving it in the air. The clapping crowd exploded below me, jostling, dancing, waving their hands in the air. The band climbed on the makeshift stage and started playing, and everybody jumped and danced, and then Reverend Potter and Rocker and Bigger Baby and Ralston Ford hoisted Zeke up on their shoulders, prancing all over the park with him. There's never been a sight quite like it in this world.

I watched from my perch, fascinated and shocked at once. Did this mean that George Hardy knew what had happened to Zeke last summer? Knew more than that Zeke had been arrested and beaten in Byer's Drugs? That he knew about the beating done by Virgil and Russell and Boyce Johnson and Lem and the others? And did all of George Hardy's people know? Did they know why Zeke had dropped the suit? If they did, why didn't our end of town say anything? Didn't anybody white know about this except me and those shameful criminals?

"Hey, Maggie!" I heard a voice calling over to me across the noise. I had forgotten about Pert and looked over. "What're they talkin' 'bout, Maggie?" Pert had about the loudest whisper in the world. "What do they mean about Zeke bein' beaten? What in the world's been goin' on, Maggie?"

"Shush, Pert," I said. I didn't know if I could ever talk about this, but I did know that now wouldn't be the time or place. "Be quiet. Just listen, Pert."

The crowd calmed down some. They began to sing, quiet and slow. The evening sky turned a darker blue, and the band picked up the tune, the crowd swaying to the chords. Some of the singers had their eyes closed. As if the music was a form of prayer.

After George Hardy left the platform, he moved to the edge of the park close to where Pert and I were hiding in our tree. I saw George Hardy kiss the top of Ida Mae's head, and then he shook a million hands.

Then all of a sudden the green leaves in front of me started swaying and then they were shaking and then finally the wet leaves slapped my face, dampening me with sprays of water. I felt a whoosh from the branch ahead of me and heard, "Maggie, helllllllp!" from far below. It was Pert Wilson, fallen clean out of the tree.

I clambered down after her. "Pert," I said, shaking her. She looked stunned. "You all right?"

Pert shivered, then shook her head. She took a deep breath. "Sure, Maggie," she said. Then she huddled over some kind of package she must have had in her hands when she fell and determined that it was all right. Next she got on her knees, stood herself up, and brushed herself off. Finally she marched right over to George Hardy, who was only a few feet away. "Pert Wilson," she said, extending her hand. "Nice to meetcha. That was a right nice speech you gave, sir. Just thought I'd drop in to say so."

I tagged right along behind Pert. George Hardy took us both in with his eyes and then grinned at us. "Maggie Pugh," he said. "What are you doing here?"

"I'm with her," I said, pointing to Pert. Then all three of us busted out laughing.

When we had calmed down, I said, "George Hardy, I'd like you to meet my friend Pert Wilson."

George Hardy left his group of friends and moved closer to us. "Pleasure to meet you, Pert Wilson," he said, extending his hand. Then he turned to me and frowned. "By the way, Maggie," he said. "Did I forget something? Isn't today your birthday?"

Pert looked dumbfounded. "How'd you know today's Maggie's birthday?" Pert said to George Hardy. I'd never in my life seen Pert Wilson with a dropped jaw.

"Let's say I've made her acquaintance," George Hardy said, smiling at us both. "And I know her well enough to be embarrassed that I've forgotten her birthday."

"Oh, that's okay, sir," Pert said, leading both George Hardy and me by the hand. "I remembered." She headed us over by the Ghost Tree. "After all," she said, "with all that speechmakin' on your mind, how on earth'd you even remember what day it was?" The Ghost Tree grew tall and sturdy at the edge of the clearing, its huge white blossoms floating eerily against

192

the darkening sky. Pert ducked around the thick base of the tree, pulling out something hidden behind her back.

"For you," she said, sticking the something out front. She handed me a pink package with white ribbons. "Happy Birthday," she said. "Go on, Maggie. Open it."

"Pert Wilson," I said. "You don't have the money to be spending on presents. What'd you go and do this for?"

"Shut up, Maggie," Pert said. "All you gotta be is grateful. Grateful as me for having a friend like you."

Pert bit her lip as she watched me undo the ribbon and peel back the paper. I think she was excited.

When I opened it, I gave a little gasp. It was the Retina I, a genuine Kodak, the same one I had held to my eye at the rummage sale. I never dreamed in a million years that something that nice would be something of mine.

Pert looked happy too. "There's film already in it, Maggie. Loaded it myself. There's a strap too. Come on, now, put it around your neck."

I lifted the camera from its box, winding the strap around my neck. The camera felt light in my hands. I knew what to do with a camera now, and Lord knows I had missed the one Zeke had given me ever since Betty Boggs's spiked heel had ruined it. With the Retina I it was easier to move around, to shoot quickly. I liked being able to focus with a camera with only one lens.

Pert put her arms around George Hardy's waist. "Come on, Maggie. Take a picture, now."

I focused on George Hardy and Pert through the vision finder and snapped the button.

George Hardy reached up into the Ghost Tree, pulling a papery white blossom off at the stalk. "Here, Maggie," he said. "Your first nature shot."

I trained my eye on the flower, remembering how soft it was on the underside of the leaves of the Ghost Tree. I snapped again.

"Better yet," George Hardy said, "let's adorn the photographer." He took the huge white blossom and placed it behind my ear. "You look lovely, Maggie," he said. "A natural beauty." Pert took the camera and snapped my picture.

"Here," Pert said, shooing us together in that bossy way she had. "Let's get one of the two of you."

George Hardy and I put our heads together, the papery white blossom tickling his nose and making him laugh. "Don't say 'Cheese,' " Pert said. "Say 'Happy Birthday.' "

George Hardy and I said "Happy Birthday" together and laughed. Pert snapped away.

I don't think I have ever been so happy as I was that day. I snapped again and again, feeling the way the smooth molded camera frame fit neatly in my hands, feeling the freedom of the single lens. I snapped over and over: Missy Maples burping one of her grandbabies, Cinda Samples at the head of the picnic table, Reverend Potter with his arm around Ida Mae, Zeke with a broad-faced grin giving a victory sign. The camera allowed me to move around quickly, to shoot over and over again. There was something about it that made me feel free.

George Hardy lifted me up to reach a Ghost Tree flower for Pert. It was waving like a hanky against the sky. Pert snapped the last picture on the roll. It was of me on the shoulders of George Hardy, reaching for the flower.

The music trailed against the night: washboard players and spoon tappers and the high-pitched singing of the women and the low-down crooning of the men. The sky changed colors: dark blue and then blue-black and then pitch. Then the fireworks began and the night exploded into greens and reds and yellows and blues and I felt, for the first time, for the first time in my whole life, like I'd finally been *born*.

Chapter 15

I didn't see much of George Hardy after that. After the Independence Day celebration he worked harder than ever. Usually he was away to Atlanta, doing the business I had only begun to suspect about. More and more frequently he left packages or bundles of letters for me to mail to the addresses of organizations in Atlanta and Montgomery that started with initials I didn't understand: CORE, SCLC, NAACP. After work I'd head uptown, pass the letters under the window to Elsie Fish, and set out for home. Often I had George Hardy's house all to myself. Mondays and Thursdays were still special to me, but I think George Hardy had forgotten all about them. It was like Zeke said: George Hardy had more important things to think about.

Today he had left a letter for Reverend Potter, attaching a note that read, *Important, Maggie. Get this to Reverend Potter right away. Thanks, GH.*

I hopped on my bike and headed uptown, looking

for Reverend Potter. I weaved my way down Fenwick Street, passing the Bijou, Gleason's Hardware, and Millie's Curly Q before turning onto Calhoun Street and the bus station. Often Reverend Potter could be seen ministering to the lonely people passing through the Trailways station. Reverend Potter called them "lost sheep." Mama called them "tramps." Although he wasn't in the bus depot, I decided to stop in at Byer's Drugs; he had two slices of Cinda's pecan pie nearly every day of his life. Elmer Byer was setting the CLOSED sign out on the counter as it was near on five o'clock, but Reverend Potter wasn't anywhere in sight.

I read the note from George Hardy again. *Important,* it said. *Right away.* So I headed south across the tracks, feeling the railroad ties bump beneath me, passing Oscar Lemaster's colored barber shop and the South Side All Nite Grocery and the tomato stand on Edmonia Jennings's front porch. I pedaled in the direction of the Tabernacle Baptist Church.

Tabernacle Baptist was an all-brick structure, and the bricks were an assortment of colors that gave the church a checkerboard look. They were salmon red, sienna red, rust red, mud red; a few had been painted white. Zeke said Reverend Potter built that church brick by brick. Those that could afford to give money bought batches of bricks for building; those who couldn't brought their own bricks one by one from the dump or the sagging chimney of their house or the worn patches of old brick sidewalks up in town. Zeke said the bricks of the church building were just like the people who prayed there: no two alike.

197

There were patched cracks in the sidewalk in front of the church, and the pansies that lined the walk looked thirsty. The title of last Sunday's sermon was still on the blackboard nailed beside the church door. The chalk letters said: SIN KNOWS NO COLOR LINE.

Since this was a Monday, it was strange that there were so many cars and baby buggies parked outside the church. After working hours I expected folks to be home. Maybe somebody had died and this was a funeral held late in the day. I slipped around the side of the building, heading in the direction of Reverend Potter's office in the back. The church windows were open wide against the afternoon heat, and as I passed them, I heard the loud and powerful sounds of someone preaching. When I looked in the window, I saw lots of coloreds inside. Nearly everyone I knew and a few I didn't.

The fans were on overhead, whirring the air. A group of people was sitting up front on a makeshift stage as if practicing for a play. They were Missy and Bigger and Georgia and Rocker and Stumble Martin and Zeke. They were facing the congregation on stools lined up before a long picnic table. Reverend Potter was moving around them, talking, gesturing, acting like he was the director of something. Sometimes he talked to the people onstage. Sometimes he talked to the audience. But he was talking to both actors and audience in the tones of a sermon, and his voice was booming.

"Thank you for your gifts," Reverend Potter was saying. "Your gifts of time. Your gifts of money. Your willingness to volunteer yourselves in this great cause. In the spirit of Christ who taught us it is more blessed to give than to receive, God will surely bless your good gifts."

The church responded to him with words like "Amen, Reverend," and "God be praised."

Reverend Potter raised his arms high and looked up at the ceiling. When he did, the congregation looked up too. "And thank you, God," he said, "for the gift of our brother Frank Alhambra. I've just received word that Mr. Alhambra has mortgaged his taxi service and served up another six hundred dollars into our food and bail bond fund to the glory of God and the greatness of our cause." When Reverend Potter said "God" he strung it out a stretch and it sounded like "Gaawwwd." When I looked up at the ceiling, following Reverend Potter's eyes, I saw that the paint was peeling off in chunks.

"Let me ask you some questions now," Reverend Potter said, leaving off looking at God for a moment and looking back at people. "We're going to do what we've set out to do because all our past efforts have failed, haven't they?"

Every voice in front of him and the few behind answered, "Yes, Reverend."

"And haven't we asked Mr. Byer politely if we could have a seat at his lunch counter?"

Again, "Yes, Reverend."

"And wasn't our lawful petition, stating our wish to have a seat at Byer's lunch counter and signed by three hundred of our good citizens, turned down the morning it was delivered?"

"Yes, Reverend." I hadn't known anything about a petition, but I did know that Reverend Potter was smart. Like a good teacher he helped you get the right answer by the way he asked the question.

"And didn't we have our only success when Cinda Samples, our good sister and an employee of Byer's Drugs for over ten years, threatened to quit?"

"Yes, Reverend."

"And can you call it success when Mr. Byer says we can have a seat if we order from a separate menu, a separate menu that charges us three dollars for a hot dog and a white man twenty-five cents?"

They were listening carefully. You could tell. They knew it was time for a different answer. "No, Reverend," they chorused. "No, it surely ain't."

Then Reverend Potter swiveled on his heels, taking another tack. "Our brother the Reverend Dr. Martin Luther King, who has been such a help to our efforts here in Kinship and our efforts all over these United States, can't even sit down to lunch at Rich's in Atlanta. And you know what happened to our friend Mr. Freeman over here." I saw him point out Zeke, his big body overflowing his stool on the stage. Everybody was nodding and clapping. Bigger Baby was making punching movements with his fists. Even from my distant window at the side of the church, one thing was clear to me: everybody seemed to know what had happened to Zeke last summer.

"But you got to remember the rules," Reverend Potter said, cautioning his actors as well as their audience. "This is something like a dress rehearsal for a play. We want it to come off smoothly, without a hitch. So let's go over the rules one more time." Moving back and forth across the stage he was as light on his feet as a tap dancer.

I hadn't noticed Ida Mae Thatcher at first. She was standing off to the side, where it was hard for me to see. When I stood on tiptoes and stretched my neck, I could see her beside an easel holding a big poster board with letters on it. Ida Mae pointed to the words on the poster board while Reverend Potter talked.

"There are only two rules. We want to keep it simple. They're not hard to remember. Our brothers Floyd McKissick and Bayard Rustin made use of them in their work in other states. Rule number one," he said. "Conduct yourself with quiet dignity." Ida Mae's pointer poked at the words *Quiet dignity*.

"What you mean by that, brother?" Rocker held his hand in the air, his white robe flapping.

"It means you need to be quiet, Rocker. You need to be calm. Don't let them rattle you. You keep your pride. You hold your head up. It's your right. All you're asking is to sit down and eat, same as white folks."

Reverend Potter looked out into the congregation. His eyes lighted on Ralston Ford and they turned fiery. In a flash Reverend Potter had taken off one of his shoes and began banging it on the picnic table. Missy Moses and Georgia gave a start, and everyone in the congregation perked up. "Now, Brother Ralston," he said, banging away. "Brother Ralston Ford," he said, calling out into the congregation. "I don't want you sleeping through this message like you did with my sermon Sunday last. You wake up, brother, you hear?"

Gladys Ford, Ralston's wife, poked him in the ribs, and Ralston's head snapped to attention. "Yes, sir, Brother Potter," Ralston said, looking sheepish.

Without missing a beat Reverend Potter put his shoe back on and kept on talking. I'd heard about his preaching. If he got mad, he was known to throw the Holy Bible into the congregation. Zeke told me how one New Year's Sunday he'd made everybody in the church stand up and say their resolution, and he told Ira Gaines in front of everyone that he'd better put leaving off women not his wife at the top of his list. Lord knows, church at Reverend Potter's Tabernacle Baptist was a far sight more fun than church at Mama's Mount Zion.

He peered out into the audience. "Cinda," he said, calling to her from the far end of the front pew, "you come on up here and help us practice. You can help us out here, can't you, Cinda?"

"Sure can," Cinda said. The people in the church gave a scattering of applause, encouraging her to go up front. Cinda moved slow, panting the way she always did. Breathless, she finally stood in front of the group of actors up front, and the congregation applauded.

Reverend Potter put his arm around her broad shoulders. "Fact is, Cinda," he said, "you know Byer's Drugs better than anyone. You're our stage manager, so to speak. So why don't you kind of act it out for everybody, all right?"

"All right," Cinda said, giving the thumbs-up sign. "I know Elmer Byer's store like the back of my hand," Cinda said, "so you just take your cues from me, okay?" Everybody on the stage nodded. "Now," Cinda said, "when you come in, you all just take your seats quiet-like. Missy and Bigger and Rocker and Stumble and Georgia and Zeke will be in the first shift. It lasts an hour. And the rest of you," she said, pointing to the people in the church, "have got word of your shifts from Ida Mae over here." Ida Mae nodded from her place by the stage. She picked up a different poster. This one had a list on it showing times and the names of different people listed under the different times. She set it on the easel.

"Now," Cinda went on, strolling in front of the group at the picnic table, "I'll serve you your order. Collards. Corn bread. Cup of coffee. Whatever you like. I'll just set your plates in front of you, sweet as pie. No fuss. Like I'd been doin' it every day. Make sure you got your money to pay for your order from that fund Brother Potter's in charge of." I remembered how Cinda worked the special counter for coloreds, serving them while they stood in line. She'd been serving them like that as far back as I could remember. Sounded like they'd finally got tired of standing.

Reverend Potter stepped forward again. "Thank you, Cinda," he said. "Let's just remember that we don't have enough in our money fund just yet. We got to pay for food for sure, but the biggest expense is raising bail money to cover anybody who's arrested. We're not expecting trouble and our efforts in other states have been generally peaceful, but there's been enough violence and arrests that we need to come prepared." I noticed that Reverend Potter's sleeves were rolled up past his elbows.

"You remember," he went on, "that we figured on three hundred dollars a person for bail and that we've got the SCLC and the Youth Council of the NAACP matching what we raise, but we still got to do our part. Even with Frank Alhambra's six hundred, we figure we still need another three hundred dollars before we can move forward with this plan. Brother Lemaster, will you do the honor of passing the hat today?" Oscar Lemaster ran the colored barber shop but was bald as a billiard cue himself. He went up front, took the porkpie hat from his own head, dug in his pockets for a couple of dollar bills, slapped them into his hat, and then passed the hat down the first row.

"Thank you, Mr. Lemaster," Reverend Potter said. Then he turned to Ida Mae. "We need the Rule Two chart, Miss Thatcher," he said. Ida Mae took the list of times and people off the easel and replaced it with a different sign.

"Rule two," Reverend Potter said, pointing to the letters on Ida Mae's chart. "It's time to go over rule two. NO VIOLENCE." He let the words thunder, the way our own Pastor Mullins did. Pastor Mullins practically made clocks stand still whenever he said, "Thou Shalt Not."

Reverend Potter's shiny black eyes scanned the

church. "No violence, you hear?" he said. "This may be the hard part. You must absolutely refuse to use force. No force in any way. It's the part you can't afford to forget."

Bigger Baby was tapping his feet under the table. He was nervous. "But what if somebody knocks you off your stool, brother?" he asked. "You can't be saying that we can't fight back, can you? You can't be serious about that?" There was an edge to his voice that made me uneasy.

"Good question, Mr. Goolsby," Reverend Potter said. "And I am serious. I'm dead serious when I say that you can't fight back." I noticed the way Reverend Potter never called his people by their nicknames. Zeke was "Mr. Freeman." Bigger was "Mr. Goolsby."

Reverend Potter began rubbing his earlobe the way he did when he was thinking on something. "But it's a good enough question, Mr. Goolsby, that I think we need some practice with it. Let's say that happens, okay? Let's imagine somebody comes along and knocks you off your stool."

Everybody nodded. Missy. Rocker. Stumble Martin. Georgia. Zeke. Even Bigger Baby. "Let's say it's Elmer Byer or Boyce Johnson or one of them that lets people do what they did to Zeke. What are you going to do?"

"Knock him on his white ass?" mocked Bigger.

Everybody laughed and cheered. The walls of the Tabernacle Baptist Church rocked and shook. Stumble Martin stomped his cane on the floor, and Rocker waved the arms of his white robe around like a flag.

"Wrong!" shouted Reverend Potter, banging his

hands on the table. The way he looked made me think of Moses smashing those tablets. "No violence. Remember the rules. Remember the Bible. Remember that you've got to turn the other cheek. 'Return to no man evil for evil,'" Reverend Potter said. I couldn't place it, but Daddy would have known the chapter and verse.

The women nodded, and the men followed along.

"If that happens," Reverend Potter continued, pacing now, "if that happens, brothers and sisters, you go back to rule number one. 'Conduct yourself with quiet dignity.' If that happens, brothers and sisters, I want all of you to come up with the answer to this one question: *'What will you do?'*"

I knew that Reverend Potter had done a lot of things in his life. Zeke told me that he had farmed behind a plow, sold encyclopedias, recited poetry for money, manned a fruit stand, and traveled the back roads preaching, carrying a peach basket for luggage. But even from this tiny square of window at the side of this checkerboard church, I could tell that teaching was Reverend Potter's calling. He managed to lead his students by a combination of wonder and shame.

He paused and looked out over the church, his voice full of thunder. He repeated his question again, striking his audience with it like a lightning bolt. *"What will you do?* Everybody in this church needs to know the answer to that question. I want to see you raise your hands if you know the answer, now."

One by one the hands in the church went up. First a few. Then a larger scattering. Ralston Ford looked like he'd fallen asleep again. His wife elbowed him in the ribs, and he woke up and raised his hand. Finally the entire congregation was waving their brown hands in the air. They looked like cattails rustled by a gentle breeze out by the swamp.

Then Reverend Potter looked satisfied. He turned to Missy Moses, seated on a stool behind him. "Okay, Mrs. Moses," he said. "I'm calling on you. If somebody knocks you down, *what will you do?*"

Missy's tiny feet were crossed at the ankle under her stool. She placed them carefully on the floor, slumped to the ground with a pretend injury, and then stood up, tall and erect. She said, "You get up, and then you set yourself down again and keep on eating." Her voice was quiet but strong.

The congregation applauded. A few people shouted "Amen" and others said, "Yes, Jesus." Reverend Potter smiled, nodding approval in Missy's direction. "You've got only two rules. They're not hard to remember. Rule number one: Quiet dignity. Rule number two: No violence."

Digger didn't seem satisfied. "Let's say they don't hit us or nothin'. But what if they start with the names?" he asked. "Let's say they start calling us names. We 'sposed to just sit there and take it?"

"Yes, you are," Reverend Potter said. "It's part of rule number one. Quiet dignity. And it's part of rule number two. No violence. You'll need to remember that by staying peaceful," he continued, encouraging all of them. "You'll keep them off guard. Being peaceful shames the whites. Now," he said, turning on his heels again, "come on up here, Mrs. Moses. We're going to practice some more."

He took an empty chair and swung it to the center of the stage in front of the long picnic table. "We're going to practice with Mrs. Moses here, okay?" He motioned for Missy to take a seat. "Come on over here, Mrs. Moses," he said. "We're going to practice with you."

Tiny Missy Moses turned the chair around and straddled it backward. Her feet dangled under her skirt.

"Now, Mrs. Moses," Reverend Potter said, "you just pretend you're eating." Missy picked up a pretend fork and took pretend bites from the pretend plate in front of her.

"Good," Reverend Potter said, his face lighting up in a smile. "Now, Mr. Goolsby. You come on over here and start calling her names."

Bigger came over with a strut. "Spook," he said, sticking out his lower lip.

Missy kept right on eating.

Bigger moved closer. He reminded me of Virgil, the way he came forward on his hips. "Spade," he said. "Coon."

Missy wiped her lips with a pretend napkin, sweet as you please. Everybody laughed.

Then Bigger Baby got right up in her ear. "Jigaboo," he said. "Mau Mau. Kinkhead."

Missy reached for the pretend salt, shaking the pretend shaker all over her plate. Cinda Samples piped up, "It's plain she ain't eatin' my green beans. I cook 'em with a ham hock on the stove all day. They're plenty salty already." The congregation busted up laughing at that. They were clapping and hooting and slapping their knees. Cinda was laughing fit to pop.

Finally Bigger Baby took a deep breath, shouting in Missy's face. "Nigger," he yelled. "Nigger, nigger, nigger."

Lordy, but Missy Moses could act. She never moved a muscle. Kept right on eating. You'd have thought she was deaf.

"Good job, Mrs. Moses," Reverend Potter said. Missy took a bow. People were standing and shouting and cheering for her.

Then Cinda, her shoulders still shaking from laughing, moved to the center of the stage. She rubbed her hands excitedly. "I've been workin' for Elmer Byer near on ten years now," she said, "and I can't wait to give you all a seat and serve you all my buttermilk pancakes."

The church was with her. They were shouting things like "Say it, Cinda," and "Hear her, now." I wished Pert Wilson could be here. She always appreciated free entertainment.

Then Stumble Martin rose from his stool and leaned on his cane, making his slow way over to Cinda. "And I'll take one pretend stack right here and right now," Stumble said. He held out a pretend plate from his open palm.

Everybody in the church hooted. "Yeah, Cinda," they said. "Cook for Stumble."

Cinda smiled, tied a pretend apron around her waist, and turned up a pretend stove. She dipped a pretend ladle of buttermilk pancake batter into a pretend skillet. Stumble stuck his nose over the pretend pancakes and sighed. "Lord, Cinda, don't that smell fine!" Everybody was clapping. Even the kids were turning to each other and giggling.

Then Cinda flipped pretend pancake after pretend pancake into the air and onto Stumble Martin's pretend plate. With each pancake that was caught by Stumble, the congregation gave a cheer. Stumble Martin was shaking with laughter. Cinda too. Lord, I always did think Stumble was sweet on her.

When Stumble had his plate loaded, Cinda ordered, "Now go on over there and sit, Stumble. You don't have to stand up to eat no more."

The people inside stood up and cheered. Reverend Potter took off his shoe and banged the table with it. After that it took him a long time to quiet everyone down, but after Reverend Potter said, "Now settle down," about a hundred times, they finally did. Then with a smile that ran the length of his pencil moustache, Reverend Potter said, "You did a good job. That's how it's done, people. Good job. No violence. Quiet dignity."

Cinda and Stumble went back to their seats, and Reverend Potter checked his watch. "Oh, yes, people," he said. "We'll get a signal to start after we get all the bail money together and an okay from Atlanta. So don't forget to keep adding to our food and bail fund. As you know, Frank Alhambra is providing transportation to the drugstore with his taxi for anyone working a shift and needing a ride."

Ida Mae Thatcher signaled to Reverend Potter. "What about the books, Reverend?" she asked.

"Oh, yes," Reverend Potter said, remembering. "You'll be sitting down for a long time, and you'll need some reading material. Everybody's going to need a book. I don't care what it is, but you need to carry one. You may be spending a long time at Byer's lunch counter. You can open a book and read to pass the time. A book'll make you look peaceful, respectable. It'll send a message. The message says you don't mean any harm. You just want your rights. Hold up your hand if you need a book, and Ida Mae will get you one."

Ida Mae Thatcher gathered up books from the piles at the front of the stage and passed them out. I wondered if any of those books came from the piles George Hardy had in his house. When Ida Mae came to Zeke, he waved her away and I felt proud. I'd checked lots of books out of the Kinship Public Library for Zeke. I had tried to get him his own library card, but Miss Marquis told me coloreds couldn't use the library, so I checked out the books for Zeke on my own card and went away mad, wondering what was so all-fired public about the public library.

I slipped away from the window. I had seen enough. Quickly I headed toward the back of the church and found Reverend Potter's office. His desk was loaded with papers, and some of them looked like the papers I'd seen at George Hardy's house. It looked like they all belonged to the same organizations. I recognized the initials like CORE and SCLC. I put the envelope on Reverend Potter's chair, thinking he was more likely to notice it there than on his mess of a desk.

Then I headed home, deciding to take the long way along the Crooked River. I dodged puddles most of the way, and when I got to the Crooked River Bridge, it looked like the rain had washed out some of the iron posts that served as side rails. Lem Patterson's pickup truck was pulled up to the side of the bridge, and Boyce Johnson and Russell Simmons were in rain slickers, pointing to a mule that stood stock-still in the middle of the bridge. When the rain swelled the river, he must have been washed downstream and through the broken iron side posts. The men had been working to get him off.

Although they had thrown up some Army blankets to cover his shivering body, now they had two-by-fours and sticks in their hands and were beating him like crazy. When the mule refused to budge, Lem got some rope from his truck and the men tied him up. They rigged up a network of ropes and pulleys that looked like a giant cat's cradle. I guess they thought they'd finally be able to pull him off that way, but the mule shook his head fiercely and whinnied, not moving an inch. Then they went back to hitting the mule again, flailing at his haunches and flanks. They shouted and yelled at him, roaring into his pointed ears.

Watching them, I saw how stupid they were, and I thought of Reverend Potter's words. No violence. Quiet dignity.

Chapter 16

More and more Pert Wilson stopped by to ask if I could spend the night. Mama always said I could, and I think she was glad to have me gone. She needed time to rehearse Gardenia for the pageant. Every night after supper she'd lock herself and Gardenia in the bathroom for singing practice. Mama believed any kind of singing sounded better in the bath. Something about how the sound bounced off the tiles. Mama went wild whenever Daddy knocked on the door, interrupting because he had to go.

I loved sleeping in Pert's trailer. It was like living in a dollhouse. Sometimes we painted our toenails. Sometimes we brushed our hair one hundred strokes like they said you were supposed to in the magazines. Sometimes Pert fixed candle salads. That's where you put a pineapple slice on a bed of lettuce and then stand a banana up in the middle of the pineapple for the candle. Then you put a maraschino cherry on the tip of the banana for the fire.

Pert was my best friend in the world, and she was dying to know more about George Hardy. Ever since the Independence Day celebration she'd been nagging me for all she was worth. It was hard for me to keep my secrets, especially when Pert kept up her questions all night long. How did I know George Hardy? Where did he live? What was he doing in Kinship? The worst question of all was this: If I was her all-time best friend, what was I doing keeping secrets from her? She didn't know that I had kept secrets from her before, most of them about my mama and the way she treated me. All I could tell Pert was the truth. I said that Zeke got me the job and it required me to pay attention to two words: *Don't ask.*

Lots of times Pert and I just walked uptown. On days when Pert had to work, I checked on my pictures. They should have been back by now. Pert had dropped them off for me right after the Independence Day celebration. It had been nearly ten days. Hazel Boggs always rooted through the big drawer behind the counter. "Sorry," she said. "Not back yet." She closed the drawer with a flip of her hip like Elvis Presley. She didn't sound sorry at all.

"Well, gotta go," said Pert. I walked her to the counter. She put on her apron and wrung out a rag, wiping down the counter.

"Me too," I said. "Mama needs me to baby-sit Gardenia."

I walked home quickly, knowing Mama would be

mad if I was late. Daddy was going out looking for work again. Uncle Taps had got him a few part-time jobs installing plumbing out in Fenwick Acres, but Daddy had a chance to get a handyman job full time at the textile plant now, and he was keeping his fingers crossed. Mama was going out to look for work too. She was headed for Troy this morning to apply for a foster kid. She was hoping to get a retarded one. Regular foster kids were ten dollars a week. Retarded were fifteen.

But when I got home, there was a big commotion in our yard. I rubbed my eyes, not believing what I saw. Sheriff Keiter's cruiser was pulling up and a crowd had gathered to watch. Uncle Taps was hanging on to Daddy's shirttails and Mama was running around like a crazy person, flailing the mop. I had heard such scenes before, but the sounds this time were different from the wailing and screeching I had come to expect from Mama; instead, they were like something I had heard on TV. From the shows I watched with George Hardy like *Gunsmoke* and *Palladin* and *Wyatt Earp*. I knew those sounds too well; they were the unmistakable sounds of shotgun blasts.

Gardenia was huddled under the pecan tree, her white nightgown pulled up to cover her eyes. When she saw me, she rushed over and clung to my legs. "Maggie, Maggie," she cried. "It's Daddy. Daddy gone wild with the gun on account of the fence. When Mama saw him like that, she called Uncle Taps, and when Uncle Taps saw him like that, he called the sheriff, and now Sheriff Keiter's here and so's everybody in

Kinship, Maggie. Here to watch our daddy, our daddy as crazy as our mama."

What Gardenia said was true. There was my daddy, my sweet daddy, my daddy who never carried anything more dangerous than a Bible in his hand, my daddy with his shotgun, the shotgun that he never fired at anything more than a rabbit or a squirrel. He was like some outlaw off TV, firing, shooting, going wild.

And there was Uncle Taps, holding on to Daddy's belt, pulling at him, trying to get him to stop, the belt buckle cutting into Uncle Taps's fingers, the look in Uncle Taps's eyes cold with fear.

Daddy had fired over a dozen shots at the fence, stopping only to reload. He was firing still; the tall wooden planks were filled with holes like a Chinese checkers board.

I looked at the fence, seeing red. Red like Edmonia Jennings's burst tomatoes. Red like the bricks that made up Reverend Potter's church.

And then I read what was written on the fence. The red letters were spread across its length, left to right, top to bottom. *Nigger Lover,* they read. *Coon Sucker. Black Ass Kisser.* The words streaked across the pine boards like messages in blood.

Red paint covered everything.

The fence.

The base of the pecan tree.

The blossoms of the purple periwinkles along the stoop had turned the color of the poppies you got when you put a penny in the Salvation Army bucket.

I moved to the fence for a closer look. And there they were. My pictures. Every one. Nailed to the plywood all around. Stumble leaning on his cane. Bigger flexing his muscles. The flower, white and bursting, from the Ghost Tree. Cinda at the head of the picnic table. Zeke and Pert and Reverend Potter and the rest. My pictures.

And there he was. George Hardy. The picture of George Hardy and me on his shoulders as I reached for a Ghost Tree flower for Pert. It was nailed to the boards, a square of red paint serving as frame. I put my fist to my teeth, biting hard against the shame.

Sheriff Keiter had his handcuffs open and was mumbling something like "disturbing the peace." My heart dropped. Virgil Boggs had never spent a night in jail and now they were fixing to arrest my daddy, who didn't even step on ants.

Uncle Taps tried to reason with Sheriff Keiter. "I'll calm him down, Sheriff," he said. "Just give me some time, sir. I know my brother. Let me handle this. You know this has got to be upsetting to him. You know he's out of work, Sheriff, and he's got an important job interview this morning. He's not going to want to miss that. Come on, Sheriff. Give me a little time."

Sheriff Keiter shuffled his feet. "I guess I'd be upset, too, if all this business with the coloreds had happened to me." He moved closer to the picture of George Hardy and me, taking out a notebook and writing something down. "Haven't seen this character around here before. Maybe he's one of those outside agitators who's been makin' the coloreds around here so uppity lately. We'll have to check it out." He motioned to me, flipping over a page in his notebook. "Who's this man, Maggie?" he said.

I swallowed hard and looked in the direction of Daddy. Uncle Taps had turned to him. He was saying, "For the love of Jesus, Henry Pugh, stop it now. Put down that gun, brother. Stop it now before you hurt yourself."

And then the shotgun blasts stopped for a moment and Daddy pulled away from Uncle Taps, trying to run for the house. "I got to reload, Wilbur," he blubbered. "Let me back in the house. I need more ammunition. I got to reload."

I squeezed my eyes shut after I saw Uncle Taps wrap himself around Daddy, holding him down. "Henry," he was saying like someone calming a hysterical child, "Henry, you got to calm down."

Then I answered Sheriff Keiter. "Don't know the man, Sheriff," I said. "Don't know him at all."

Sheriff Keiter frowned at me. "So what're you doin' up on this stranger's shoulders and havin' your picture took with him, Maggie?" You could tell he wasn't believing me for a minute.

My heart was pounding, and I was trying to think fast. I stalled for time by watching Uncle Taps. He was pulling Daddy's belt clear off the loops, taking another tack. "Here, Henry," he said. "Let's take a look at this nice belt buckle here. Looks like it's made out of gold or something special, now."

Daddy turned to Uncle Taps, distracted. He

blinked. Behind his eyes was an empty look. "It's brass, Wilbur," he said. "Ain't gold. It's brass."

Uncle Taps gripped his slender victory and kept on talking. "Come on now, Henry. Ever spend a mornin' polishing it up, brother? I always did love the way brass gleamed after a good rubbing, don't you? You can get it to shine and shine. Rub it fine like something magic, like something from the lamp of a genie."

Daddy blinked again, and I saw Uncle Taps steadying him so he could sink into the lawn chair. Then I saw Daddy dip his head into Uncle Taps's shoulder and start to sob.

I turned to Sheriff Keiter. "Like I say, Sheriff, I don't know the man. But Pert and me—that's my friend Pert Wilson—we were in the big horse chestnut tree over at the Negro Park. The coloreds were having their Independence Day celebration like they always do, Sheriff, and Pert and me snuck up in the tree to listen. We know we weren't 'sposed to be there, Sheriff. But then Pert got stuck in one of the high branches and I had to come down and get help. That man there put me up on his shoulders so I could reach up and help Pert out."

"Hmmm," Sheriff Wilson said. He was scribbling furiously in his notebook. He seemed to be buying my pack of lies. Then he frowned and questioned me again. "But how'd you get in those pictures, Maggie?"

I shrugged my shoulders. "It was a picnic, Sheriff. Folks was snapping pictures right and left." I could see him nodding his head. Sheriff Keiter had sawdust for brains.

Then he asked, "Don't you have a camera, Maggie?"

I took a deep breath. You needed air for telling whoppers. "Used to, Sheriff, sir. But Betty Boggs busted the lenses with her high heels after we finished the fence and went out to take pictures. I've still got the broken pieces up in my room if you'd like to see 'em, Sheriff."

He flipped the notebook closed and waved me away. I think he bought it hook, line, and sinker. "You hang tight, Maggie," he said. "I might need you for questioning later on."

"Sure, Sheriff," I said, sweet as pie. "Be glad to."

As I watched his back moving away from me, his holster slapping at his hip, I let out the air all at once like a pin to a balloon.

Uncle Taps was still taking care of Daddy, so I ran to the pecan tree, swooping up Gardenia in my arms. She had the hem of her white gown balled up in her fist, and I could feel her tiny body shaking under the white cotton. Mama had disappeared into the house. I looked back over my shoulder before I went in, seeing the red letters of the fence thrown like a bloody curtain across the yard.

Mama was standing in front of her jelly-glass case, a pink glass in her hand. When I came through the door, it narrowly missed me and shattered against the kitchen cabinet. Before it tinkled to the ground, it hovered for a moment in the air like fireworks before they explode.

I put Gardenia down, and Mama picked up another glass, a blue one this time.

"Mama," I shouted. "No, Mama! Stop, Mama!"

She had the glass raised over her head. Her eyes glowed red. She seemed to me like an animal running wild in a deep wood. "For shame!" she shouted, her teeth bared at me. "Shame, shame, and nothin' but shame, Maggie Pugh!" she shrieked. "Shame! And from you, my own daughter, my own flesh and blood!" She hurled the blue glass at the wall. I heard the glass shatter against it and saw in my mind the fireworks at the Independence Day celebration, exploding against a sky that seemed light-years away.

Mama picked up a yellow jelly glass and held it ready to hurl straight at me.

"I didn't mean to shame you, Mama," I said, working as hard as I ever worked in my life to keep my voice calm.

"I knows Cinda and Zeke and those other coloreds, Maggie," Mama said, the glass poised still, "and I guess it's shameful enough you 'ssociatin' with them, but you pile shame on shame when you rides around on the shoulders of a colored stranger."

"He wasn't a stranger, Mama," I said.

The yellow glass exploded right behind my left ear. "Don't you lie to me, girl," she said, gathering up a group of glasses and cradling them to her chest.

Gardenia's voice sounded high and breathy, like flutes tuning up. "Maggie ain't no liar, Mama," she said. Gardenia had tiptoed carefully across the floor, avoiding the shards of glass, and she tugged at Mama's skirt as she talked.

My sister was only half right. I didn't want to be a liar. But I had lied to Mama about George Hardy, letting her think I was working somewhere else. I had done it to keep all those secrets. And I was tired of the lie and sick of the secrets. Sick of keeping quiet. Sick of the things I knew but couldn't tell.

"He's no stranger. Leastways to me, Mama," I said, feeling like some kind of window had been opened. "Maybe to Kinship, Mama. But George Hardy's no stranger to me. George Hardy's my employer, Mama. George Hardy's been putting bread on this table for a couple of months now, Mama." It felt like a tiny breeze was beginning to drift through.

For a brief instant Mama's grip loosened around the glasses in her arms. One of her jelly glasses escaped her grasp, rolling across the countertop; another dropped with a thud to the floor.

Mama had a look like dawn rising on her face when she faced me now. "You mean you've been cleanin' all this time for a *colored* man?"

I nodded.

Mama's face said it all. That in spite of how hard she tried, Pughs had finally slipped south of the tracks.

"I just wanted to help you, Mama," I said, struggling to help her hold on, to hold on to whatever might make her feel she still lived north. "We needed the money, Mama. I needed the work. I knew you wouldn't want me working there, Mama, but I knew how much we needed the money, and he was a good employer and a good man. George Hardy put food on the table here. He's not a bad man. He's just colored, is all. He's my friend, Mama. George Hardy's my friend." I held on to a slim length of hope. If I explained it just right, maybe Mama would understand. But I could feel hope slipping from my fingers as I talked.

Suddenly the anger returned to Mama's face. "No daughter of mine's friend to no colored man, parading her shame for all the world to see," she said.

"Listen to reason, Mama," I said, moving closer to her. "What you're thinking isn't true. Coloreds can be friends. You like Cinda, Mama. You never thought bad of Reverend Potter. Zeke's the one who got me my job and returned that laundry basket after what Virgil did. Lord knows half the stuff in this house was got on trades from Zeke, Mama." I hated the note of pleading that had crept into my voice. Begging was almost as bad as lying.

As I watched her lay the jelly glasses one by one on the countertop, I saw for the first time how frail my mama was. I saw that my mama's hips were as fragile as chicken bones. I ran my sweaty palms down my own hipbones. I was tired of all this fighting, and I saw that my bones were different from Mama's. They were wide and strong.

I moved to Mama, putting my face to her cheek. "There's no shame in friendship, Mama," I said. "There's no shame in that." I felt her bobby pins prick my cheek as she pushed me away and then began wildly reaching for the glasses she had just set down.

I saw that my mama couldn't be reached by reason.

I saw the look wild and staring in her eyes. They reminded me of the eyes of the patients in the sanitarium over in Lutzville.

Suddenly she had glass after glass in her hands, and she was hurling them at me. I felt them knock against my head and beat against my back, and I slipped on the shards that shattered beneath my feet as I ran outside, bent on escape. Behind me I could hear the glasses shattering against the door one by one, and I saw one thing clearly: Mama's madness could be the end of me.

From the top of the pecan tree I rubbed my temples and arms. I could feel the knot starting at the back of my head, and I knew the bruises would raise up soon. I looked down at the red world of Kinship, Georgia, spread out below me. The red earth sprawled at the base of the tree. It stretched out across our lawn and under the fence. It passed across the Boggses' chickweed and between the ties of the railroad tracks up town. It stretched its way north and south, from Clifton Hill to Pearl Lake. The children to the east in Fenwick Acres played in it, and the dead to the west in the cemetery slept in it. The red earth of Kinship seeped into crevices and soaked into cracks. And I was beginning to see that the Pugh family lay in its ruins.

Chapter 17

They made me paint the fence.

They watched from the window as I dipped the brush into Daddy's old can of red that Pert and I used on that sneak, the one where we put our red hand-prints up all over town.

I wiped the brush across the plywood slats for hours, up and down, side to side. The sun scorched my face, marking my own red shame.

I traced over the letters, one by one. N-I-G-G-E-R-L-O-V-E-R. B-L-A-C-K-A-S-S-K-I-S-S-E-R.

Daddy and Mama hunched inside, watching. Some-times Gardenia would run out, bringing me a glass of ice water. I'd wipe my forehead with my sleeve and drink it straight down.

Everybody in Kinship came out to look. They drove by in their pickups. They strolled by after supper. Some of them wouldn't look at me; they just glanced at me sideways out of the corners of their eyes. Others of them stood and plain out stared. Some of them shouted names from their cars; others whispered the names under their breath. When Olive Shriner came by she clucked and wagged her finger. Sheriff Keiter found out that I did take those pictures and came by to say that he should have me arrested for obstructing justice but that painting the fence was a better punishment for such as me.

Although Mama and Daddy kept inside, they felt the shame too. Of course, Daddy didn't make it to the job interview at the textile plant, but when he called to set up another date, Mr. Orville Hearn, the plant manager, said they'd decided not to hire anyone just yet. The social worker in Troy contacted Mama when she didn't show up, but instead of asking when Mama could come again, she said she needed to set up a time to come to our house and look us over. Said homes for foster kids had to be the right kind. Mama slammed the phone in her ear.

Pert brought me the stories from town. When she got off work, she'd stand right by me as I slapped on paint, and she didn't seem to mind the folks who stared or shook their fingers. She said that the more people snubbed her, the less it bothered her. She said it made her famous in a way. Besides, Pert said, she got back in little ways. She filled a special sugar dispenser with salt to set out in front of Boyce Johnson when he ordered coffee. She made Olive Shriner's milk shakes with one less scoop of ice cream now. Pert said that after the pictures appeared on the fence Elmer Byer threatened to fire her, until she asked him where he

227

was like to find someone willing to work as hard as she did for what he paid.

Of course, I couldn't leave the house, but Pert often came over at night. She'd sneak up to my window and pass jawbreakers through the loose screens, and I finally told her all about George Hardy. How I'd come to be his friend. What he'd said about words being fences. How he said you could understand a person by looking at their fears. I think she shared my wonder at how your heart could ache so much and still beat.

Sometimes Gardenia joined us at night, slipping out of her room after Mama thought she was asleep. Lord knows Gardenia was trapped just as much as I was. Only, she was a canary in a cage, and I was a crow. One night Pert and Gardenia and I played Old Maid, passing our hands through the rips in the screen when we had to draw. Pert set us laughing at the characters on the cards. They had names like Fifi Fluff and Baker Benny and reminded me of the families in Fenwick Acres, mothers in high heels and sundresses gossiping over fences, fathers in chefs' hats and matching aprons cooking over grills.

Painting the fence was powerful hard. My arms would grow sore and heavy after a couple of hours, and my fingers and knees were streaked with red. When the sun blazed at noon, the lump on the back of my head throbbed and swelled. But there was one good thing about painting the fence: it gave me time to think, and a lot of what I thought about had to do with George Hardy.

In the evenings, when the sky was black and it was

too hard to see to paint, I disappeared into my room. Of course, Mama had sworn that I would never see George Hardy again, so I'd take his notes out of the cigar box shoved under my bed, turning the papers in my hand, trying to concentrate on the words: *splendid, highly recommended*. They seemed like phrases from a foreign language I'd been struggling to speak. I folded up the Santa apron into a neat red square, stuffing it into the bottom of the dresser drawer. I stuck the photographs pulled off the fence into the pages of the *National Geographics*; they were reminders of life in another country. I held the flower George Hardy had picked for me in my hand. It was still white and full, just starting to brown at the edges, but the smell was gone. I remembered how the leaves of the Ghost Tree were soft as felt on the underside and how the white blossoms waved like hankies against the black sky. As I pressed them between two pieces of waxed paper, I felt the tears smart. Then I mashed the flowers and paper between two bricks.

I thought about Zeke too. About how he said you had to see things clear and about how then you had to say them. As I moved the paintbrush up and down over board after board, the folks from Kinship clucking and sneering outside the gate, I saw what it was to hold your head high in the face of shame. When I first began to paint the fence, all I could do was duck my head and blush, but as the days went by, I saw that I could say, "Hey," to Lem Patterson's kids when they came by to gawk and look Olive Shriner straight in the eye. The longer I worked and the longer I thought, the more I knew what I had to do.

I had one more day to finish the fence, and I determined to do it right. After all, wasn't Maggie Pugh known for her splendid work? I checked off the finishing touches from the list in my mind: dab on the last drop of paint, tack up the WET PAINT sign, clean the brushes, put everything back in the garage. I had worked everything out with Pert. All I had to do was tell Mama.

When I came in, she was ironing the blue velvet coat she had bought for Gardenia from the First Presbyterians last year. She intended for Gardenia to wear it to Savannah. I saw Mama's bent shoulders and the force of her will on the iron, and I knew that Gardenia's trip to Savannah was the only sunshine in Mama's rainy life. That and the hope that the papers would come back from Richmond any day now and she'd be approved to join the UDC.

Mama picked up the sprinkling can and began to spray light drops of water across the blue cloth. I saw that the coat was turned inside out; Mama knew to press velvet on the wrong side.

"Mama, I need to talk to you," I said, lacing my fingers together to hold them quiet and still.

"Can't you see I'm busy with your sister's coat here, Maggie? Then I've got shoes to polish and a suitcase to pack. Can't you see I'm busy?"

I swallowed and began again. "This won't take long, Mama."

"I ain't got any time for jabberin', Maggie," she said.

She never took her eyes off her pressing. "Besides, you got to get on out and finish that fence."

"I did finish, Mama. Just now."

"Did you put the lid back on the paint can?"

"Yes, Mama."

"Did you put the can back in the garage?" The point of her iron was moving steadily between hem and waistband.

"Yes, Mama."

"Did you clean the brushes?"

"Yes, Mama."

"Did you twist the lid back on the turpentine tight? You know that turpentine evaporates as quick as money around here, don't you?"

"Yes, Mama. I did," I said. "I know." I laced my fingers more tightly. I thought the pressure of them might help me to begin. "Put down your ironing, Mama," I said. "I said I needed to talk to you."

She gave a sigh like irritation and set the iron on the ironing plate. The silvery click of metal on metal made the same sound as Gardenia's tap shoes. "Be quick about it," Mama said, turning to me. "I ain't got all day."

"Just need to tell you two things. Two things is all, Mama."

"Well, make it snappy," she said, turning away from me again. She had put her hand back on the iron.

"Take your hand off that iron and listen, Mama," I said.

Then she whirled around like the wind. She had the look she got in her eyes every time she thought I was sassing; the look was usually followed by a slap or a belt.

Before I spoke, I reminded myself of Zeke's proud head held high. I took a deep breath. "First thing is that I wasn't wrong. It wasn't wrong to be friends with Mr. Hardy, Mama. He was good to me and to this family and he's my friend, no matter what you say. I'm sorry that you felt wronged and shamed. I truly am. I've painted the fence and taken my punishment and done the job from start to finish. But I'm not sorry for what I've done. And I wasn't wrong."

I could see her body tense. The muscles in her jaw twitched, and her shoulders stiffened.

"The second thing I need to say is that I'm leaving, Mama."

I had expected the anger. I had never expected the sneer. Her lips made a curve that was half up and half down, and she gave a snorting sound partway between laughter and disgust. "Where you plannin' on going, Miss World Traveler?" Mama said. "What you plannin' on payin' for your food and shelter with, Maggie Pugh? Only free place around here for that is jail." The look on her face said she thought she was clever; then the look turned mean. "Come to think of it," she added, "that's likely where such as you belongs."

I bit my tongue against the words that would say I *had* been living in jail. "Going to live with Pert," I said instead. "Going today."

She folded her arms across her chest and threw back her head. "Ha!" she laughed. "I should of knowed it. Life in a trailer with a no-account bunch of

232

RCs! Shaming your own family even more. Leavin' your own family one less set of hands to look for work or bring in money. Surely you know how hard it is to find work in this town, Maggie Pugh. And who north of the tracks would hire you?" Her sneer turned sour. "Or maybe," she went on, "you could get a job with your colored friends down south!"

I struggled to stay calm, to keep my hands from trembling, to finish what I had to say. George Hardy had spoken the truth: it was hard making the words come out right.

"I don't care what you say, Mama. It doesn't matter anymore. And you're right. It *will* be hard to find work, I know. But you need to know the reason why I'm leaving, Mama."

"Already know the reason, Maggie," Mama said. "It's so you can go live with RCs and colored and shame your own family."

"No, Mama," I said. I held my head up and looked right at her. "It's not so I can go with them or shame the Pughs. It's because I won't live with you, Mama. I'm going because it's not good for me to live with my own mama."

Her hand moved quick as a blink. It had wrapped itself around the handle of the iron, and as the iron sprang from the plate and moved toward me, it hissed like a cattle brand.

I fought the urge to back away. I made myself stand my ground. "Look at you, Mama," I said, willing my shoulders to straighten and my head to lift. "Look at you with that iron in your hand. Look at you ready to strike your own daughter. Mamas don't act like that, Mama. Seems you've always got something in your hand, something ready to strike at me. A jelly glass. A rose stem."

I saw her step back and blink. It reminded me of people coming out of a dark movie theater into the light. As I lifted my voice, my eyes filled up. "Don't you know it's not me you're mad at, Mama? Don't you know it's not really me?"

I could feel my chin quivering. I bit my lip and thought of Zeke. Then I lifted my chin to keep my head held high. "But it doesn't matter to me that you're mad anymore, Mama, or why. I just know that mamas don't act like this. And that daughters can't live with them while they do."

I saw the muscle in her left cheek twitch as she turned away. Her right arm, which held the iron, dropped its heavy load onto the ironing plate, but her hand continued to grip the handle. Then Mama shrugged her shoulders, loosened her fingers from the iron, and sighed. Her bony fingers began to straighten the blue velvet cloth at the other end of the ironing board. Then she picked up the iron, touched it to the edge of the skirt, and pressed down.

"Good-bye, Mama," I said.

She didn't say a word, and as I closed the door behind me I saw only her stiff back and her tilted neck and her arms making slow careful motions across blue cloth.

Chapter 18

I moved into Pert's trailer right away. Daddy came over and tried to talk me out of it, and Gardenia came over and cried. She brought a paper sack filled with my clothes and the cigar box filled with my George Hardy memories.

Pert and Jimmy and Rae Jean Wilson were awful nice to me. Pert shared her bed and tried hard not to take all the covers and Jimmy brought home free bottles of Nehi from the Texaco station and Rae Jean let us live like tramps, eating out of cans. But I was restless. Like George Hardy I thrashed and tore at the sheets at night.

Of course, I needed a job. My palms were empty, but I knew I could work and wasn't afraid to. And Mama was right: people north of the tracks didn't seem to be hiring. I asked Bucky Gleason for a job, thinking all the years of watching Daddy fix stuff might have equipped me for selling hardware, but Bucky just kind of stumbled over his words after he said no and never really did give me a reason. At Millie's Curly Q Salon, Millie was real sweet, but she said my presence there would remind all her ladies of what happened to me. Millie said ladies came to a beauty parlor to feel better, not worse. I knew in my heart that George Hardy would take me back, but I didn't want to ask; Sheriff Keiter was on the lookout for him, and I didn't want to add to George Hardy's troubles by leading the Sheriff there.

The only luck I had was with Martha Leonard. She hired me to sit with Charlie, her retarded boy. Martha made Charlie wear his hair clipped short as a hedge, and he looked like a reject from the Army. His full name was Charles MacAlister Leonard, and I called him Charlie Mac. I liked sitting for him.

Charlie Mac was all that Martha had. Her husband Ralph had died soon after Charlie was born by falling into a silo full of grain and suffocating to death. That was why Martha spoiled Charlie so. But I thought it disgusting the way a ten-year-old boy was still fed with a spoon and said so.

"Here," I said, taking the spoon from Martha at supper. "Charlie Mac can do it himself."

The first time he tried, the loaded spoon misfired, hitting him in the side of the cheek. But when I propped his elbow on a book and got him to grip the spoon closer to the bowl, he slipped the wiggly tapioca into his mouth himself sure as the world. "See, Mrs. Leonard," I said. "If you treat him like a baby, he's going to stay a baby. Lettin' him try things is how he grows up."

Sometimes Gardenia would come to Martha's to visit. She'd tell me she missed me and then Gardenia, Charlie Mac, and I would read a book or make fudge. Martha Leonard was pleased as punch when Gardenia visited. She said Gardenia was the first friend Charlie Mac ever had. When it was time to go, Gardenia always said she missed me and clutched my neck.

Things had begun to get a little better when they began to get worse, and it was all on account of Pert, although it wasn't Pert's fault. She had said it might be fun to go to the drive-in, and she said we ought to take Gardenia. "She's been livin' in solitary confinement ever since you left, Maggie," Pert said.

She was right. I knew Gardenia was lonely at home all by herself.

So we raced across the fields to the place in my window where the screen was torn away, and Pert slipped inside and then I followed after, and we tiptoed into Gardenia's room, where she lay sound asleep surrounded by her dolls.

I gently shook her awake, and Gardenia's eyes got as big as saucers. "The drive-in, Pert?" she asked. "Why, that's all the way to Troy!"

Pert nodded her head. "I know it is, but *A Summer Place* is playing and my brother Jimmy's taking Sue Ellen. Said it's the best make-out movie to come down the pike."

With all my cleaning and delivering and painting fences this summer, I'd never even heard of *A Summer*

Place, but Gardenia had. "Oh, Maggie," she said, clapping her tiny hands together. "I've been hearing about it on the radio. Sometimes late at night the station in Atlanta plays the violin music from it."

"You'll love the story, Maggie," Pert said as the three of us ran back across the fields to Pert's trailer. "It stars Sandra Dee and Troy Donahue and it's about how they spend the night together and walk barefoot along the beach and how he gets her pregnant and *now* what are they going to do?"

"It sounds like a good movie, Pert," I said, and suddenly stood stock-still, remembering. "Lordy, Pert," I said, slapping my head. "What'll we do for money?" I asked.

"We'll get in for free," Pert said. "Leave everything to me."

Jimmy picked us up at the trailer. He was driving his friend Arnold Hardin's old car, the one that made grinding noises when it started and clunking noises once you got going. Gardenia and Pert and I hid under a yellow blanket on the floor of the backseat so we wouldn't have to pay admission. Jimmy and his girlfriend, Sue Ellen, sat up front. Then Jimmy insisted on setting a cooler and a tool tray on top of us. Said it made us look less suspicious. We went clanking up and down all the hills to Troy, the soda pop in the cooler rattling on top of Pert and me and the tools in the tool tray jangling and clanking on top of Gardenia.

When we pulled up to the admission gate at the Troy Drive-In, Jimmy told Pert to shut up with her giggling right now or he was going to put her out of the car. Jimmy had his right arm around Sue Ellen and she was sitting real close to him. Made it look like it was just the two of them in the car.

After he had given the boy the admission for two, he pulled away to find a parking spot, and Pert jumped up from under the blanket, sticking her fingers in her ears and signaling to the admission boy. Luckily he didn't see her. He was busy. There were a lot of cars behind us in line to see *A Summer Place*. Pert said it was going to be about the best movie ever was.

The Troy Drive-In was packed that night. There were cars pulled up at just about every speaker, looking like horses hitched to posts. It was getting black as pitch out, so we knew it was about time for the show. There's just nothing worse than a drive-in movie when it's even a tiny bit light out.

We kept watching the numbers count down on the screen. The screen showed a clock with a smiling face, the hands moving around to tick off the minutes. The clock blinked its eyes every time it switched over to a lower minute and made this tick-tock sound like Mickey Harris did by clucking his tongue off the roof of his mouth. "Five minutes to show time," it said. "Four minutes to show time."

Pert kept us all laughing. She did an imitation of a radio announcer's voice. "Show time," she croaked. "Five minutes to showtime, folks. Git your seats and shush your babies. Ladies, kindly remove your hats. You got about five minutes to go pee. Show time, folks," she said, holding a make-believe microphone to her mouth. "Five minutes to show time." In between

Pert kept bugging Jimmy and Sue Ellen by turning the volume up real loud on the speaker so that it squawked in their ears.

And then it started. The Percy Faith music and the strings and the scene of the long stretch of beach and Sandra Dee and Troy Donahue. I felt as excited as a bridesmaid just before the wedding march. I don't think Jimmy and Sue Ellen cared about the movie much. After a while it looked like they had lain down in the front seat to take a nap.

When it was about half over, I whispered to Pert. I was sitting between Pert and Gardenia. "Pert," I said, "I just never really liked Sandra Dee. She can't act half as good as Debbie Reynolds." I had seen Debbie Reynolds in *Tammy and the Bachelor*. When I heard her sing that line that went, "Tammy, Tammy, Tammy's in love," I'd never in my life heard anything so sad except for train whistles at dawn.

I didn't get to hear what Pert thought about Debbie Reynolds because the intermission was starting up. You could hear car doors slamming shut and people's feet crunching on gravel on their way to the snack bar. On the screen were pictures of popcorn boxes and soft drinks and candy bars. They all had faces on them and stick arms that were holding on to each other's white-gloved hands. Their stick feet were tap-dancing and they were singing "Come on out to the lobby, Come on out to the lobby, Come on out to the lobby, And have yourself a treat." Then the popcorn and the drinks and the candy started whirling each other about and at the end they put their stick arms around each other and made a cancan line.

Gardenia had fallen asleep on my shoulder. She had on her white nightgown, the one with the border of lace at the bottom. She looked like a sleeping angel.

Jimmy came up for air and told us to go get him and Sue Ellen a snack. He gave us a wad of money and said we could get a snack too. Jimmy Wilson spent every penny he ever made pumping gas at the Texaco station.

"Wake up, Gardenia, honey," I said. "It's intermission. You want a snack?" Jimmy and Sue Ellen each wanted a 7-Up. I wanted some popcorn and Pert wanted malted milk balls.

"I ain't hungry, Maggie," Gardenia said, pushing her curls back off of her forehead. "I just gotta go pee."

The popcorn line was half a mile long. I saw Virgil Boggs and Bubba Ziegler and some of their buddies in front of the line. The big vat of popcorn kept dumping a new load of popcorn out every five minutes or so. The snack bar was close to the rest room, and the place stunk of pee and salt.

Virgil and Bubba and the others turned and stared at us. I was still pretty far away from them, so I wasn't sure. Maybe it was a glare more than a stare. Then I saw Virgil leer at me and run his dirty fingers through his wet, greasy hair. He looked at me again and took a pocket knife out of his pocket, picking his fingernails clean with the tip of the open blade. I remembered those grimy hands with the half-moons of dirt up under his fingernails.

"You stay in line, Maggie," Pert whispered to me. "I'll take Gardenia to the rest room. We don't want to miss the show." I saw Pert disappear with Gardenia, her gown white and clean as one of Mama's ironed sheets.

Finally it was my turn. I ordered one popcorn, one malted milk balls, and two 7-Ups. Then I ordered a bag of red licorice for Gardenia. If she wasn't hungry, she could have it tomorrow.

I picked up my stuff to go and saw Pert in the corner, talking to Russell Simmons, Junior. He had his hand stuck in the hip pocket of her jeans and was whispering something in her ear. Lord knows Pert Wilson had no fear of boys.

"Here, Pert," I said, heading over to her. "Help me with this stuff."

Junior Simmons whispered something else in Pert's ear, and Pert gave a giggle. I didn't see how she did it. Boys didn't scare Pert a lick.

"Hey, now, Pert," I said, looking around. "Where's Gardenia?"

Pert turned beet red. "She was right behind me just a minute ago. She's around here someplace. You know how she dawdles, Maggie. Maybe she's back at the car." Then Pert kept quiet and kind of hung her head.

I headed back to the car, a tiny speck of fear scratching at my throat. Everything was quiet except for the gravel grinding under my feet.

Jimmy and Sue Ellen were sitting up. "Have you seen Gardenia?" I asked, handing them their 7-Ups.

"Naw, Maggie," Jimmy said, ignoring me. He was

taking his ice cubes and snapping the elastic on Sue Ellen's halter top, tossing ice cubes down her front.

Then I heard the shrieks. They were coming from the side of the snack bar, outside of the shack where the concrete ended and the gravel started up. Cars were honking their horns and people were shouting, "Shut up. We want to watch the movie."

I ran like the wind and then stopped in my tracks. There stood Gardenia in front of Virgil Boggs, his hateful hands on her sweet shoulders, his open knife at the top of her head. She looked stunned, her eyes wide and pleading like you see in photographs of victims in concentration camps. Her nightgown hung down in strips like Red Cross bandages.

I heard her helpless shrieking. And then Virgil Boggs made quick movements with his knife, and they fell to the dirty concrete, white and round and quiet as snow, one by one, the curls, the curls, Mama's sweet baby's curls. The top of her head was now shorn. It looked like a stubbly field.

Virgil gave me a twisted smile. "Looks just like Angel, now, don't she?" he said.

Anger washed over me as I remembered Gardenia's doll, her torn white dress, and Buster sniffing at her fallen curls.

I lunged at Virgil Boggs, beating him with my clenched fists. People were running to the snack bar, shouting, yelling, knocking over boxes of popcorn, kicking over trash cans. "Call the po-lice," Simon Nolan ordered the girl behind the snack bar.

Virgil pushed me an arm's length away from him. "I

just got one thing to say to you, Maggie. Consider your-self warned. First the fence. Now your sister. You'd better feel warned. My friends and I've been snooping. We've found that nigger in the picture with you. Ain't gonna be another warning, Maggie. You pick up your sister's curls and take 'em over to him, Maggie. Say it's a greeting from Virgil Boggs. He'll know my name."

It was true. George Hardy did know Virgil. But I had thought Virgil didn't know him. At least not yet. I hurled myself at Virgil, beating him again and again. Then I felt thick palms around me and Simon Nolan pulling me off him. Simon towered over both of us, his huge frame separating me and Virgil. "You get your trashy ass out of my movie theater, Virgil Boggs," Si-mon yelled. "And don't you let me catch you settin' one foot onto my property ever again."

Then Virgil flipped his knife shut, gave a sneer, and slunk away into the darkness.

Gardenia was shaking. Her face was white and pasty. Her short stubbles of hair stuck straight up like someone stumbling on a ghost in a forest.

Simon Nolan turned to me. "You and your friends'll get yourselves out of here if you know what's good for you," he said. "I've called the po-lice for a report. I'll send them over to your house to talk to your folks. And don't you plan on coming back to my drive-in anytime soon, you hear? You trashy kids is bad for business."

I didn't like the name he called us. We weren't trashy kids. I didn't like the way people in Kinship put a name on everyone. Worst of all, I didn't like the fact that the name Simon put on me was the same name he put on Virgil Boggs.

I ran to the car, Gardenia's trembling body in my arms.

"Get in quick, Maggie," Pert called to me. She was already in the backseat. I shoved Gardenia next to her, and Jimmy tried to start the engine. It sputtered and died again and again. When it finally kicked over, Jimmy looked like he was about to cry. He threw the car in drive and gassed it out of the lot.

Sheriff Keiter's cruiser was out front when we pulled up.

It was dark inside the house. As I stumbled into the living room, squeezing Gardenia's hand in mine, I saw something flash white in the darkness. It was Mama's hanky, flickering as she dabbed at her eyes.

The only light in the room came from the fixture in the hall. Daddy's pajamas and Mama's nightgown glowed eerily against the blackness. And in the darkness Daddy, Mama, and Sheriff Keiter looked like cellblock prisoners in an old prison movie.

Mama rose from her rocker and moved quietly to Gardenia. My sister's mouth hung open like a person in shock, and a thin line of drool trickled from the corner of her mouth. Mama reached out to touch the shorn hair, running her fingers across it like someone strumming a guitar.

"Oh, Gardenia, sweet baby," she crooned, kneeling before her, tracing her fingers through stubble. Then Mama kissed her own bony index finger, touching it to all the places on Gardenia's head that were once curls. Mama knelt beside her for a long time.

I started to explain and then thought better of it. I heard Daddy and Sheriff Keiter whispering in the corner. I heard "Virgil" and "Bubba Ziegler" and "Simon Nolan" and names like that. I heard, "What did you expect, Henry, after what they're sayin' about your family?" and "You sure can press charges, but that ain't no guarantee Boggses'll leave you alone" and "If he were colored, you'd have an easier time in court."

Then Mama gathered up Gardenia in her arms and moved to the rocker. She never once spoke to me. She rocked and rocked, singing.

> Hush, little baby, don't say a word.
> Mama's gonna buy you a mockingbird.
> And if that mockingbird don't sing,
> Mama's gonna buy you a diamond ring.
>
> If that diamond ring turns to brass,
> Mama's gonna buy you a looking glass,
> And if that looking glass gets broke,
> Mama's gonna buy you a billy goat.

After Daddy showed Sheriff Keiter the door, he took my hand and led me outside. We stood under the pecan tree under the black night. Daddy never once blamed me and did what he always did when he couldn't find words: he talked about the War.

"What all's happened put me in mind of General Gordon, Maggie," he said. He meant John B. Gordon,

246

the Georgia general who sat on his saddle at the eastern end of Fenwick Street. "General Gordon never gave up. Was wounded five times and got up to fight again and again. Fought the whole War through and lived to tell about it." I knew that Daddy was talking to me, but somehow it felt like he was saying the words just to himself.

Through the open window I could hear Mama's voice from the front room and the creak of the rocker. After every few lines Mama gave a tiny sob, breaking the melody like a plate being chipped.

> If that billy goat don't pull,
> Mama's gonna buy you a cart and bull.
> And if that cart and bull turn over,
> Mama's gonna buy you a dog named Rover.

I listened to Daddy's voice and the words about General Gordon and they failed to comfort me. I tried to think of Madagascar and Malaysia, those far-off foreign places I had read about in George Hardy's magazines, but they seemed as far away as Mars, and I feared that, in spite of everything, I would never escape Kinship.

I heard Mama's voice and pictured her moving the white hanky between her lap and her eyes, dabbing and wiping, wiping and dabbing, stroking Gardenia's head, grieving for the loss of her sweet baby's curls.

> If that dog named Rover won't bark,
> Mama's gonna buy you a horse and cart.

247

And if that horse and cart fall down,
You'll still be the sweetest little baby in town.

It didn't seem to matter what we did or didn't do. Trouble haunted Pughs like a ghost. I tried to concentrate on Daddy's words, on what he was saying about General Gordon. At Chantilly. Seven Pines. The Wilderness. And all I really heard were the words about that time in Sharpsburg. How he was wounded in the face. How General Gordon buried his head in his hat. And how he was almost drowned by his own blood.

Chapter 19

Martha Leonard was lonely and loved to talk, so at her house I got to hear what was happening in town and at home. Mama and Daddy decided not to press charges against Virgil because it wouldn't bring Gardenia's hair back in time for the pageant. Pastor Mullins made a lot of trips to our house to get Mama to stop weeping. Miriam Simpson was the only one of the UDC ladies nice enough to visit Mama. She said that what happened to Gardenia shouldn't have happened to a dog even if the dog had a stray for a sister that ran with colored. The latest was what Martha heard while she was getting her shampoo and set at Millie's. Mayor Cherry was looking for a substitute for Gardenia in the pageant, and it would likely be Dawn Deems.

I didn't miss Mama as much as I longed for her. It was like a favorite thing that you loved but had misplaced somehow. I kept hoping I might find her someday. I was sorry about Gardenia's curls, not so much for Gardenia but for Mama. With Gardenia's curls went Mama's hope.

When I walked back to Pert's trailer after a morning with Charlie Mac, I was sad to think that the only place for me now was with the outcasts of Kinship: the retarded, the RCs. The click of the handle on the trailer door was the most lonesome sound in the world to me, and I wondered if Daddy and Gardenia missed me like I missed them.

And then one morning early she was there. I saw the smudges on her nose that meant she had powdered it, and she was wearing her best black dress with the brass brooch and carrying her pocketbook under her arm like she did that time she marched up to the bank and asked for a loan.

I walked down the concrete steps from the trailer to the patch of brown thatch that passed for a yard.

Mama cleared her throat before she spoke. "I got a call from Mayor Cherry this morning, Maggie," she said.

"Yes, Mama?" I said. I guess Mama wasn't going to say hello or ask how I was doing or apologize for the way she treated me. She was getting right down to business.

She pursed her lips and reached in her purse for a hanky. "That two-bit politician called to remind me that the bus left for the state pageant in Savannah tomorrow. Said he 'figured' Gardenia wouldn't be on it. Said he 'figured' she wouldn't be making the contest after what-all's happened to her," she said. "Said he 'figured' Dawn Deems and her flaming batons would make a good showing instead."

You could tell Mama was making an effort to stay calm. I just knew she was itching to wring Mayor Cherry's neck, but she wrung the hanky instead.

Then she started pacing like I'd seen her do so many times. "Well, I swanee," she said. "The nerve of that man." The heels of her shoes as she paced dug tiny holes in the grass. "I'll teach that man about 'figuring' if it's the last thing I do.

"You see, Maggie," she said, punching the air with her index finger when she talked, "I got this idea about calling Millie up at the Curly Q and finding out how much she sells one of her wigs for. And it was five dollars." As she punched at the air with her finger, she reminded me of Elmer Byer, toting up numbers on his adding machine. "Five dollars includin' styling."

Suddenly her eyes lit up. She stopped pacing and pounced on me. "Maggie," she said, grabbing me by the shoulders and shaking me, "does you reckon you could be gettin' yourself over to that no good colored man's house to clean for one more day?"

You could have knocked me over with a feather. Clean for George Hardy? See my friend again? With my mama's *permission?* My thoughts raced. It sure seemed likely that his place would need cleaning. I pictured the spilled tobacco, the empty soup cans, the gold bathrobe spilling onto the floor. I thought about it for a minute before I nodded. "Yes, Mama," I said, whispering the words. "I reckon I could do that."

I could see the tight muscles in her shoulders relaxing into relief. "I think that's a good idea, Mama," I said. "And I'll see if I can get you your five dollars today." There was a hopeful look in Mama's eyes that made me glad. I knew that you were dead when you ran out of hope.

Then her lips smacked me on the cheek in something like a kiss. "You, Maggie," she said, catching the strap of her pocketbook on her brooch in her excitement, "if you can get us that five dollars from that awful colored man you called a boss, you, child, is gonna save this family's life!"

As I pedaled to George Hardy's house on my way to save my family's life, my heart thumped hard inside my chest. Lord knows I'd never seen anything like my mama. She was like someone who could be killed dead and brought back to life. Like Jesus Christ Himself.

I turned the key in the side door lock and heard the newspapers rustling under my feet when I reached the mudroom. When the scent of his pipe tobacco caught in my nose, something behind my eyes began to smart. I slipped into the kitchen, happy to see his familiar mess. Inside, it was quiet as dawn.

I began with the dishes in the sink. One thing's for sure: George Hardy still didn't know beans about dishes. There they sat, egg coated and grease slicked, dried milk clinging to the sides of glasses, coffee grounds floating in empty cups. I thought about leaving him a note, telling him to let them soak if he hadn't the time to wash them right off. Mama, of course, didn't believe in soaking. Said water was too dear. I didn't care what Mama said. I could decide on things my own self. Mama wasn't always right. I did things different today, different from Mama. I put the glasses aside, tossing in the silverware first, making my own order to things.

I let the water run real hot and put in extra soap. It was going to be my last time here and I wanted George Hardy to remember that I always did splendid work.

The bubbles were rising high and pink when I heard the front screen door slam. The sound went through my heart like a shot, and I gave a little start.

And there he was, peeking around the kitchen door, his face the warm brown color of morning toast, a smile spread across his cheeks as inviting as a blanket thrown down for a picnic. There he was, looking like he always did: like my friend, like my friend George Hardy.

"Hey, Maggie," he said as if I'd never been gone. George Hardy looked tired, but he was smiling still.

"Hey, yourself," I said, biting my lip. Something inside me had made it start to tremble. I thought that if I bit it hard enough, I could get the tremble to stay still. I had finished with the silverware. The glasses clattered under my hands.

I turned to him and wiped my hands on my jeans, biting harder. "I just wanted," I stammered. "I—I—I just wanted," I stammered again. "I wanted," I said, "I wanted so much to explain things to you, to explain what happened, to say I was sorry about the way things turned out, George Hardy."

He stood and looked at me the way he always did,

studying me carefully as if I were a math problem. "No need, Maggie," he said. "I heard about what happened. I knew what you must have been going through. No need for explanations between friends."

And then they came. The tears I had held back all summer, all my lifetime. They streaked down my face and made my nose run, and I wiped them on the sleeve of his shirt as he held me, shaking, to his chest, and I wiped them on his collar, his sleeve, his hands, pouring them out like oil.

He took a clean white handkerchief from the back pocket of his jeans and swabbed my swollen face with it.

I turned away and began to finish my work at the sink, embarrassed. Maggie Pugh wasn't one to cry. My chest was still heaving and I could barely see through the suds. "I came today because my mama said"—I offered the words, still shuddering—"that I could come one last time."

"She must have needed the money," he responded. Out of the corner of my eye I saw him swabbing his glasses, polishing at the wet spots made by my tears.

I dried my hands on my jeans again and turned to him. "You got to listen to me about something, George Hardy," I said. "You got to do me a favor."

He stopped his wiping, hooking the ends of his glasses up over his ears. "Sure, Maggie. I'll do anything you want."

"You promise?"

"Sure."

"George Hardy," I said—I put my face right up in

his and grabbed the front of his shirt. This was important—"you got to get out of Kinship."

He knit his brows together and backed away from
me. Then he folded his arms across his chest and
leaned against the counter, listening.

I told him about Virgil Boggs and Gardenia's curls
and the threat Virgil made about him, my words rushing out, spilling like one of George Hardy's own ink
bottles tipped over.

"Calm down, Maggie," he said. He had put out his
hand to stroke my head the way Daddy always did.

I brushed his hand away. I didn't want comforting.
I wanted his promise. "Will you go soon, George
Hardy? Please?"

"I can't do that, Maggie," he said. "There's too
much unfinished business here."

"Like what, George Hardy?"

"Like the business about the way Kinship treats my
people. With its Jim Crow laws and its 'colored' rest
rooms and water fountains and swimming pools and
bus stations and everything else rigged up against us.
And the violence, especially the violence of places like
Kinship, whenever you try to take those fences down."

I wondered if I could ask. I wondered if George
Hardy knew. I drew in my breath, looking up under
the canopy of his eyebrows into the dark-brown eyes.
"George Hardy," I asked, fumbling with the words like
a key in a lock, "how much do you know about what
happened to Zeke? Not the part about when he tried to
use Elmer Byer's rest room. Everybody in Kinship
knows that. But the part after that, the part about Zeke

and the reason he dropped his suit. Do you know about that part, George Hardy?"

George Hardy's eyes were fixed on me. They reminded me of cowboys in the TV westerns, aiming through their rifle sights. "Maggie," he said, "yes, Maggie. I know about that." His voice was sure and steady. "It's the reason I came back to Kinship. It's the reason I'm determined to finish the business here. But you, Maggie. That's what I need to know about. What do you know?"

"I was there, George Hardy."

"There? What do you mean?" His eyebrows were squeezed close together.

"I was there when it happened, George Hardy. Up in the horse chestnut. I saw it all."

He reached for me then while I told. I told him about the shadowy figures below and the truck pulling up and Zeke with his hands bound and Virgil Boggs and Boyce Johnson and the rest and what they did and what they said and about how Zeke passed out and what happened after that.

When I had finished, George Hardy asked, "And you never told anyone, Maggie? You never told anyone about it?"

"Never before this very day, George Hardy," I said. "Kept the secret all to myself. It's been like an ache in my heart ever since. And it's why you've got to leave Kinship, George Hardy. Before they do the same to you."

He held me at arm's length, his hands at my shoulder. "I'm not going to leave, Maggie," he said firmly. "I can't. Besides, I'm not afraid of Virgil Boggs."

"How can you say that? How can that *be?*" I thought of what Virgil had done to Zeke, to Gardenia, and to me. Hadn't George Hardy listened to what I just said? Hadn't George Hardy heard a word of it?

"Truth is, Maggie," he said, "Virgil's afraid of me. Remember how I told you how you could understand a person by figuring out the things they were afraid of?"

I nodded, remembering.

"Same thing applies to Virgil Boggs. Virgil does everything out of fear, Maggie. I'm not afraid of *him*. I understand him. I understand Virgil and his type. He's afraid of *me*."

I moved again to the sink, confused. I still had so much to learn. I hadn't yet learned all I needed to know about how to stand up to fear, how to face it, how to stare it down. I held a glass up to the light, rubbing at a ring of milk that hadn't come clean.

I felt him behind me. "Maggie," he said, taking a five-dollar bill from his wallet and laying it on the damp counter beside me, "take the money and forget the work for today. You've got a lifetime of work ahead of you. Besides, I want to show you something."

He took my hand and led me out the back. We walked behind the house, out to the big dark woods that bordered it, and he took me down a tangled path through evergreens and scrub oak and deep pine scents into a clearing, in the middle of which was a pond.

The pond was clear and clean, unlike the other ponds I had stumbled on in the woods around Kinship. George Hardy had obviously been working on the pond, for there was a big net lying on the ground filled with pine needles skimmed from the surface of the water. Beside it were hammers and chisels and all manner of saws and wire and screws. I saw, too, that there was a bandage across George Hardy's left hand.

He walked around to the wide open space in the clearing and pointed to a little wooden bridge that spanned the surface of the water. The pine planks looked like they had been sawed by hand, and the railing had been given some fancy touches. "I wanted to show you this, Maggie," he said, indicating the bridge. "I'd always hoped I could. I'm kind of proud of it. Built it myself."

"Your-*self?*" I asked, laughing quietly. "Your-*self,* George Hardy? Why, you told me you were never any good with your hands. Weren't you the one that always had to labor with your mind?" I gave him an upturned smile that was a question mark.

"You inspired me, Maggie. I learned a certain amount of confidence from watching you. The way you worked. The way you used your hands. The way you did things so efficiently. It was something I respected, something I always wanted to do. I always wanted to build something myself. From scratch. The way my mama made her cakes."

"It's lovely," I said, a catch in my breath. "It's beautiful, George Hardy." I caught his hand and looked at it, turning it over, laughing still. "George Hardy, there's calluses *everywhere,"* I said, rubbing at the hard places on his palms. "And your *hand!* You've cut your hand!"

"Earned those bruises and cuts, every one. Got them sawing all these boards."

"And there are cuts and bruises all up and down your arm," I said, pointing to the red and purple badges that marked his battle with the bridge.

"Don't worry *too* much about it, Maggie. I got to use my head a lot building this thing too. Bridges are built of mathematics as much as brawn," he said. He picked up a stray pine branch and said, "Want to try it out?"

"Sure." I nodded.

The planks felt secure under my feet. The pine railing was wide and sturdy. We came together in the middle of the bridge, George Hardy and I, and gazed over the railing into the clear green water. Our two reflections wavered on the surface.

After a moment he said, "This bridge was a kind of solution for me, Maggie. My own kind of answer to the puzzle that was everything in Kinship." He paused, patient and calm like he always was, weighing his words.

I knew what he meant. "I've been wondering about the puzzle that was everything in Kinship, too, George Hardy," I said. "Only, I don't have any solutions like you."

I looked down into the water and could tell from his reflection that he was studying my face. His profile was turned toward me. "I want to ask you something,

Maggie," he said. "Something important. But I don't want you to answer me right away. I want you to take as long as you need to think about it."

"Sure, George Hardy," I said, turning my profile to him.

"I think you may have a solution, Maggie," he said. I could see the sunlight filtering quietly through the pines behind him. "A solution better than this bridge."

I looked at him, wondering. The sun was at the top of the trees, rising to noon.

"I want you to think about telling what happened to Zeke. Telling in court."

"Telling, George Hardy?" I gasped, breathing hard. "In front of every—" He broke off my words by putting his finger to my lips.

"I don't want you to answer me right away, Maggie," he said.

I moved his hand away. "But, George Hardy," I said, "how could I—?"

He silenced me again with his finger. "Shhhhh, Maggie," he said. "You don't have to say anything. With your testimony Zeke can make a case for himself against those men who beat him. With your evidence and all and Ida Mae's efforts to get the trial moved someplace else like Troy or Macon, there's a real chance that you could help him, help all of us, Maggie."

I kept quiet this time. Of course I wanted to help Zeke and George Hardy, but this was a different kind of help. This kind of help was going to be harder than teaching Zeke to read or teaching Charlie Mac to use a spoon. I dove down deep into myself, thinking. I could think for a long while. I could take all the time I needed. It was all George Hardy asked of me now.

We walked back across the bridge, and for the first time in my life I only half heard what George Hardy was saying. "I'd hear you tell of your daddy hoisting that *fence,*" he said, picking pine needles one by one from the branch in his hand and tossing them over the rail to float away on the surface. "I'd look at the bruises on your body, at Zeke's swollen face. I'd look at the way my people had to stand at the takeout counter or sit in the balcony. The fences made me furious."

My mind was racing with images. They were black and white like the images on a strip of film: Zeke's black body as it stretched across the dock to read, Gardenia's white organdy dress flounced stiff with Niagara starch, Reverend Potter's shirtsleeves rolled up as his black hands worked, Jack Bailey placing a white robe around the shoulders of a lady that looked like Mama.

"Fences. Bars. Fortifications. Stockades," George Hardy was saying. "They don't make any sense. Whether the fences affect white or black, it's enough to drive you mad, Maggie. This bridge was my response."

The sun was high in the sky. It was beating down hard on me as my mind thought on responses of my own. I remembered what Zeke said: that it made everybody in Kinship sweat, black and white alike. Zeke and Daddy and Reverend Potter and Martha Leonard and Missy Moses and Virgil and Mama and George

Hardy and even me. I looked up to the dome of sky, at the sun spinning way up in the middle of the air like a wheel, and I thought of Zeke. Of what Zeke had said. About never being afraid of the truth.

Chapter 20

I biked over the next morning to put the five dollars on the table, and for the first time since I can remember, our house seemed to hold a sense of happiness. I could hear Gardenia splashing in the tub and Mama scrubbing her like she was a pot or a pan. Daddy was dancing to "Alley Oop" on the radio, making caveman motions and scratching himself. When Daddy saw me, he stopped his dancing and scooped me into a gorilla hug.

"Bless you, Maggie," Daddy said, "for all your help. It's good to have you here."

I wanted to say, *It's good to be here,* but it wasn't exactly the truth, so I said, "Thank you, Daddy."

"Your mama's real pleased, Maggie," Daddy said. "Millie styled the wig all over with ringlets. Gardenia looks cute as a button."

Lord knows she did too. They came down the hall together, Gardenia giggling and Mama grim. When she saw me, Gardenia ran over and hugged me around the waist. "Ooops, Maggie," she said, hugging me with one hand and adjusting her hair with another. The wig had slipped down over her left eye, and she tried to straighten it with her fat fingers. Mama looked up from the checklist she had made and said, "Thank you for your help, Maggie." Then she called out the following items, putting checkmarks next to each: petticoat, bobby pins, hair spray, shoe cloth, nail file, soap, hairbrush.

She turned to Daddy. "Think I need that rabbit's foot, Henry?"

Daddy looked from her to me and shrugged.

"Sure, Mama," I said. "It couldn't hurt." I went to the big oak dresser in their room and rooted around in the corner of the drawer. Then I slipped the rabbit-foot chain over Gardenia's neck.

Then it was time to go.

"You're going with us, Maggie, ain't you?"

"I don't know, Mama," I said.

"Well, I need someone to take a picture of your baby sister at the bus station, and your camera's sittin' right there on the table waitin' for you to pick it up if you can stop all this shilly-shallying around."

It was the closest thing to an invitation I'd ever gotten from Mama, and the camera sure felt good in my hands. She had taken it away from me after the letters appeared on the fence. I had missed it, like so many other things.

On the way out the door to help them put their things in the car, I accidentally let Gardenia's dress hanger trail on the floor. Mama pulled her foot back, fixing to give me a swift kick in the shins, and then she stopped when my eye caught hers.

I biked over, meeting them in the asphalt lot behind the Trailways station. Through the viewfinder Gardenia looked lovely. She was framed in front of the silver bus in her blue velvet coat and matching bonnet. They underscored the color of her eyes and reminded me of the song called "Blue on Blue, Heartache on Heartache." Daddy pressed three quarters into her hand and told her she could buy whatever she wanted with them in Savannah.

"Watch the birdie," I said, tripping the shutter.

"Now, why don't you get her and me in the picture together, Maggie," Mama said. "A nice mother-daughter." Mama gave Gardenia a proud mother-of-the-bride kind of look.

When Alma Jenkins, who worked the ticket counter and chain-smoked, announced the bus for Savannah, Gardenia clutched my neck, pressing her cheek to mine. I could feel the rough strands of her curly wig itching my cheek. On the jukebox in the station Frankie Avalon was singing, "Oh, Venus, make my wish come true."

Mama gave instructions all the way up the steps to the bus. Don't forget to water the periwinkles. Keep a lookout for the genealogy papers from the UDC; they're due from Richmond any day now. Try for that job over in Troy with the cotton-yarn company. Meet us here on Sunday at one. Cross your fingers for good luck.

The bus started up in a puff of smoke, and then the smoke trailed away, disappearing as it rounded Front Street. I saw Gardenia's tiny face in the window and Mama's big one behind it. Gardenia's fingers gave a wave, and I saw that my own fingers were crossed tight.

I took a deep breath, then let it out. I was dog tired.

"You want to come back over to the house, Maggie? I can put some corn bread in the oven and cook up some beans and we can turn the radio up as loud as we want."

"Thanks, Daddy," I said. "Maybe I'll be over later. I'm thirsty right now. I think I'll meet Pert over in Byer's for a Coke. Want to come?"

"No, thanks, Maggie," Daddy said. "But I'm expecting you for supper later on, you hear?"

"I'll be there, Daddy," I said, giving him a kiss on the cheek.

As I biked to Byer's Drugs, the streets of Kinship seemed somehow different to me now that I was no longer living at home. Smaller. Less comfortable. Like an old shoe that had suddenly grown too tight. On the way back to town I passed under the Civil War statue. Even it seemed less grand. Someone had carved some letters into the granite, and white bird-do streaked General Gordon's face. At the pedestal a flock of pigeons pecked for food.

I heard Elmer Byer's bells jingling behind me and saw Pert working the counter. She waved when she saw me. "They get your sister off, Maggie?"

"Just did, Pert," I said. "Mama asked me to go to

take pictures, and Gardenia looked swell in her blue coat. I think she's nervous as a cat, though, Pert."

"Well, I hope she wins, Maggie. I think she's got a chance, don't you?"

"I hope so, Pert," I said, watching Cinda Samples. She was dipping a basket of french fries into the grease. "How 'bout a Coke? Easy on the ice, now."

"Comin' right up," said Pert, filling a glass.

I saw them out of the corner of my eye. They came in single file, threading through the aisles to the lunch counter, holding books and magazines and newspapers. It wasn't quite lunchtime yet, so there was only me at one end of the counter and Russell Simmons with a cup of coffee about halfway down.

They sat down quietly on the stools. It was me, then Missy Moses, then Georgia, then Stumble Martin. Next was Russell Simmons, Rocker, Bigger Baby, and Zeke. Every seat was taken. George Hardy stood alone at the very end by me. "Here, George Hardy," I said, passing him my Coke. "You can have my seat. My Coke too."

He looked me in the eye. "You better get on home, Maggie. I don't want you in here."

I got up to leave and he took my stool.

Cinda came right on over. "Here, Pert," she said, pushing her gray hair back off of her broad face. "I'll help you take orders."

Pert's eyes got as big as saucers. Then she took a pencil from behind her ear and flipped to a new page in her order book. Lord knows Pert Wilson never got her feathers ruffled one day in this world. She crooked one hand on her hip and set about taking orders. Chili and corn bread. Beet greens. A hot dog and a vanilla milk shake. A slice of sweet-potato pie. A cup of coffee for Georgia. Missy took toast and tea.

Russell Simmons gulped down his coffee, burning his tongue. Then he slammed the cup down in the saucer, hopped off of his stool, and headed for Elmer Byer's office in the back. When he passed the register, I saw Hazel Boggs dialing the phone. I moved to take Russell's seat, and George Hardy looked down the counter at me, stern as a teacher. "I said to get on home, Maggie," he said.

Elmer Byer stormed down the beauty aids section, heading our way. "You get on off of them seats," he said, sweeping the stools with his eyes. "You gots your own special section for orders," Elmer said. "Right over here." He pointed to the place where coloreds usually stood in line.

George Hardy turned to Elmer. "We're paying customers, Mr. Byer," he said, swiveling on his stool, "same as everybody. And paying customers take a seat."

"What's the matter with you niggers?" Elmer said. The top of Elmer's head was bald with a fringe of curly hair at the sides: like a clown at the circus. "Ain't a special section all your own good enough? Ain't it enough for you that you've got your own schools and your own cemetery and now your own park? Ain't a special section all to yourself enough?"

George Hardy stared him down. "No, Elmer," he said, pulling a copy of *The Atlanta Constitution* from his hip pocket. "A special section isn't good enough. We'll sit down like the rest of your paying customers."

Elmer headed back behind the counter. He pulled the cord out of the toaster and shut off the milk-shake machine. He flipped the button on the hot-dog cooker, and the hot dogs stopped turning. "Well, then," he said, red faced. "We ain't open for lunch yet. It's only ten-thirty."

George Hardy opened his paper to the editorial page. Calmly, he said, "Well, then, Mr. Byer, we'll wait."

All up and down the lunch counter, books fell open one by one like dominoes. When I saw Zeke open his Bible, I was proud. He had moved far beyond our first simple words.

George Hardy's people sat quietly, reading.

Elmer Byer fumed. Over my shoulder I saw Hazel Boggs and behind her a crowd of people flying through the door. I stood stock-still. I knew those people. Virgil. Cecil. Jim Bob. Bubba Ziegler and Boyce Johnson and the rest. I knew them all. I wished I didn't.

They moved through the store to stand behind the people seated at the counter. But George Hardy's people kept right on reading. Rule number one: Quiet dignity.

Virgil was the first to speak.

"Coonhead," he said into Missy's ear. She didn't blink.

Then he moved down the counter to Zeke. "Jigaboo," he said. Zeke's Bible was open to Romans.

It looked like Chapter 12, and I remembered my daddy's words: "Recompense to no man evil for evil." Zeke didn't flinch.

Then he went down the line, taunting. "Blue gum. Jungle bunny." When Virgil came to Bigger Baby, you could see Bigger Baby tense. The muscles rippled under his shirtsleeves; he was breathing hard. "Rule number two," I said silently, under my breath. "No violence." Then Virgil balled up his fist, knocking Bigger Baby on the head. "Coconut head," he said, and kept on knocking.

That was all it took. Bigger Baby swung on his stool and punched Virgil in the stomach. I heard an ugly thud, and Virgil doubled over with pain. Then I saw the white arms flash with hammers, chains, tire irons, baseball bats.

George Hardy tried to get up, his voice firm. "Rule number one, brothers. Rule number two." Bubba Ziegler shoved George Hardy down.

Then Bigger picked up the sugar canister and threw it at Bubba, raising a welt on Bubba's head. Zeke jumped up and started shouting, "Whosoever shall smite thee on thy right cheek, turn to him the other also." Cecil dumped my glass of Coke on Zeke's head.

They went crazy. They went wild, everything a blur.

But something changed inside of me as I watched. No more secrets, I told myself. I would trust myself: to see the truth and to tell it.

I held up my camera and tried to focus, but somebody pushed into me, and the camera jerked. I refused to give up. *Remember your big strong hands, Maggie Pugh*. I tried again.

Somebody was throwing drinking glasses across the counter. Fists were flying. Missy Moses was kicking with her tiny feet. I steadied the camera in my hands, tripping the shutter.

A rack of comic books was sent spinning as Zeke was shoved into them. *Cock the shutter. Trip it. Advance the film.*

Plates and dishes were thrown at the counter. Cinda ducked, and they smashed against the wall. My hands were shaking as I held the camera to my eye. *Steady, Maggie,* I told myself. *Steady your hands. Focus. Shoot.*

Bubba Ziegler had grabbed some knives and was slashing the air. He caught Rocker across the cheek, and a line of blood sprang up. I trembled as I held my eye to the viewfinder. *Remember your hands, Maggie. Remember your big strong hands. Cock the shutter. Trip it. Advance.*

Bubba was slugging like a madman, sending bodies flying. Cecil somersaulted across the counter, landing in a heap. His hand caught the handle of the fryer basket, and a hot stream of grease flew out, burning foreheads, faces, arms. *Trip the shutter, Maggie. You know what you're seeing here. You've got to get it down.*

Everything was out of control. The colors melted together like a watercolor gone wild: Missy's purple scarf, Bigger's yellow vest, Virgil's black pants, Cecil's blue neckerchief. I saw that it didn't matter what side you were on. When it came to this, it was wrong, wrong. Every bit of it was dead wrong. I thought of Daddy's belt buckle, the one of Joe Hooker bringing Union mules to fight the Confederates at Lookout Mountain. At the first sound of gunfire the mules bolted, running wild, turning mad, attacking anything in sight. It didn't matter whether it was blue or gray.

And then I saw George Hardy.

Virgil's fist slammed into George Hardy's face. George Hardy reached to protect his glasses. They had slid to his chin, the glass shattered into a spider's web. He stood up, facing Virgil, a river of red blood running from his nose. He kept his hands to his side, refusing to fight back. I held the camera to my eyes, steadying it against my shaking fingers. The image before me swam red, filling up the lens. *Trip the shutter, Maggie Pugh*. What filled my lens was more than the blood gushing from my sweet friend. It was the red color of the fence, the red color of the earth on which I stood. It was red, the color of my life this summer. *Cock. Trip.* Red: it was the color of Kinship.

Everybody in town had come to look. Olive Shriner, Elsie Fish. Martha Leonard even brought Charlie Mac. Lenny Tubbs watched between the skirts of Sarah Deems and Margaret Matlack.

Somebody passed Virgil Boggs a baseball bat. He gripped it in one hand, raised it over his head, and slung it at George Hardy. George Hardy hadn't even raised a hand to him. I heard the thudding sounds of the bat and saw George Hardy slump to the ground.

Something like terror rose in my throat. *Dear God,* I prayed. *If you're there, sweet Savior, please help me. I know I haven't been faithful. But he has been good to me, Lord, a faithful friend, a friend and a blessing. Please protect George Hardy, Jesus. I swear on all that's holy that I will do your work as a child of Jesus if you just protect him. Watch over him, Lord. Protect him. Keep him safe. Let him live.*

Sheriff Keiter pushed his way through the crowd, hauling George Hardy up. His eye was swollen black, and he had passed out. Sheriff Keiter put handcuffs on George Hardy's wrists, and he and Elmer Byer and Boyce Johnson dragged his rag-doll body off to the cruiser.

I followed them every step, pushing through the crowd, whispering loud. "Hold on, George Hardy," I said. "You're going to be all right. The Lord can't be cruel enough to let them kill such as you. Hold on, George Hardy. Hold on."

I held the camera to my eye and snapped. Sheriff Keiter dragging a man passed out. *Cock the shutter. Trip it. Advance the film.* Elmer Byer shoving him into the cruiser. *Steady your hand, Maggie. Snap.* The white folks on the sidewalk holding ropes and chains, tire irons and bats. *Snap. Click.*

After they pulled away, I biked with all my might to the drugstore in Troy. I wouldn't trust Hazel Boggs with my film for one blessed minute. I thought of the stories told by the pictures in George Hardy's magazines, animals moving in the wild, the earth itself heav-

273

ing and shifting, the people of the world creating natural forces of their own. For the first time that long, wet summer, I knew what I was seeing. And I intended to tell the world.

Chapter 21

At one sharp I arrived at the Trailways station. I knew they had won by the way Mama came prancing down the steps of the bus. They were carrying shopping bags filled with brand-new clothes from their all-day shopping spree. Gardenia looked more relieved than happy. She had stuck her wig up under her arm and the top of her stubbled head was damp. Lord knows that scratchy wig must have been hot.

Mama talked a mile a minute. They'd won two hundred dollars, and she proved it by spreading the green bills out like a canasta hand. Daddy's eyes looked fit to pop, and he cautioned the money back into Mama's pocketbook. Lord knows I was glad I had got out that rabbit's foot.

A photographer from the *Troy Tribune* showed up. Gardenia frowned and put her wig back on. Then he snapped some pictures while Mama talked. It was beautiful in Savannah. The stage looked just like Tara, with white cardboard columns tacked to a chicken-wire frame. The boxwoods and shrubs were green tissue paper. Gardenia had to come in through the back of the set to descend the front steps of the mansion. When she stood at the threshold of the doorway and gave the judges her smile, you just knew she had won. In addition to the two hundred dollars and winning the state pageant title, Gardenia now got to compete in the national pageant in Washington, D.C., this fall where they'd get to see the Washington Monument and the Lincoln Memorial and the wax museum. It was the first time I ever heard Mama say anything good about Washington.

The fact was that Mama's present happiness made me as nervous as her past anger, because I knew about the letter from the UDC. It had come from Richmond while Mama and Gardenia were away at the contest, the day after the strike at Byer's, the day that Kinship was swirling with reporters and TV cameras, the day I learned that George Hardy and his friends were all right, beat up for sure, but, Praise Jesus, all right.

Pert told me how you could open a letter without anyone knowing. You stuck it in the freezer so it got good and cold and then the glue that sealed the envelope got brittle and you could open the letter right up without tearing the envelope. Then you read what was inside and glued it back down again after you held your head in your hands awhile, wondering how you would ever tell your mama that her soldier ancestor was a traitor. Not a traitor, exactly. But not General Lee, for sure. The papers from Richmond said that

Mama's great-grandfather, Ermal Vesey Merritt, my great-great-grandfather, had fought for both the North and the South. They had papers showing pay vouchers from both Washington and Montgomery. He fought at Gettysburg for the North and at Manassas for the South and at a bunch of places in between.

I stuffed the letter in a drawer in Pert's bedroom to give to Mama sometime later. Miriam Simpson had brought a group of the UDC ladies to the house after they heard the news about Gardenia, and I didn't want to be the one to ruin her happiness. Mama's heart would break when she got the letter, but I could understand about Ermal Vesey Merritt. Pughs were hungry even back then.

After Mama and Gardenia got back from Savannah, I visited now and again, but I still lived at Pert's. The fact that I hoped to find my mama someday didn't mean I had to live at home to do it. In fact, I was glad the letter from *Life* magazine arrived at Pert's trailer instead of my house.

It came in a thick manila envelope with the big capital letters of the magazine in the left-hand corner. I read the cover letter quickly. It was from an editor, a Jacqueline Steinmetz, and they were using my pictures from the lunch-counter strike in the enclosed issues of the magazine that featured similar activities in similar places like Greensboro and Nashville. They sent $250 and six free copies. I flipped quickly through the pages of the magazine, past the advertisements for Buicks and Camels and Palmolive soap. And there they were. My pictures. Bubba Ziegler catching Rocker across the cheek with a knife. The swirl of thrust fists and thrown punches. The river of blood running down George Hardy's face and across his smashed glasses. The swollen openmouthed faces on the sidewalk outside Byer's Drugs, shouting and angry. George Hardy's limp body stuffed into a police cruiser. Jacqueline Steinmetz said the issues would hit the magazine stands soon.

A reporter came all the way from Macon to talk to me. I showed him my camera and took out my treasures from George Hardy: the *National Geographics*, the notes, the flower from the Ghost Tree. I even modeled my Santa Claus apron for him.

I was glad that the envelope from *Life* came to Pert's trailer, for I wanted to tell Mama and Daddy and Gardenia about it myself, to explain about it in just the right way. I hadn't figured that the reporter would go there too. Martha Leonard told me all about it. How Mama let him in all smiles, thinking he was writing about Gardenia. How the smiles continued when he explained about the money. How she said she knew her daughter was right handy with a camera. How after that she looked at the pictures. How then she said she shouldn't have been surprised. How she'd been shamed more than once by her own daughter. How she threw the magazine after him as she chased him out the door.

I didn't need Martha to tell me all this, for Pert confirmed how Mama felt after she stomped over to the trailer park. I was baby-sitting Charlie Mac when she arrived, but Pert said Mama made a scene in front of all the park residents, with Jimmy and Rae Jean looking out the kitchen window. Pert tried to explain that I had won a contest and that I was something like Gardenia now. It wasn't like that at all, Mama said. I had shamed her, but Gardenia made her proud. Said everybody in town was talking about how Pughs were Communists.

Mostly I tried not to care. I told myself that Mama didn't make sense and never would. Why I still secretly hoped that some kind of peace would come to us I'll never know. I thought about General Gordon. How it was possible to drown in your own blood. But I also saw that some kind of escape might be possible. Things were different now. I knew that things took will and money. From Mama I had been given the will. From *Life* magazine I had been given the money. They allowed me to go to Atlanta.

Pert and I had to leave in the dead of night to get to Atlanta by eleven in the morning. When we arrived, a man sat alone at the counter in front of the small grill drinking black coffee and sprinkling ketchup and pepper over a plate of french fries. He was the only other person in the station besides Alma Jenkins. We paid for our tickets and waited outside. The lights glowed blue in the darkness.

When the bus pulled up, we took our seats near the back, leaning our heads against the greasy headrests. I felt wads of gum sticking up under the armrests. Then we heard the voice of Alma Jenkins one more time. "Departure for Atlanta. Departure for Atlanta," she said. "Departure for Athens at 4:05. Milledgeville at 4:15." When the bus started up, it sounded like Arnold Hardin's clunker.

The signs flashed white in the night. Madison. Social Circle. When we reached Lithonia, the sky streaked orange and pink. The crests of the hills turned from brown to rust. The engine churned.

Pert and I talked and dozed on the way. She told me how Elmer Byer had printed new menus and raised all of his prices. I already knew that he'd consulted a fancy lawyer in Macon who asked him to think about what meant more: a slew of lawsuits or his business. I told her about my decision to testify for Zeke. I had made it that day when the sun was beating down on me and George Hardy standing beside his bridge. I hadn't told anyone but Pert yet, and I'd tell George Hardy when I got to Atlanta. I also wanted to ask him if I could keep his key. I still wore it around my neck, even though I didn't need it anymore, but I wanted to keep it as a reminder, a reminder of the world outside of Kinship.

When we reached Decatur, we saw the signs for Stone Mountain. I wished Daddy could be here. He'd die to see Stonewall Jackson up on that mountain. I felt the strap of my camera around my neck and promised to take some pictures for him.

The sun was gold and climbing when we arrived in Atlanta. My fanny ached from sitting so long. Cars honked, and the people moved so fast. It wasn't anything like Kinship. There were trees everywhere and traffic circles. There were statues of generals on horseback. Every street seemed to be named Peachtree. Peachtree Street. Peachtree Battle Avenue. Peachtree Hills.

We had to hurry. The service started at eleven. When the bus ground to a halt, Pert and I dashed into the rest room marked WHITE WOMEN. I washed my hands with some pink soap that came from a pump, and then we got dressed in toilet stalls that cost a nickel. I slipped into my navy skirt and white blouse. Pert put on a polka-dot shift with the back cut out. We stood before the harsh light of the mirror, making up.

"Here, Maggie," Pert said. "You can use my Tangee."

Mama never let me use anything stronger than Vaseline on my lips, but Mama wasn't here. Besides, I could decide things for myself. I smeared the waxy orange color across my lips, smiling into the mirror, wondering if I looked better.

Pert took some polish from her purse and dabbed at her nails. "Want some, Maggie?"

I looked at my hands. "No, thanks, Pert," I said. I had stopped biting my nails down to the quick and was proud of the way they looked. But I liked them plain just fine.

"Ooooooo-eee!" Pert said, clicking her purse closed. "We's late, Maggie Pugh. It's ten forty-five," she said, looking at her watch.

"Lord have mercy!" I said, brushing out my hair one last time. It was long and auburn and shiny. I liked the way I was wearing it now. Loose. Falling all over my shoulders. "I promised George Hardy I'd be the official photographer. He wants me to get Reverend Potter holding the Bible and marrying them. Plus one of his mother and her father and all of their cousins." I adjusted the camera strap around my neck. "We'd better run, Pert. We can't afford to be late."

I unfolded the map with the directions to the college chapel. I saw that we'd get there faster if we cut through the alleys.

"Take off your shoes, Pert," I said. "That way we can run faster."

We dodged taxis and businessmen in suits. We ran in and out of traffic. Flower stalls whizzed by. I saw snatches of newspaper headlines: GEORGIA NOT COMPLYING WITH DESEGREGATION, JUDGE SAYS. People on benches pointed and stared at us. Our suitcases banged against our thighs. My camera jerked at my neck.

We were only a block away, but the big clock over the chapel archway was already striking eleven.

There was an accident in front of the chapel. Two taxicabs had collided, and a fire engine was blocking the path. People were shouting, crowding around to look. I knew I'd never make it through that crowd.

I saw what I had to do.

The fence surrounding the chapel was a sturdy wrought-iron square. I eyed it thoughtfully. Then I motioned for Pert to follow me, and I threw my suitcase over the top. I made a long running jump, pulling up with my strong hands, throwing myself up and over, landing on both feet. I brushed myself off, satisfied.

I looked up and saw that George Hardy had been watching me. He was standing in the archway under the clock. He had seen me climb the fence and sail over, without a rip or a tear. Quickly I raised my camera to my eye and I caught him through the lens, grinning to beat the band.

A lot of people we knew were there. Georgia. Rocker. Bigger Baby. The ceremony looked like a pirate's wedding. The groom wore a patch over his eye, and Zeke, the best man, leaned on a pair of crutches.

George Hardy and Ida Mae repeated their vows, and I made some promises of my own, fingering my gold key as I listened to Reverend Potter. I saw that the one thing I had left to do was give Mama that letter from the UDC and I saw that I needed to be there to help her understand. What would happen after that I couldn't say.

I saw Stumble Martin slip his arm around Cinda when Reverend Potter talked about how it took a lifetime to build both a relationship and a community and thought how the world was a curious place, full of change and wonder. I believed that if Mama could be made to understand, anybody could. Mama would be ashamed, of course, but I was proud. Ermal Vesey Merritt knew it didn't really matter what side you were on. Somehow, we're all kin.